ALF

the Sea

Melissa Bailey read English at Oxford, before studying law in London and then pursuing a career in media law. *Beyond the Sea* is her second novel.

Other books by Melissa Bailey

The Medici Mirror

Beyond the Sea

MELISSA BAILEY

arrow books

1 3 5 7 9 10 8 6 4 2

Arrow Books
20 Vauxhall Bridge Road
London SW1V 2SA

Arrow Books is part of the Penguin Random House
group of companies whose addresses can be found at
global.penguinrandomhouse.com

Penguin
Random House
UK

First published in paperback by Arrow Books in 2015

www.randomhouse.co.uk

A CIP catalogue record for this book is available from the British Library

ISBN 9780099584957

Typeset in Baskerville MT by Palimpsest Book Production Ltd, Falkirk, Stirlingshire
Printed and bound by CPI Group (UK) Ltd, Croydon, CR0 4YY

MIX
Paper from
responsible sources
FSC
www.fsc.org   FSC® C018179

Penguin Random House is committed to a
sustainable future for our business, our readers
and our planet. This book is made from
Forest Stewardship Council® certified paper

B000 000 015 7496

To Parvais

Acknowledgements

Thanks to my agent, Luigi Bonomi of LBA, for all his assistance and for sharing stories of mermaids with me. From those exciting early discussions the landscape of a novel began to emerge. Thanks to everyone who read early drafts of it and for their valuable commentary and insights.

Huge appreciation to all the team at Penguin Random House and especially my editor, the exceptional Gillian Holmes, who seamlessly blended perceptiveness, honesty and sensitivity and helped transform this into the best book it could be.

I am especially grateful to Nicola Goldfinch-Palmer, who gave me help when I needed it, and Angela Woods – dear friend, wise counsel and all round superstar – for her boundless encouragement and advice.

A big thank you to my mum and dad for their unstinting support and, most of all, to Parvais, for everything.

Prologue

The boat glided effortlessly across the water. Not bad for an old wooden tub, Jack thought. Whatever Freya said about it, he loved this boat. No doubt it needed a new motor, but it would last another summer. Angus at the boatyard had assured him of that. He listened carefully but all he could hear was a contented purring. Perhaps it would last the winter season as well.

The sea was peculiarly peaceful for this time of year, as if it were a lake rather than the open Atlantic. One of those perfect days, with a deep blue, cloudless sky reflected in the calm water. He grabbed his binoculars and looked towards the horizon. But even further out, where the rise and fall of the waves should be more pronounced, there was little movement.

He turned around to Sam, seated at the back of the boat, nose down in a book about seabirds. 'Do you want to come into the cabin to steer the boat for a while?' Jack called.

'No,' his son replied without looking up.

'Well, are you warm enough out there?' Even though the sun was shining, it was still spring and there was a cold breeze on the water.

'I'm fine.' Sam looked up this time and grinned.

'So what have you seen so far?'

'Well, I think they were fulmars. Although they look quite like gulls or kittiwakes so it's not easy to tell. Dad, do you know what fulmars do to protect themselves from predators?'

'No,' said Jack, increasing the motor's speed. The thrum of the engine became more pronounced.

'They squirt the contents of their stomachs out through their noses at them. It's a gross, smelly liquid.'

'Sounds like a pretty good way of keeping things at a distance.'

'They learn to do it as chicks. Pretty cool, huh?'

Jack smiled. 'Certainly is.' He increased speed again and could hear the slight strain of the motor. But it was nothing it couldn't handle and now they were really moving faster. He grabbed the binoculars again and surveyed the horizon. Clear. Nothing out of the ordinary. It would all be plain sailing.

A few minutes later Sam shouted, 'Hey Dad, look at this.'

Jack turned to see his son, his own set of binoculars in hand, pointing skywards. But he couldn't make out anything from inside the cabin.

'What is it?' he said.

'A big white bird. Very high up. On its own.'

Jack twisted around but again couldn't see. 'Any ideas?' he said.

Sam was scrutinising his book of seabirds once again.

'It's got a big wingspan and black wing tips. I think it might be an albatross.'

'An albatross? I don't think so. They're generally found in the south and the Pacific. In which case it's a long way from home.'

'But it says here that they range over huge stretches of ocean and regularly circle the globe. So it could be.'

'Well maybe,' Jack conceded. 'But I think it's more likely that it's a gannet. They're common around here.'

'Yes, but they don't really fly alone. Albatrosses do. It also says that gannets glide low over the ocean. And this one isn't doing that.'

Jack smiled. This seabird book his father Alister had bought had fast become the ornithological bible. But he had to admit that it was very accurate. 'Maybe it's going to feed. Gannets fly high and circle before diving into the sea.'

Sam was silent for a while, and Jack hoped perhaps that was the end of it. But, knowing his son, he suspected not.

A few moments later, Sam spoke again. 'Well, I don't think this gannet is all that hungry. He's still just hovering high up on the thermals. Come and have a look, Dad.'

Jack still couldn't see the bird from inside the cabin and he knew that his son wouldn't be satisfied or move on unless he had seen it properly.

He powered the engine down, but as he slipped it into neutral it stalled. 'Shit,' he said. It had a nasty habit of doing that. But it wasn't usually a problem, so perhaps

3

rather than fiddle with it now, he'd leave it until they were ready to go again.

'Ooh. You're going to be in trouble with Mum. She'd kill you if she knew the engine was off way out here.' Sam was smiling and laughing as Jack stepped out of the cabin.

'Well, no one has to tell Mum,' said Jack, looking upwards. For a moment he couldn't see anything, the glint of sunlight catching in his eyes. But finally he made it out. A solitary white bird, high up in the sky.

'Let me take a look with your binoculars.'

Sam passed them to his father and then moved impatiently from foot to foot while he waited.

'Hmm. I know what you mean. The colour of the wing tips means it could be either. It's big for a gannet, but it's pretty difficult to see the beak and tail feathers clearly.' Jack lowered the binoculars, blinked hard and then tried again. But the bird was partly obscured by the glare of the sun. 'I still think it's unlikely to be an albatross, Sam.'

'Aww.' His tone was one of disappointed sulkiness. 'It would have been really cool to have seen one. Mum would think so. She read me "The Rime of the Ancient Mariner".'

'Did she now?' Jack frowned. For God's sake, he was only ten. But Freya had always done that. Read him stuff that was way beyond him. 'And can you remember any of it?'

'Hmm. Not really.' Sam laughed.

Jack pulled his son to him and ruffled his hair. 'Well,

while we've stopped shall we have our lunch? It's about time.'

For half an hour Jack and Sam talked, ate and drank on the deck at the back of the boat. When they were finished and ready to carry on, Jack grabbed Sam's binoculars again. The bird, whatever it was, was still hovering above them.

'Strange,' Jack muttered, and continued to scout the sky. It was only then that he noticed a black cloud growing on the horizon west of them. 'Where did that come from?' He watched it for a little while longer and then scanned around them three hundred and sixty degrees. Every horizon showed nothing but sky and sea. He handed the binoculars back to Sam and looked over the ocean. It was building swell, the once-still blue water now rippling and murky. Then he caught sight of shadowy trails of movement, swift blurs of grey here and there.

A moment later, Sam's voice rang out excitedly. 'Dolphins.'

Jack nodded as he looked. It was quite a big pod if he wasn't mistaken. 'Are they feeding? Looks like they might be.'

'I think so,' said Sam, hanging over the side and trying to touch them.

'Be careful,' shouted Jack.

'I will, Dad,' said Sam, rolling his eyes.

They watched the dolphins jumping and playing, criss-crossing beneath the boat from one side to the other. Sam shouted and pointed as he caught sight of them dancing beneath the surface, leaping momentarily into the air and then disappearing once more into the darkness. Eventually the pod overtook them and vanished.

'That was sooo cool,' said Sam, still dangling over the edge of the boat.

'Yes it was,' said Jack. But he had already turned his gaze back to the horizon. The cloud was growing and he didn't like the look of it. He dropped his eyes back to the ocean. Could he still see traces of grey flashing beneath the surface? Perhaps, he wasn't sure. But surely the pod had moved on by now? He scrutinised the surface of the ocean, tried to see beneath it, but he couldn't tell. As he looked he felt a strange dizzying sensation, suddenly conscious of the miles of water beneath them. His skin prickled. Ridiculous, he said to himself.

Moving into the cabin, he turned on the radio and listened. Cloud was building, the weather turning and heading their way. 'Sam,' he shouted, 'I'm afraid we're going home. There's a storm coming.'

'Aww,' he heard his son cry again from the back of the boat. The sound gave him comfort. It was fearless and indifferent.

He wrapped his fingers around the ignition key and faltered for a moment as he felt an odd sensation of giddiness and nerves. What had got into him? They had plenty of time. With a bit of luck they would be home in an hour. He breathed in deeply and exhaled slowly. But the vertiginous feeling was still there, lurking in his stomach.

From the back of the boat he could hear Sam chatting

away to himself. 'Well, I think it has webbed feet, which gannets don't have. So I'm still not one hundred per cent convinced.'

Jack looked out of the cabin window and caught sight of the bird. It was still hovering above them but it was lower now. It seemed larger, darker. He frowned. And he was not one for omens. But as he turned the ignition key, the words of the poem he had been trying not to think about jumped into his head.

> Day after day, day after day,
> We stuck, nor breath nor motion;
> As idle as a painted ship
> Upon a painted ocean.
>
> Water, water, everywhere,
> And all the boards did shrink;
> Water, water, everywhere,
> Nor any drop to drink.

1

The ferry ploughed across the Firth of Lorn, churning the still, grey waters beneath it. Waves crashed against the broad hull of the boat before sliding down, mingling with the foam and once more disappearing into the depths. Freya, standing upon the deck, head bent in concentration, had been watching this violent collision, this unceasing ebb and flow, for some time. The movement of the water was compelling, the hard smack then the retreat was like a lithe, endless dance. And the sound of the waves, harsh yet hypnotic, was so familiar to her despite her absence. She breathed in deeply and, sensing a shift in the air, looked up.

A storm was on its way. The signs of its approach were in the increasingly darkening sky, a flinty hardness massing around its edges and the hint of electricity in the air. But it was still some way off. Freya looked at her watch. It was only three o'clock but it looked much later. It also felt much more like winter than spring. But that was just it. The weather could change in these parts in an instant. Rain could be followed immediately by sunshine, sunshine by snow. You never knew what was coming.

Freya blinked hard and, to distract herself, surveyed the land. To her left, she could make out Duart Point, and before long she would be able to see the castle. Perched on a rocky outcrop, it guarded the entrance to the Sound of Mull. Behind it the hills rose steeply. Now they were green and brown, the result of a long, cold winter, but by the autumn they would be burnished rust, red and rose with the setting sun upon them. Dazzling in their beauty. She remembered the last time she had visited there. It had been with her son, Sam, just over a year and a half ago. She couldn't take her eyes off the colours of the hills, but she knew without turning that he was staring out over the Firth, a dreamy look in his eye, far more interested in the sea and the wreck off the coast.

'What was the name of that ship?' she asked.

'The *Swan*, Mum,' he said, the slightest hint of impatience in his tone.

She smiled. 'And when did it sink?'

'During a storm. On the thirteenth of September, 1653.' He was now, she knew, doing calculations in his head. Her heart constricted slightly. 'Three hundred and sixty years ago.'

'Hmm,' she said. 'Almost to the day. And when was it built?'

'In 1641. It was a small warship, remember?'

She nodded, still looking northwards. 'And who had sent it?'

'Oliver Cromwell. To crush Royalist sympathies in the Highlands.'

Now she laughed. He sounded as if he were reciting from a history textbook. Who knew whether he really understood what it meant.

'What's funny, Freya?' He only ever called her Freya when he thought he was being patronised, mocked or derided in some slight, sly way he couldn't quite understand.

'Nothing, darling. That's very good.' But still she hadn't turned to face him. Why hadn't she? 'And what did they find when they excavated the wreck?'

'Silver coins, an anchor, flagons, seven iron cannons, a pocket watch, clay pipes, a sword hilt, leather shoes and human remains.'

She smiled at the way he pronounced 'human remains'. With the unique combination of diffidence and fear that perhaps only a nine-year-old could muster.

'They only found the bones of one man, though.'

'And what did they name him?'

'Seaman Swan. He was only five feet tall but he had a really big chest like King Kong. His legs were bendy. From rickets.'

'That's right,' said Freya, nodding. She had heard all of this before. But Sam found it endlessly fascinating.

'I wonder what happened to all the other men,' he said pensively. 'And the cannons. Granddad said that the *Swan* had twelve to start off with.' Her father-in-law, another shipwreck enthusiast, had taken Sam to the National Museum in Edinburgh to see the excavation finds.

'Well, perhaps it did.'

'But if it did, then what happened to the others?'

'Maybe people took them.'

Sam contemplated this for a moment, as he always did, before dismissing it.

'Or they disintegrated in the water.'

This met with a more favourable response, she could tell. Even though it still wasn't quite right.

'What do you think happened?'

'The sea took them.'

Freya nodded. It was the most likely. That the sea had claimed them, as it seemed to claim most things in its path; taken them away to the Land under Waves.

The sound of metal grinding against metal then, as the anchor dropped, a whirring free fall before a hard smack against the surface of the water. Freya sat inside her car, waiting to leave, the clangour of iron ringing in her ears, imagining the anchor sinking into the silent, cold darkness. She had put on a hat and dark glasses, as she did not want to be recognised. She did not want to see it just yet, in the eyes of anyone she knew, how much she had changed, how very different she now looked. She did not want the sympathy or the attention of people just yet, did not want to hear their condolences for the loss of her husband and child. The horn sounded and the large iron doors began to slide apart. She turned on the ignition and waited, impatient, to exit.

2

Freya had already passed the low hills to the north of Loch Spelve when the thunder sounded. Like a whip crack, sharp and swift. Before too long the lightning would break. If the storm was still in full spate when she reached the western side of Mull it would be reckless to take the boat. Her father had warned her to leave in good time, to use the daylight to make the journey and not to finish it if the weather was bad. She had given the impression of listening but, in truth, like so often now, the words fell around her unheeded. She didn't really care. Besides, with any luck, the storm would have passed by the time she got to Fionnphort.

It was at the left bend in the road, following the sharp turn of the Lussa River, that the rain began. Fat drops fell heavily from the blackening sky, spattering onto the windscreen. She slowed down and looked out over Glen More. With the downpour, its desolation was complete. She looked across the barren landscape, the undulating scrub that even the sheep now seemed to have abandoned. She knew her father hoped that encountering such isolation once again would push her to turn around. He had said as much. That this place would make her long for home. But as Freya looked at the dark clouds scudding low over the Glen, glancing over the surface of the three lochs, obscuring the mountains beyond, she felt something else entirely. Comfort in the solitude; solace in the emptiness and singular beauty around her. There was much more of home about this place. And she had missed it. As she followed the turns and bends in the road, she thought that perhaps this might have been the right decision after all.

The road appeared on her right, illuminated in the first crack of lightning. For a moment, Freya considered taking the turning and visiting Torin, her old friend, waiting out the storm with him and only then setting off. As she deliberated, the turning came and went, the rain-spattered tarmac disappearing untaken. No. She wasn't ready to see him yet. She needed a little time to settle herself and then she would make the journey.

Freya tried to focus on the road, clinging to the southern shore of Loch Scridain, partly veiled by the deluge of rain and low cloud. On a clear day, she knew that the loch was a brilliant blue. But today its waters were dull, slate grey. Another lightning bolt fractured the sullen sky. It's Thor and he's angry, Jack would always say if they were caught driving in a thunderstorm. He's wielding his hammer, isn't he, Sam? But Sam, staring out of the window into the raging darkness would never answer. He was always deep in thought, his lips partly open, his mind thinking perhaps about gods and strength and power.

As the road began to forge inland, the strength suddenly

went out of the rain. The pinnacle of the storm was past, she knew, and it was waning. Thor's anger was abating.

Freya sat silently for a moment, behind the wheel of the car, looking down towards the harbour. The sky was brightening and the sea looked still, waves lapping softly against the sides of the moored vessels. Her eyes moved over them one by one and she doubted for a second if she would recognise her own boat. But it didn't take her long to pick it out – old, blue and white, battered by wind, rain and saltwater. The *Valkyrie*. It sat perky and oblivious, bobbing upon the water, its paintwork flaking a little, lifebuoys roped onto its sides. Freya stared at the wooden boat, at its mast with the incurable bend three-quarters of the way up and then shook her head, incredulously. It looked flimsy, like a toy. Not a craft sturdy enough to navigate these sometimes-treacherous waters. Beside it was a space normally occupied by her husband's boat, *Noor*. But it was, of course, absent. It was a small gap, no doubt about it, between her boat and the next one along, but it seemed to her in that moment incomprehensibly large. She closed her eyes, suddenly dizzy, and a strange sound burst from her throat, unbidden. The grief erupted unexpectedly, swiftly, stripping her of breath. As if she too were drowning. She felt lightheaded, about to pass out, and then moments later the opposite – weighty, sinking, her stomach sick and churning. It was often this way. But she had grown used to the feelings now and she knew what to do. She opened her eyes, breathed deeply, and waited for them to pass.

A knock on the driver's window startled her. She turned to see a man's face on the other side of the glass, staring at her. His eyes were soft, a pale grey, and he wore a striped black-and-white woollen hat pulled down low over his forehead. His face was lined from years of being exposed to the elements at sea – wind, rain, hail and sun, making him look older than his forty years. Yet it was still handsome: a Roman nose, defined cheekbones, a strong jawline, thick lips with laughter lines etched into their corners. But he wasn't smiling now. For a few moments Freya simply stared at him. Then slowly, she wound down the window.

'Hello, Callum.'

The man nodded. 'Freya.'

Then neither of them spoke; they simply looked at each other. Freya wasn't sure she trusted herself to say anything more. Her voice had sounded flat, empty. As if the life had been sucked out of it. But then she supposed that wasn't surprising. She tried to distract herself, to think of something to say to Callum, a man she had known for more than fifteen years, but couldn't. The mere act of thinking exhausted her.

Callum looked out to sea and studied it for a while before turning back to meet Freya's eye. 'So you're going to take the boat out?'

She blinked. 'Yes.'

'There was a big sea running not long ago, but it's settling now. You should be fine.'

Freya nodded. Callum knew what he was talking about.

For years he had been a fisherman before he began running boat trips to Staffa, the Treshnish Isles and beyond. He knew as much about the rocks that lay beneath the surface of the water in these parts as he did about the ones above it. She remembered that he had taken Sam fishing and lobster potting the last time they were here, and the thought made her smile.

'You changed your hair colour.' Callum's words sounded bizarre, unconnected with any kind of reality. Slowly the smile vanished from her lips.

'What?'

'Your hair.' And he gestured somewhat awkwardly towards his woollen hat.

'Oh, right,' said Freya, recollection dawning. She had forgotten that she had taken off her hat in the car and cursed herself now for not thinking about it. 'I didn't exactly change it,' she muttered. 'It changed itself. The shock, they say.' Her words petered out and she looked to the horizon to avoid looking at Callum. But she could still feel his eyes upon her. Was he taking in the white hair on her head, comparing it to the lustrous black it had been the last time he had seen her? She turned back to face him, suddenly filled with anger and defiance. But there was nothing but kindness in his eyes.

'I was very sorry to hear the news. Very sorry indeed.'

The rage went out of her as quickly as it had come. She nodded, looking away, again not trusting herself to speak.

'Will you be all right to take the boat?'

'Yes, of course.'

'Will you be all right to take it?' he said again.

'What do you mean?' she said turning to face him. Freya was an accomplished sailor, so she didn't understand what he was driving at. But as her eyes met his again, she took a deep breath and paused. 'Yes, I'll be all right.'

'Are you sure?'

'I'm sure.' Then, as if to reassure him, 'I promise I won't do anything reckless.'

Finally, he nodded, as if satisfied with her answer. 'Give it half an hour before you set off.' He looked at her one last time then raised his hand in parting and strode away.

Freya wound up the window and sat very still for a few moments. By the time she had unloaded the car, packed the boat, checked the engine and fuel and set off, thirty minutes would have passed. She thought of Callum, his unsmiling face, his dour concern. She would be careful for him. Luckily she too knew what lay beneath these waters. Almost as well as he did. She could sail to the island in the dark, in a storm – blindfolded, perhaps. It would pose only a slightly bigger threat to her safety. But she had promised him she would not be reckless. Her father too.

It wouldn't be long now before the sun disappeared below the horizon. Freya imagined journeying through the dark, the blackness of the sea closing in around her, until suddenly she would see it, the beacon flashing, drawing the boat homewards, guiding her. Finally, she was going home.

3

As Freya approached the island's jetty, she thrust the boat's engine into reverse. Seconds later, she killed it altogether. For a moment she was surrounded by a silent darkness. Then the lighthouse beam swept over the bay. It moved for three seconds over the sea before it disappeared for a further seven. Then it emerged and vanished again in the same revolution. As Freya watched, a long-forgotten memory emerged from the deep.

She was young and newly in love, on her way to the island for the first time with Jack to meet his parents. She would have followed him to the ends of the earth, and she told him so.

'Well, Frey, where we're going isn't all that far from there.'

His blue eyes had twinkled as he said it, his light hair flurried by the breeze, sitting beside her on the fishing boat driven by Callum.

She had laughed as she looked at Jack, then turned her attention once more to the ocean and the darkening evening light that fell upon it. In that instant, in the gloaming, the lighthouse lamp had come alive. It was the beginning of its nightly vigil. As light danced over the bay, the beauty of it took Freya by surprise. She watched again and again, the expansive sweep across the ocean, captivated by the thought of its endless repetition, until Jack pulled her face back towards his. For a moment he simply stared at her. Then he had kissed her and she had forgotten about the lighthouse entirely.

Freya pushed the memory down, jumped out of the boat and tethered it to the jetty. Then she grabbed her bags and began the steep climb up to the lighthouse. With each sweep of the lamp she could see the dark tower briefly illuminated, and from time to time, as she ascended the path, the squat outline of the cottage around its base. Before long, she reached the gate in the wall of the lighthouse enclosure and, moving through it, crossed the garden. At the cottage door, Freya searched in her pockets for her keys. By now her heart was pounding, and not just from the climb.

She unlocked the door and pushed it open. The peculiar mustiness of an abandoned space greeted her. She peered into the darkness of the interior for a moment and then stepped over the threshold into the kitchen. Ignoring the pile of letters scattered over the doormat, unopened and unanswered for the last year, she put down her bags and moved to the wall lights. She flicked them on and turned to look at the kitchen once more.

Under the hard yellow light, everything seemed smaller, emptier, more colourless than she remembered; the ceiling low, the table bleached and bare, the kitchen worktops narrow and naked. It was all so devoid of life. Beyond the kitchen stretched the hallway. She could just make out the locked door to the lighthouse tower on the left and beyond it, she knew, although she couldn't see, were the bedrooms – the guests' furthest away, then hers, Sam's closest. As she thought of her son's room, reeking with the same cold, forsaken smell now hanging in her nostrils, Freya's stomach lurched and she struggled to catch her breath. Maybe this had been a mistake after all.

She turned and switched off the overhead lights and rested her forehead against the wall. Its coolness soothed her and eventually her breathing slowed. Looking into the darkness, the deeper smudges at its edges, she crossed the kitchen into the sitting room and lay down on the sofa. In front of her was the large picture window built into the western wall, with its magnificent view out over the sea. She caught the sweep of the lamp and watched it over and over until a small feeling of comfort balled inside her. She would stay here for a while. She would stay here, quietly watching the light, until she was ready to go to bed.

4

She felt his hands upon her, bringing her out of the depths of sleep, those unmistakeable hands that she would know anywhere, simply by touch, in pitch darkness. He never spoke, never whispered her name, but she felt his breath hot against her ear, at the back of her neck, teasing her awake. As she rose quietly back into this world, she groaned softly, feeling his fingers sliding down her back, across her skin, over her hips. She turned towards him and opened her eyes. But she couldn't see him, couldn't find his face.

'Jack. What are you doing?' She always said this, even though she knew exactly what he was doing. The rote phrase was always followed by a smile. 'What *are* you doing?' she gasped, as his fingers slid between her legs.

She closed her eyes again and surrendered to his touch, feeling the gradual rise of pleasure deep within her, growing, until it burst, shattering the comfort of sleep once and for all.

Freya opened her eyes. She was wide awake but it took a moment for her to place the strange familiarity of the room, the pale blue walls, the whitewashed floorboards, a wooden dresser covered in rocks and seashells which stood opposite the end of the bed. Sunlight was streaming through the windows, there was the raucous call of seabirds close by and, faintly, in the background, the sound of waves breaking upon the shore. The next instant it fell upon her – the shattering remembrance. For a second, as ever, she tried to delay the flood of knowledge, the spill of darkness and death. She closed her eyes and turned onto her side. But the knowledge bubbled upwards, permeating every nook, every space inside her, moving through her veins like swift, slick poison. She opened her eyes again and looked at the cold, empty side of the bed. She thought of Jack, of the dream, always so vivid, so real and intoxicating, memory alive with desire. She thought of her son, of the empty bedroom next to the one in which she lay. And she remembered, as the tears began to fall, that they were both gone, both taken from her.

The sun was shining, the sky cloudless, but the air was cold. It was spring, after all, and summer was still some way off. But when the weather was like this, bright and clear, the sand glowed white and the sea was vivid blue and brilliant green. Freya walked along the beach at the southwest tip of the island, close to the water's edge, breathing in the salty air, meandering amidst the driftwood and seaweed. From time to time she bent down, her eye catching upon something in the sand, but mostly she gazed towards the horizon, across the sea. From this point on the island, if you sailed directly west, you would not meet land again until America. The thought of such remoteness, such splendid isolation, was both thrilling and terrifying. When it became too much, the other side of the island afforded a more reassuring view. Mull could be glimpsed to the northeast and a spattering of land beyond and to the south. Today, however, Freya was content to stare out into the wildness of the Atlantic.

At this moment, it did not look as savage as she knew it could, neither dangerous nor threatening. She ambled along the beach, her pace unhurried, familiarising herself with the land and its watery borders, hazy, forgotten. She bent down and tested the water, but it was cold, too cold still for swimming. As she reached the giant stack of rock at the southern end, she paused momentarily. Then she began to scale it. She was tall, five feet nine inches, and svelte, thinner than when she had last been here. Yet it still took her twenty strenuous minutes to get to the top. From there you could survey the island in its entirety, in all its diminutive glory. It was roughly half a mile from here to the northern tip, a quarter of a mile from east to west at the broadest point. But Freya did not want to study it all, the shingle beaches, the wild machair, the glistening burns catching the sunlight as they drained into the sea. For now she was content to see just one thing. It had been dark the previous day by the time she arrived. So she hadn't seen it properly. As she reached the summit of the rock, stood and turned inland, there it was, towering before her, majestic on the northern cliffs. The lighthouse.

It had been built over the course of two years in the

mid-1800s from rose-coloured granite quarried on the Isle of Mull. Its beauty wasn't confined simply to its colour and texture, but to the grace and symmetry of its outline – it was over 150 feet in height, soaring into the sky, from a base width of around 40 feet to just over 15 feet at the top of the tower. Even now, having seen it so many times before, Freya was humbled as she looked upon it again.

'It was designed and engineered by Alan Stevenson.' Freya remembered Pol's words as clearly as if he'd uttered them yesterday. But it was more than two years since she'd watched him clambering up the internal staircase of the tower. 'He was the uncle of Robert Louis Stevenson. I expect you know him better?'

Sam nodded, almost overwrought with excitement, following closely like a dog at Pol's heels. 'Yes, Mum's read *Treasure Island* to me a few times, and *Kidnapped*,' he managed, somewhat breathlessly, trying to balance his elation with the exertion of the stairs.

Anthony Tipol, or Pol for short, had once worked as a keeper at the lighthouse. After it had been automated, he had continued to be employed by the Northern Lighthouse Board, the body responsible for the upkeep of all lighthouses in Scotland, to check that everything was well maintained and ran smoothly. Pol visited every three or four months. But this particular visit had been a special one. It was the first time that Pol had allowed Sam to accompany him on an inspection. And the last time that Freya had seen Pol.

'Aye. That'd be about right. But Robert wasn't keen on

spending his life in the family business. Did you know the Stevensons built most of the lighthouses in Scotland?'

Sam nodded but Pol didn't turn to look at him. The question, Freya realised, was rhetorical. Pol was simply talking to himself on the subject closest to his heart. Following slowly behind the two of them, she was there ostensibly for the tour, but more to keep an eye on Sam.

'And for a rock lighthouse, like this one,' Pol continued, 'they had to ship all the granite out to the island already dressed and shaped, the slabs ready to fit one on top of another and then be anchored together.'

As they climbed upwards, Pol would shout out periodically what the rooms on each level of the tower had been used for – rope, lifebelts and a rubber dinghy in one, detonators and chargers for the fog gun in another. 'And this was where the tanks of paraffin for the light were kept. When they abandoned oil in favour of electrical power for the lamp, they built an engine shed down below, Sam, next to the keepers' cottage that you now live in. It generates electricity for the light, and for the machinery which makes it revolve, and for your home.'

Freya listened to see if she could make out the tone of disapproval in his voice that usually became so obvious by this turn in the conversation. But she couldn't detect it. Perhaps Pol had decided, after all these years, to finally forgive them for now living there. Perhaps he had also decided to forgive her for the automation of lighthouses in general for which she felt, acutely sometimes, that he also blamed her. Still, it was too early to tell.

As they climbed higher, Freya began to feel claustrophobic. The stairs clung to the sides of the lighthouse wall, ascending in a clockwise direction, and the internal space was narrow, becoming increasingly so as they rose higher. It was also much darker than she had imagined. But then the windows in the tower were small, allowing in only a little light. They spiralled upwards, this unlikely threesome, to the omnipresent mutterings of Pol.

'This room, see, the last one before the lamp room, once contained the air-pressure tanks for the oil. Me and the other keepers – when it was their turn to light the lamp – would pump the paraffin up to here by hand from the tanks down below; then it was vaporised and the vapour went up to the burners above.' Pol practically ran up the last flight of stairs into the lamp room, unable to repress the thrill of his remembrance, with Sam still at his heels. 'And here, at the light itself, we'd light the paraffin vapour.' And Pol would strike an imaginary match with his hands. 'But what really gave the light its power were the lenses that revolved around it and magnified it into the beam.' For a moment both Pol and Sam were silent, mouths open slightly as they marvelled at the sheer magnificence of it all.

'Anyway,' Pol continued at last, finally focusing on the real lamp in front of him rather than the older imaginary one he still carried in his mind, 'the oil lamp was eventually replaced with this electric one.' Pol pursed his lips and Freya braced herself for the tirade against modernisation that usually followed. But when it finally came, Pol's damning finale lacked both lustre and length. 'Then automation came shortly after.'

Fortunately, perhaps, Sam was as obsessed with the long-vanished days of lighthouse keeping as Pol. 'Pol,' he said, with that inimitably inquisitive look on his face that always made a small part of Freya's insides melt, 'did you have to sit up all night and tend the lamp? To check that it didn't go out.'

'Aye, that I did. When I was stationed here as a principal keeper, there was me and two others. We kept watch in turns, but when I had the night watch – from twelve to four o'clock in the morning – I would always sit up here in the lamp room. I mean you had to keep your eye on the lamp throughout the night – check the paraffin pressure was keeping up and that the burners weren't clogged. That sort of thing. But it wasn't really necessary to sit up here the whole time. But I always did, see.' And he turned to gaze at Sam, looked at him properly for the first time, scrutinised him intently to see if he understood the sacred piece of knowledge that was being shared with him. 'I would sometimes write my log, in that quiet time. It was crucial, you see, Sam, for a lighthouse keeper to maintain his log, to keep it bang up to date. But more often than not I would simply watch the flash of the light.' He paused, pensive. 'A man can have strange thoughts, alone at night, sitting at the top of a tower, in the middle of the ocean, miles from family and friends. He can begin to imagine that he is the only man left in the world, stranded and alone, or that the world that he knows has vanished entirely and is gone from him for ever.' Pol was nodding and Sam was watching him, mesmerised. 'Yes, it can do odd things to a man's head to be in a lighthouse alone at night, especially at night, looking out over the sea.'

Once more Pol descended into deep thought; to change the subject, Freya spoke for the first time. 'Perhaps Pol would let you go outside onto the gallery, Sam, and see how far you can see.'

'Aye,' said Pol. And without looking at Sam, he moved silently to the gallery door, unlocked it and pushed it open.

As the crashing sound of the sea came rushing in on the air, Freya felt the mood of existential melancholy that had been building disperse.

'Thanks Pol,' yelled Sam, already on the gallery, looking up at the seagulls, which were squawking as they orbited the tower. 'Come on, Mum, come and see with me.'

Freya smiled at Pol as she moved towards the door to the gallery, but he didn't return her smile, simply turning towards the light to carry out the checks that were required of him. Perhaps she had offended him. But then she always thought that she'd offended him by the end of his visit, one way or another. Sometimes she thought she offended him simply by being there.

Outside on the gallery the air was fresh and they could see for miles. The views from the island were magnificent on a clear day, but towering one hundred and fifty feet in the air they were staggering. There was a panorama over the western islands. To the north they could see Coll and Tiree and Skerryvore lighthouse, a mere dot on the horizon. To the southeast was Colonsay, and beyond it Islay, then Jura stretching north and eastwards towards Scarba.

'If you look closely,' she had said to Sam, 'perhaps you can see the whirlpool of Corryvreckan.'

'It's too far away, Mum. We can't see that. Silly.'

Then he had turned and smiled at her. Such a beautiful smile.

5

'What the fuck are you doing *there*?' Marta's voice, approaching a shriek, competed with the crackle and fizz on the line.

Freya removed the receiver from her ear for a second before speaking. 'I thought it would be good for me.'

There was a momentary pause. 'And why did you think that?'

In spite of having to defend herself, Freya couldn't help smiling. Marta was always like this – direct, foul-mouthed, uncompromising – and the familiarity of it was reassuring. 'Because wherever I've been in the last year, wherever I've gone, simply to avoid being here, it hasn't helped. So I thought I might as well come back. Grasp the nettle, you know. I thought it would be good for me,' she said again.

There was another, longer, pause on the line. 'But it doesn't feel right for you to be there – so . . . close to everything that happened.'

'Perhaps that's what I need.'

'But to be alone there?'

'I think I need that too.'

'You sound very certain of yourself all of a sudden,'

said Marta tartly, and they both started to laugh. 'Are you sure you don't want me to come up and keep you company?'

'Really, I'm OK,' said Freya, hoping to imbue the words with more certainty than she felt.

'Suit yourself. There was a time, you know, when you couldn't get enough of me.'

Her tone was light, mocking. But Freya was silent, thinking of the seemingly endless dark nights not so long ago when Marta had stayed up with her, through the tears, the despair, the agony. Without Marta, she was sure, she wouldn't have made it.

'Are you still there, Frey?'

'Yes, I'm here. Just thinking. You know . . . ' She stopped. 'I never thanked you properly . . . not really . . . '

'Forget it. We're not going there. Not with you so far away and me on my own here. You'll have me weeping into my Chablis.'

Freya smiled again as the line renewed its fizzing, and for a moment the sisters were silent.

'But, how is it to be back, really?'

Freya took a breath. 'Memories everywhere, of course. But there were memories everywhere even when I wasn't here.' She closed her eyes. 'I haven't been able to go into Sam's room yet. But I will. Soon.'

Marta was quiet but Freya could imagine her nodding at the other end of the line. After a moment she asked, 'And are you dreaming there?'

'Uh-huh.' Freya paused. Going to bed was like reliving

her life with her family. A steady replay of all her memories. Everything she and her family did together. Was it
a blessing? Perhaps. And then there was the other thing.

Marta read her mind. 'You haven't had the nightmare,
have you?'

'No, not yet.' But Freya knew that sooner or later it
would come.

'The doc said that would fade, become more and more
infrequent, the longer it is.'

Freya nodded. 'As everything works itself through.'

'And you're still taking the pills?'

'Yep.'

'And avoiding the booze?'

'Of course.' Freya looked at the glass of red wine
standing on the table beside the sofa. It was just the odd
glass now and then to calm her nerves, make her sleep.
And God knew she needed help with those things. But it
wasn't worth telling Marta about. It would only worry
her.

'Have you been for a swim yet?'

Freya had always loved the water; just after the news
of Jack and Sam, it had become a lifebuoy to her sanity.
She had swum almost every day, mile after mile, until she
was so exhausted she couldn't think any more, couldn't
feel anything. It had become a salvation, a dulling oblivion.
'No, I haven't been able to. The water's too cold. But
before long I'll get out into it. Still, Marta, I'm OK. I
think the really bad days are behind me.'

There was a short silence on the line, during which

Freya knew Marta would be assessing whether her older sister really was okay or just placating her. Not for the first time in their recent history, she wanted everything to be different. She settled for changing the subject.

'So how's work?'

'Same as. Depending on the mood of that cock of a partner I work for.' Marta sighed and then started to laugh. 'Fortunately he's quite a cock in other departments.'

'Oh no. Tell me that isn't still going on?'

''Fraid so. Try not to judge me. At least I'm single, so it's not double adultery.'

As Freya laughed, she felt a lightness she only rarely experienced these days. As if, for a split second, the events of the past year had never happened and she was her old self again. But then Marta, suddenly serious, went on. 'Claude's been asking about you, you know. She's phoned me a couple of times lately.'

'Oh yeah,' said Freya, the heaviness pressing around her once again. It had been her boss, Claude, who had suggested that Freya accompany her on that trip to the south of France over Easter. She hadn't wanted to go, especially over the holidays, but then she had changed her mind. After all, it would be good to play such a prominent role in the marketing campaign for their new client's perfume. So she had departed for two weeks with Claude, reluctant but smiling. It was the day before she was due to come home that she got the news from Scotland. A boating accident. They had found the boat but not the bodies. She had left immediately, the scent of night jasmine still thick in her nostrils. Now she always associated that smell with death. And sometimes she could sense it, she thought, heavy, on the air of her dreams. She swallowed, her throat suddenly dry, and reached for the glass of wine.

'Anyway, I think she'd like to talk to you. When you're up to it.' Marta's tone was breezy, the way it became when she knew she'd strayed into dangerous territory.

Freya said nothing. She had now, more or less, stopped blaming Claude for the theft of those last weeks with her family. She knew it was irrational. But it didn't mean she wanted to speak to her. For the second time in the conversation, Freya changed the subject. 'You know I'm thinking of selling the flat.'

'Mmm. Mum told me.'

Freya groaned. 'Oh God. Did she ask you to try and talk me out of it?'

'Of course.' Marta laughed. 'But I hope you know me better than that.'

'I hope so too.' Freya took a sip of wine. 'I just didn't want to be there any more. And I don't have a job in London now, so I don't need it.' Freya thought of the life insurance money sitting in a bank account, as yet untouched. Perhaps if she ignored it for long enough it would disappear, cease to have ever existed. She would do anything to have it gone, to have her family back in its place. She closed her eyes and tried to banish the thought. 'Anyway, I know I've only just got here, but I already feel better, more right. Or less *not right*, at least. Does that make sense?'

'I guess. Just think it over for a while. Don't make any hasty decisions.'

'I won't.' Pause. 'How is Mum?'

'Fraught. Nothing new there, eh? But I sense she's really trying. She's worried about you, Frey, that's all. And she doesn't know how not to be a cold fish. So it just comes across as criticism rather than concern. Go on, make her day. Give her a call and try not to get mad at her.'

Freya smiled. Marta was always the one who could manage their mother best. 'And Dad?'

'Worried sick. But he'd never say it.'

'Yeah. I know. Don't worry, I'll call. I promise.'

For a few moments the static crackled down the line as the two women sat in silence. Freya stretched out her long legs on the sofa and scrutinised her bare feet sticking out of the end of her jeans. The red nail varnish on her left big toe was chipped, a sudden absent chunk of colour. Something about it struck her as intensely sad. Then she felt her insides twist.

'You know, it's funny,' she said at last. 'Sometimes when I wake up, for the first few moments, maybe a minute sometimes, I don't remember what's happened. And in those moments, I'm floating, blissful, without memories.' She paused. 'I just don't remember that they're gone,' she said, incredulity in her tone. 'And then it crashes in on me all over again, new and fresh and devastating every time. It's like torture, the morning ritual of feeling like my body is free-falling from a great height, my heart ripping out.'

She let out a hard little bark of a laugh, and the line, suddenly free of static, was quiet, as if embarrassed by her outburst. Marta said nothing, but Freya could hear her breath, heavy at the other end. Suddenly, more than anything in the world, she wanted to cry out. What had happened to them? While she was away, Jack had told her that he and Sam had been out a lot on the boat. But she remembered only fragments of conversations, interrupted snippets told as the phone was passed excitedly between her husband and son. What she didn't know is where they had been heading on that last day. What had they been doing when they disappeared? Why hadn't they radioed for help when they got into trouble? Had they been too far from land? Where were they now? These were questions she had asked a hundred times a day. But no one knew. And now she mostly asked the questions only to herself. It drove her mad, the not knowing, pricked hotly at her brain; sent her into a downward spiral of imagining. Now, thinking of it in this moment, she wanted to let out loud, racking sobs of grief, uncontrolled and unabashed. But, for once with Marta, she held it in. 'I'm sorry,' was all she said, her voice muffled with emotion. 'I'm sorry.'

'Don't be sorry. It's okay. You can say whatever you like to me.'

'I love you. You know that, don't you?'

'Sure I do. I love you too.'

They both lapsed into silence once more. Freya waited but she could no longer feel the tight black clutch of grief around her heart. She had ridden the tide of her emotion and not been entirely swallowed by its darkness. Perhaps she was making progress. She looked at her watch. It was still early but she didn't want to talk any more. 'So. Much as I'd like to stay on the phone all night to you, I must go to bed. And, after all, you've got a cock to serve in the morning.'

Marta laughed out loud. 'Don't remind me.' She hesitated, as if there was something else she wanted to say. But when her voice came again it was final and light. 'Sleep tight and call me often. Okay?'

'Okay. Good night.' And Freya hung up.

6

It began as always.

'Dark Queen Beira, the mother of all the deities of Scotland, was old and wild and fierce. When she was angry she was as biting as the wind and as terrifying as a storm-filled sea.'

Freya paused, resting the book in her lap for a moment, and looked down at Sam, who was half sitting, half lying under the bedcovers. It was night-time and they were leaning against each other on Sam's bed, both propped up by pillows. The lamp gave off a warm yellow light and, through the open window, Freya could hear the soft sound of waves breaking upon the shore. It was her favourite part of the day – a time of late summer sunsets, wishes and possibilities. She raised the book and continued reading.

'Beira had lived for hundreds of years. But she never died of old age because, at the onset of every spring, she drank the magic waters of the Well of Youth on the Green Island of the West, a place where it was always summer and where the trees were always full of fruit. The island drifted on the Atlantic, and sometimes, it is said, appeared close to the Hebrides. Many sailors have searched the ocean looking for it in vain – for often it was just beyond their vision, hidden by mist or having sunk beneath the waves.'

'Is that true, Mum?' Sam craned his head to look at her. He was wide-eyed, puzzled – his literal father's literal son.

'Perhaps,' said Freya, gazing back at him. 'But more likely it's just a myth.'

'What's a myth?'

'A story, a legend. Something that might not be fact, that can't be proved.' She paused. 'But it still might be something we choose to believe in.'

'So the Green Island might not actually exist?'

'No, perhaps not. But then again, perhaps it's just that no one ever finds it.'

'Maybe you and Dad and I will find it when we're out in the boat sometime.'

'Yes, maybe.'

Sam was silent for a few moments, perhaps thinking of a voyage over the waves. 'But Beira always knew how to find the Green Island, didn't she?'

'Yes, she did.' Freya smiled and kissed the top of his head. 'And what happened when she got there and tasted the magic water of the Well of Youth?'

'She grew young again. Then she came back to Scotland, where she was a beautiful girl once more with long, flowing hair.'

Freya nodded. 'That's right. But with each passing

month, Beira aged fast. And by the time winter returned, she was an old woman again, beginning her reign as fierce Queen Beira.'

Sam turned to Freya once more and pulled a face. 'But that can't be true, can it, Mum? That must be a myth.'

'Yes, I think perhaps it is.'

'Although certain things can undergo a metamorphosis. Like flies and other insects. Crustaceans and molluscs.'

'That's right,' said Freya, slightly taken aback. 'Have you been talking to Granddad again?'

'Uh-huh. He called Dad the other day.'

Freya nodded. 'I see. Yes. But Beira's was more of a magical transformation. Rather than the change of a caterpillar into a butterfly.'

'Do you believe in magic, Mum?'

Freya looked at him. 'Perhaps.'

'Well, I don't believe it. Beira couldn't grow old that quickly and then become young again. I think it's really just a story about the seasons.'

Freya suppressed a laugh and dropped the book onto the bed. 'Yes, most likely, Sam. Your father would certainly agree.' And *his* father would be shocked at the mere contemplation of anything out of the ordinary. She kissed Sam's head again then stood, gazing at him for a few moments, before turning out the light.

The dusk of summer cast a shadowy light through the windows. Freya heard Sam shift his head down into the pillows, getting comfortable in anticipation of sleep. 'Sing that song, Mum.'

She smiled. 'The one about the storm?'

'Hmm. I like that one.'

Because even though it came from a magical tale, it was about a shipwreck and all things below the sea fascinated him. So in the half-light, beside her son, watching his small body lying safely in bed, she sang:

> Full fathom five thy father lies;
> Of his bones are coral made;
> Those are pearls that were his eyes;
> Nothing of him that doth fade,
> But doth suffer a sea-change
> Into something rich and strange.

But then the room began to fill with water. Quietly, innocently almost, as it always did. And, as always, she couldn't tell where the water was coming from. She heard its low trickle and then watched it climb slowly up the legs of the chest of drawers, over the tops of Sam's small shoes lying haphazardly across the floor where he had just pulled them off and left them, urgently moving on to the next thing.

She saw the water rise gradually over her own feet, up to her ankles and beyond, ever rising. She watched it soak the dirty clothes piled in the corner, saw it rising inexorably upwards. She was powerless to stop it. She felt that clearly. She looked towards the window, saw the pale light gaining access there, spilling over the rising tide within the room, the water inching its way up the walls. Where was it coming from? She couldn't understand it. Before long it spilled over the bed and covered the sleeping form of her son. She tried to move towards him but she couldn't; her feet were cemented to the floor. She felt a flash of fear move through her body, and still the water flowed into the room, rising ever upwards. Now it was approaching her neck, and before long it would rise over her head.

The water continued to creep. Freya took a deep breath and held it as her body became entirely submerged. For a moment she stayed stock still, then she opened her eyes and looked. They were no longer within the confines of the bedroom. Instead it had given way to a vast watery expanse. Beyond the edge of her vision, there was something, she was sure. Something in the darkness. In front of her, she could no longer see Sam's silhouette, his sleeping form, and fear bolted through her again. She looked deeper. There was someone, or something there – watching her. She opened her mouth to speak but no words came. Only the escape of breath. She wanted to call out to Sam, to say 'Goodbye.' For she knew that this was goodbye. But no words came out of her mouth. And then she knew that there was no breath left in her. But it didn't feel like death. She closed her eyes and surrendered. 'Goodbye my son,' she said.

Then she woke up.

Freya opened her eyes. She felt the pillow wet with tears. It took her a moment to remember, to realise that she had had the nightmare again. But it took her turning over in the empty bed, feeling the cold absence on Jack's side, to remember everything. To feel the sickening reality claw its way out of the dark. Those are pearls that were his eyes.

Freya lay still for a few moments. She was always drained after the dream. More than that, she felt it was trying to tell her something. But quite what it was, its meaning, always eluded her. Finally she looked at the clock. It was only 9 p.m. She flicked on the bedside lamp. Yellow light spilled into the room, and with it the last clutches of the dream – any resonance it might have had – vanished in an instant. Besides, what was there for it to tell her? Her husband and her child were dead, drowned. And there was no way anyone could feel anything beyond despair at the remembrance of that.

Freya closed her eyes and swallowed. Her throat was parched and she had a bitter taste of saltwater in her mouth. It was simply fallout from the dream, she knew – her doctor had told her enough times. It was her mind playing dirty tricks on her. She climbed unsteadily out of bed and made her way slowly across the creaking bedroom floor. The wood felt warm, reassuring against her feet, and yet she still felt cold to her core, had the sense of being disconnected from her own body. In the hallway she paused at the threshold of Sam's room, her hand resting lightly upon the doorknob. But still she could not open it. Ridiculous as it seemed, she placed her ear upon the door and listened. What was she trying to hear? she wondered. The sound of her son breathing? His voice calling out to her in the night? Or perhaps it was the absence of sound she needed to hear. For a moment she listened intently. All was quiet. The only noise was the faint sound of waves breaking on the shore. Freya's hand fell back down to her side. Perhaps tomorrow, she thought. Perhaps by then she would be able to do it. To look at everything that was still there, that was exactly as he had left it.

Turning away, she made her way down the hallway into the kitchen. Even in the dark, she could manoeuvre her way around it effortlessly – the long table against the north wall, the island in its centre, work surfaces along the eastern wall. She walked to the sink in front of the kitchen window, turned on the tap and stuck her head beneath it, greedily drinking the water down. She became conscious of the dull ache in her throat, as if all the breath had been squeezed out of it. But she blinked the thought away and continued to drink. It was always this way – after the dream. As Freya turned the tap off, the sound of running water was replaced instantly by silence. Outside, there was barely any cloud in the sky and moonlight shone down into the walled garden. It was unkempt, overrun, weeds strangling the pathway, the trees and bushes overgrown. But beyond it, she knew, beyond the whitewashed wall that ran around the lighthouse enclosure, was the sea. Freya opened the door.

It was still, the wind that had picked up earlier had dropped, and it was surprisingly warm given the lack of cloud. Barefoot, she made her way across the garden and then followed the path. When she reached the gate, she unlocked it and tiptoed down the slope to the beach, over the grassy knolls and the shingle. The sea was calm, flat, and when she reached its edge she dipped her toe in. It was cold. She took a step forward until her feet were submerged and a shiver ran down her spine. It was the temperature of the water, she told herself, watching her skin shimmer and distort below the surface. She fought the urge to take another step and then another and raised her head.

After a moment, a broad flash of light arced across her gaze, reaching – it seemed – almost to the horizon. Then there was only a dark ocean. Seven seconds later it came again. One, two, three, Freya counted in her head. It was magical, beautiful, this interchange of light and dark, making it possible for things to be saved from the clutches of the sea. After a time, Freya realised that she was looking for something to emerge. A boat, perhaps. She smiled and a tear slid silently down her cheek. Yes a boat, bearing her son and her husband back to her once more. She narrowed her eyes. Perhaps if she longed for it enough it might just be possible, if she simply wished for it enough. The lamp arced to the horizon, dissipated the darkness for three seconds, and then was gone.

7

When she returned to the cottage, Freya poured herself a glass of wine and sat, drinking it, at the kitchen table. She was tired, her thoughts sluggish and dull, but she knew that she would be unable to sleep if she went back to bed. Her hands played with the pile of letters in front of her, the mail that had accumulated at the cottage in her absence and that she had stacked on the table to be dealt with when she was ready. She picked the letters up now, one by one, scanned them cursorily and then placed them slowly back down on the table. At the bottom of the pile was a thick brown envelope addressed to her. She picked it up and turned it over in her hands. It was heavy and on the back was a stamp indicating that it came from a Dr MacCallister at the National Museum in Edinburgh. She frowned, wondering what it could be. She had no idea who Dr MacCallister was or why he would be writing to her. Curious, she turned the package over one more time and then ripped it open.

Inside were a number of typed A4 pages, held together with a bulldog clip, and on the top of the pile was a letter addressed to her. It was dated three months previously. Intrigued, Freya read it.

Dear Mrs McPherson,

My name is Rory MacCallister, and I am a curator at the National Museum in Edinburgh. I have long been a friend of your father-in-law, Alister McPherson, and as such I hesitated to write to you, knowing as I do the tragic circumstances of the passing of your husband and son, for which I offer my most heartfelt sympathy. I hope that this letter will not prove to be unwelcome as a reminder of that time. Rather I hope that it will serve as a touchstone to a happy time your husband and son shared together. It is with this in mind that I continue.

As you may know, last Easter Jack and Sam discovered a Bellarmine jar sandwiched into a crevice in the Torran Rocks while they were sailing in the area. Your husband sent it on to Alister, who in turn passed it to me. A number of these jars – made in the sixteenth and early seventeenth centuries in the Netherlands – have been recovered from shipwrecks off the Scottish coast, the *Swan* being one of the most famous in the Western Highlands. What was most striking about the jar recovered by your husband was how amazingly well preserved it was, Cardinal Bellarmine's face – on the outer surface of the jar – being clearly visible and whole, the glaze practically unscathed, the neck of the bottle stoppered and still sealed. It really was quite remarkable given the journey the object must have taken.

As many of these jars were used as means of carrying liquids, beer and wine in particular, I passed the find on to a colleague of mine who is a specialist in analysing items recovered from wrecks at sea. He carried out a CT scan of the jar – to determine if there was anything inside it – and this revealed what looked like a roll of paper. Now, while the jar had proved remarkably resilient and watertight, after all the time at sea the contents were in fairly bad shape – decayed and decomposed. But my colleague is exceptionally skilled and managed to remove the paper, dry it out and treat it. And he discovered that it was not just a roll of paper but letters. Quite miraculous.

To cut a technical story short, the letters have been radio-carbon dated for authenticity, treated to preserve them and a lot of the text has been salvaged – although some, as you will see from the pages attached, is missing. The letters have been transcribed into more modern English for ease of reading, but it appears that they were written by a soldier aboard the *Speedwell*, one of the six ships, including the more famous *Swan* which I mentioned above, which were part of a flotilla sent by Cromwell to quash Royalist support in the Highlands. It disappeared in a ferocious storm in 1653, presumed sunken, but the wreck was never found. Few records remain about the expedition or what happened to those who took part in it. So they are a remarkable find.

I wanted to send copies of the letters to you, as without your husband and son they would never have come to light, and I understand Sam, in particular, was fascinated by the jar and what it might contain. Perhaps he would have been as amazed as I am by what was salvaged.

With kindest regards,
J. C. MacCallister

Freya placed MacCallister's letter on the table and closed her eyes. She remembered her conversation with Sam on the phone on the day he and Jack had found the jar. He had been incredibly excited, stumbling over his words, telling her the story of Cardinal Bellarmine. She vaguely recalled him saying he would give the jar to his grandfather, but she had had no idea that he'd ever done so, let alone anything beyond this. She opened her eyes and flicked through the letters once more, breathing in deeply, as if to inhale the scent of salt and sea spray that the originals must once have contained. Letters in a bottle. She smiled. She had to admit her curiosity was aroused. Turning to the first letter she began to read.

8

6 September 1653

Speedwell

My dearest Josie,

We arrived in Scottish waters yesterday. I do not know whether you care about this now or indeed whether I will ever send this letter even if the means to do so are at my disposal. But I feel the need to write it, to make a connection with you despite the distance between us.

After departing Plymouth three days since, our journey passed largely without event. We made our way around the treacherous Eddystone rocks, around the coast of Cornwall and from there sailed northwards, first with Wales to our starboard side and then Ireland to our port. We were blessed with fine weather almost the whole of the journey and only once did a gale start up, as we approached Chicken Rock, off the southern tip of the Isle of Man. That is a dangerous spot, Josie, the rocks jutting out of a sea which is as black as pitch at night, unlit by fire or lantern, and I feared that, as with many ships, the spot might prove to be our undoing.

But while we suffered heavy rain and a turbulent sea, the storm stayed mostly on our tail and so we avoided the worst of it. From there we continued northwesterly, along the coastline of southern Scotland and shortly after emerged into Highland waters.

The first island we skirted was Islay, the southernmost of the Highland islands. It is low lying and marshy, a man named Duncan told me, one of our force and a Scotsman originally from these parts. The population, he claimed, often come to a famous well to drink, turning once sunwise around it – in a circle east to west the way the sun rises and sets – before drawing water. They believe that in doing so it will be blessed. Blessed by who exactly is anyone's guess. It seems nothing but nonsense to me. But Duncan said that such customs are not infrequent in these parts.

Islay's neighbour, the island of Jura, is by comparison mountainous. Along the middle there are four hills of considerable height. As a result of the mountains, Duncan told me, Jura is said to be the wholesomest plot of land in all of Scotland, with fresh breezes and pure air, the population rarely becoming sick and living to be extraordinarily old. One of the natives, he said, died at the age of 180 years, while others have seen at least one hundred Christmases in their homes. The more I hear these tales, Josie, and Duncan speaking with such reverence about the air, the water, the unexplainable miracles of these isles, the more I feel he believes that we have entered a magical kingdom. While his accent has no doubt faded, he clearly still believes the silly superstitions of these parts.

Leaving Jura behind, we skirted its neighbour Scarba, and arrived at the Sound of Mull. At last, the object of our mission came into view – Duart Castle, seated on a peninsular jutting out into the water. Our orders were to take the castle and quell the uprising of the Royalist Macleans. Sadly, for our Lord Protector, Cromwell, things did not go according to plan. Having surveyed the area for some time, we prepared to take Duart, and its inhabitants, by force, according to our instructions. We loaded ourselves with muskets, rifles and ammunition, and then took small sailing boats to the land. But as we approached from behind, readied for battle, it quickly became apparent that the loyalist Macleans had fled. The Castle was deserted and we encountered no resist-ance whatsoever gaining access. So it was a victory – although a hollow one.

It seems, if the small pieces of information gathered from the locals are to be believed, the Macleans sailed for Tiree some time ago. No doubt, as a result, we will set off for the outer-lying islands, but without more detailed knowledge of exactly where they are to be found, any mission to locate them would doubtless fail.

And so, for the moment, we are taking in the weather and scenery. It is a wild beauty here on Mull, a ragged splendour: crags, moorland and rocks, sea and mountains. One minute we are bathed in sunshine, the next there is cloud and then rain, the elements often following rapidly one after the other. The sunshine casts a candour, a beauty over everything. But when the weather turns sour, the cold mist and drizzle make this place utterly dreary, like quite the end of the earth. 'Dreich' is the word Duncan uses for it. And it is as perfectly miserable sounding as that which it describes.

But I must not fall into a black state of mind. Although I fear it is too late for that. Before we came below deck to sleep, as we looked out over the deserted darkness of the ocean, Duncan told me of a famous shipwreck in these parts, a wind-battered remnant of the Spanish Armada, *Florencia*, laden with gold and silver coin. When the Spanish double-crossed the Scots who had come to their aid, the *Florencia* mysteriously blew up and its cargo of coin sank into the silt of the sea bed and was never recovered. Neither were the crew. I looked at the impenetrable darkness of the water once more. It was like a veil drawn over the past, the carcasses of ships, coins, and the bodies of countless men strewn about its bed. Is that my destiny, I wondered then, floating here and there on the tide, unbound to any place, fighting and suppressing rebellion? I risk death here for a commander I feel no strong allegiance to and leave behind what has grown to be most dear to me.

I felt a hollowness inside me then. This place stirs it in me, I am sure. It has a wildness being so far north, subject to its own reason, its own remote rhythm. And that is in part due to the sea and its dominance. It is more master here than Cromwell, that is for sure.

I am haunted by what you told me before I left and I am only sorry that I was rough and that I did not speak the words that you longed for and deserved to hear. It pains me to have parted from you in such a way. But I trust now that we will return to England sooner than I had hoped. Then I will see you again and will speak all as I should have done the last time we were together.

Until then
I am your
Edward

After she had finished reading, Freya took a large mouthful of wine. She still couldn't quite believe that these letters had survived. And the contents, as MacCallister had suggested, were equally astonishing. A dangerous yet fruitless voyage, into the wind and sea-lashed wilds of the north, in pursuit of a vanished adversary. It was a journey that would have been frustrating at the best of times, but even more so for a soldier battling his own stained soul and an ever-quickening desire for home.

As Freya turned the page to continue, the telephone rang. It was shrill, invasive in the quiet of the night. How appropriate, Freya thought. It wouldn't be Marta (she had already spoken to her that evening), so that left her mother, Joan. For a moment she thought about ignoring it. But it would be better to get it over with and cut the call short. It was late, after all. Freya sighed, feeling tired at the prospect of the conversation. She grabbed the phone and answered it as she wandered back to bed.

'Hello darling, how *are* you?' Joan always got in the first words of any call, even when she was the one ringing.

'I'm fine thanks, Mum. Everything's okay.'

As Freya tried and failed, as always, to reassure her mother, she found herself telling her instead about Edward's letters in a bottle, their discovery at the Torran Rocks, and their final journey to Edinburgh.

After all, it gave them something else, besides her mental health, to talk about.

9

It was late morning two days later.

Freya was still in bed, unable to face the day, when she heard the sound of a horn rising up towards the cottage from the ocean. She closed her eyes, hoping that the boat was not signalling her and would simply pass on. But a few moments later the sound came again. She opened her eyes and waited. When the horn came a third time there was no ignoring it any longer.

She struggled out of bed, her mind as much as her body a dead weight, and dressed as quickly as she could. When she was ready, she left the room, avoiding looking at herself for long in the mirror. Still, she was aware of the dark circles under her eyes.

Outside, the day was cold and blustery, clouds scudding swiftly across the sky. As Freya walked down to the jetty, she felt the rough refreshing blast of the wind in her hair. Turning the corner, she caught a glimpse of Callum's boat, bobbing on the water, about to dock. As she raised her hand to wave to him, she saw that he was not alone in the cabin. She squinted, trying to see who his passenger was. She caught a glimpse of long dark hair, but that was as much as she could make out. By the time Freya reached them, Callum was roping the boat. Then the passenger jumped onto the jetty and began to move towards her. She caught her breath. It was Marta.

Freya felt the simultaneous sting of tears and anger as she walked towards her sister. She tried and failed to summon a smile.

'What the hell are you doing here?' she said, almost resentfully, as they met. Then Marta wrapped her arms around her and she felt an instant sense of intimacy and comfort.

'Well, that's nice. Especially after the journey I've had. And, for the record, could you live any further away?'

Freya pulled away from her and smiled. 'It was kind of the point.'

'Yeah, yeah.' Marta scrutinised her sister. 'Christ alive. You look a sight. Big night?'

'Something like that.' And, in spite of herself, Freya laughed. 'It's good to see you.'

'You too,' said Marta, and hugged her again.

Callum came up behind them, and despite the fact that both women were tall, at well over six feet he towered above them. He wasn't wearing his black-and-white hat today and his dirty blond hair stuck up in tufts from his head giving him a youthful, less serious look than when Freya had seen him last. He smiled, and it lit up his face. 'Can you believe who I found lurking around the harbour this morning?'

'Not really. But nothing surprises me with this one.'

Callum nodded. 'Marta tells me it's a spontaneous visit.'

'Indeed,' said Freya, turning her attention back to her sister. 'So when did you get here?'

'Last night. Too late to persuade anyone to bring me out. So I grabbed a room at a B&B. Callum was lucky enough to bump into me this morning.' She grinned at him and headed back to the boat to collect her things.

'It was kind of you to bring her, Callum.' Freya smiled at him. 'Will you come up to the cottage? Have a cup of tea?'

'No, thanks,' he said, shaking his head. 'I've a tour to take out soon from Iona. Besides, I'm sure you two have plenty to catch up on.' Callum paused for a moment. 'How are you, Freya?' he asked softly.

'Oh, I'm okay,' she replied, suddenly conscious of her hair being battered by the wind. She ran her hands over it and wrestled it into a ponytail. 'Good days and bad.' Good nights and bad, she wanted to add, but didn't. She didn't want to have to explain.

'Well, that's to be expected, I suppose. But just let me know if you ever need the company and I'll look in on you on my way back from a trip.'

Freya felt the sweetness of his words, their care. 'Thanks, I will.'

'Okay I'm all set,' said Marta, rejoining them, a large bag on each shoulder.

'All right then, catch you later.' And Callum turned and headed back down the jetty.

As the sisters made their way up the hill to the cottage, Marta turned a couple of times to wave at the receding form of Callum's boat. Then she grinned at Freya.

'What is it?' Freya asked.

'Oh, nothing,' said Marta, and winked at her.

10

Sitting opposite one another at the kitchen table, a pot of tea between them, Freya wondered what her sister was thinking. No doubt she had spotted the unwashed pots in the sink, among them several wineglasses, empty but for an incriminating film of red at their base. Perhaps they had gone unnoticed. But it was unlikely. Still, if Marta had seen them, she said nothing, and Freya loved her for it. She looked her sister over. She was as beautiful as ever – long brown hair, dark eyes, full, irreverent red lips. They had been chatting, catching up, nothing deep or contentious. Yet Freya was sure there was something, unspoken, lurking beneath her usual bravado.

'So how long are you thinking of staying?' She tried to make the question sound nonchalant.

'Trying to get rid of me already?' Marta answered, quick smart.

'No, no, not at all,' Freya rushed in. Then she saw Marta smile. 'I was just wondering.'

'I don't know. But I'm flexible. Could be open ended.'

'Open ended?' Freya repeated. 'How does that work with a full-on job as a lawyer in London?'

'Ah, that.' Marta paused. 'It really wasn't working out with the cock, and that meant that it really wasn't working out at work. I decided to quit.'

So that was it. 'Isn't that a little hasty?'

Marta shook her head. 'No. I've been thinking about it for a while.' She took a breath. 'He was never going to leave his wife and that made the whole thing pretty untenable. Besides, I can get a job like that anywhere else.'

Freya nodded. 'I see,' was all she said.

'So, as I'm owed holiday, it seemed sensible to take some time off during my notice period and come and see you. Two birds, one stone.' Marta's tone was light, but beneath it Freya suspected that she was hurting.

'I see,' she said again. She was longing to ask if Marta was okay, but she knew that if her sister didn't bring something up directly she didn't want to talk about it. 'And the cock agreed that this was a sensible approach?'

'I made it clear that, if he knew what was good for him, he really wouldn't mind how much time I spent up here with you. Personal time, on so many levels.'

Freya snorted and Marta smiled.

'But don't panic. I won't cramp your reclusive style. I thought just for a few weeks perhaps. And then I'll be off.' She winked at Freya, but there was something beneath the look.

Freya reached over the table and took Marta's hand. 'Darling sis, I'm very glad to see you. Thank you for coming. And you are welcome to stay as long as you like. Are you okay?'

Marta nodded briskly and kissed her sister's hand. Then she sat back in her chair, looked around and, as Freya had anticipated, changed the subject. 'It brings back a whole load of memories for me being here, you know. It's been a while since I've been to Ailsa Cleit. That's right, isn't it?'

Freya nodded. That was what Jack's father, Alister, had called it when he bought the island for his wife. And it had stuck. Everyone for miles around knew it as that. The Rock of Ailsa.

'You know what?' said Freya. 'I can still see Jack's mother, as clearly as if it were yesterday, standing by the shoreline, gazing out to sea, her blonde hair whipped by the wind.' Freya smiled. Ailsa had the wildness of the Orkneys within her bones and a greater affinity with the water than the land. She had eyes like shimmering rock pools and her skin was so pale it was almost translucent.

'She was a strange woman, wasn't she?' Marta said. 'I don't think she said more than ten words to me in total, in all the times I met her.'

'Me neither. And I saw her a lot more than you.'

Ailsa had been taciturn, unfathomable, and Freya sometimes thought that she had the cold saltwater of the Atlantic, rather than blood, coursing through her veins. But once, perhaps only once, there had been a moment of connection between them. As Freya was leaving, after her very first trip to the island, Ailsa had taken her hand and looked into her eyes. Something had passed between them, but quite what it was, Freya wasn't sure. Then Ailsa had smiled, let go of her and the moment was gone for ever. When Ailsa died, she left the island to Jack. But Freya always felt that, secretly, it had been a gift to her. A gift given with a smile and a look as deep as the ocean.

'Do you remember when you finally got round to renovating this cottage? You were pregnant with Sam. It was chaos.'

Freya nodded. She also remembered that she had never been happier.

'And I seem to recall you standing on the beach and yelling at the ocean?'

Freya smiled. 'I did.'

'What was it you kept shouting?'

'I feel like the Stevensons,' she replied, laughing.

'That's right. And every time you did it, the builders practically shat themselves. They were petrified you were going to go into labour on their watch.'

'It was a brilliant way of keeping them on schedule.'

Both women laughed. 'And then you basically lived here, didn't you, after Sam was born?'

Freya nodded. They'd spent a lot of time on the island then; less with the advent of school and careers that led to greater ties to London. But they always came back, washed in by the tide. And it had been a dream of Freya's, barely acknowledged, unrealistic after all, that eventually they would settle here and leave London behind. It had been a vain, unlikely hope. Impossible, ironically, until now.

'When I put my stuff in the spare bedroom I passed

Sam's room.' Marta's voice was soft, tentative. 'Have you been in yet?'

Freya shook her head. She had hovered at the threshold several times, but still hadn't been quite able to take the plunge.

'I really think it will help.'

The sisters looked at one another and Freya nodded her head.

'Yes. Perhaps it's time,' she said.

11

Freya flicked through the worn copy of *Treasure Island*, its pages close to her face. The smell of the old paper, its notes of grass and vanilla, rose towards her reassuringly, pulling at her memory. She heard Sam's voice, talking of pirates, maps and the search for gold, of murder and intrigue, friendship and loyalty. It had been his favourite book and he had read it over ten times. In fact, he knew it almost by heart. She flicked through the pages once more, inhaling deeply. Most of all, she remembered, he was fascinated by the black spot. How a dirty stain on a piece of paper had had the power to kill Billy Bones. Maybe he'd died of a heart attack, she'd suggested, or a stroke brought on from all the rum. Perhaps he'd simply died of fright. But Sam had shaken his head defiantly. No, he had said sadly, it was not something that could be explained like that. It was unexplainable. And perhaps that was why it bothered him. She smiled, ran her fingers over the tattered cover and then replaced the book on the shelf.

Marta had gone for a walk around the island. She said it was to get her bearings once more, but Freya knew that it was to give her some space. And, in that space, she had taken Marta's advice and ventured into Sam's room for the first time. The curtains had been pulled to, and its smell was different to how she remembered it. Faded, withered, almost like a tomb. She had immediately lain down on the bed and sought out the smell of Sam's small body on the still-unwashed sheets. Only when she was satisfied that she could detect it did the furious racing of her heart subside. For a long time, she had remained there, prone, her eyes closed, breathing deeply, feeling connected to something that she knew was gone. Eventually she had turned over and opened her eyes.

In the darkness of the room, the ceiling had glittered, tiny dots of silver spattered across its surface. For a moment Freya simply gazed at them. And then she remembered. They were stars that she and her son had painstakingly arranged into constellations. She could make out the Plough and Orion, Cassiopeia and Ursa Major. Yes, they had spent the best part of a week creating this universe in his room. She smiled as tears slid down onto the pillow. The universe wasn't quite the same any more.

For a long time Freya lay on the bed, surveying the room. She looked at the elaborate map of Treasure Island that Jack had created on Sam's wall, the train set in the corner that he had constructed with his son. She looked at the ship in a bottle that Sam's grandfather had made for him and that had always sat in pride of place on his chest of drawers. Alongside it lay an old wooden pipe that Sam had found beachcombing. It had once belonged to a pirate, of this he was convinced.

Finally, she rose and looked under the bed for the boxes she knew Sam kept there. His most treasured possessions. She pulled one out, sat down on the floor beside it and removed the lid. Almost instantly she came across the fossilised remains of some sea creatures that resembled highly elaborate necklaces. Freya loved these, and something about their ornate beauty, so delicately preserved, had always made her want to cry. But today when she looked over them her eyes remained dry.

She placed the fossils back into the box and rummaged through the books and drawings it also contained. Robert Louis Stevenson, *Kidnapped*, *Prince Otto*, *The Master of Ballantrae* and *The Strange Case of Dr Jekyll and Mr Hyde* – a book that, after much discussion, it had been decided Sam wasn't quite old enough to read just yet. The fact that it was nonetheless here was, for once, not down to her. It must have come from Jack's father. Freya frowned and continued. She found a tattered picture of the Pharos lighthouse – an old favourite of Sam's – marking the entrance to the shallow harbour of Alexandria. There were other pictures of lighthouses, Eddystone Rock, Bell Rock, Skerryvore and the Isle of May, and a well-thumbed picture of Lucy Anderson. Freya stopped when she came to this last item. It was a story that had fascinated Sam and one that he could recite by heart.

'It happened in 1791.'

Freya could hear his small voice, still incredulous despite the number of retellings.

'The keeper was George Anderson, who, with his wife

and five of his children, was suffocated by fumes from the lighthouse beacon. Only the youngest child at the lighthouse, Lucy, survived. She married the man who rescued her and moved with him to America.'

Freya had always thought Lucy's story strange and miraculous, but never before had she felt so acutely its arbitrariness; the thin pale line that separated those who lived from those who died. She placed the picture back in the box and began shuffling its contents around once more. As she did so, her eye caught upon something metallic in a bottom corner. She reached forwards, grasped it and pulled it out. It was an old copper key, long and slightly greening with age, with three teeth, two thick and one thin, and intertwining loops of metal at its end. Freya ran her fingers slowly over its length and wondered whether this was also an object discovered beachcombing. She doubted it, as Sam didn't hide things from her and she had never seen it before. She would have remembered. Then she caught a glimpse of *Dr Jekyll and Mr Hyde* and frowned again. Perhaps it was another secret gift that someone had given to Sam. She weighed the key in her hands and tried to imagine what it might open. A trunk or a case, perhaps. But the key seemed too large for that. She looked it over one last time and then threw it into the box which she slid back under the bed. That was enough for today.

12

That evening, Marta was standing at the hob cooking risotto while Freya chopped salad sitting at the kitchen table. Rain lashed the windows and a hard wind juddered the panes. But inside the wood burner crackled, spilling out heat, and the lamps filled the kitchen with a homely glow. Freya had to admit that it was nice to have the company. Especially now. Eating alone made her feel a peculiar form of sadness. She took a mouthful of red wine – which Marta had poured for her, unquestioningly and without remark – and continued to slice cucumber.

The ring of the telephone shattered the companionable silence.

Freya put down the knife, wiped her hands and picked up the receiver.

'Hello, darling.'

Freya looked at Marta and rolled her eyes. It was Joan. 'Hi, Mum. How's things?'

'Better for getting hold of you again. It seems you're elusive even on a tiny island.' Her mother let the rebuke hang on the air for a second before stampeding through her news and settling close to where she really wanted the conversation to be. 'And, darling, how are *you*?'

'I'm okay. It's nice to have Marta here.'

'Well, of course. It's important to have company.' Freya smiled. Slowly they were inching towards it. 'Which reminds me. I've been meaning to ask you for ages. Have you been in touch with Alister?'

Freya hadn't seen or spoken to Jack's father since the funeral. She found him a difficult, stern Scotsman, all facts and rigidity. In his life, everything could be explained, nothing was uncertain. And, after the accident, Freya felt that there was nothing but uncertainty in hers.

'Really, Freya, you should get in touch. He's all alone now, you know.'

Freya nodded. This was her mother's way of saying that Alister had lost his son and his grandson; that this was a family tragedy and not just Freya's personal loss. 'I know,' she said. 'I promise I'll call him.'

'Well, you should. Especially as he sent that jar on to the museum. That was so nice of him.' Her mother paused and Freya waited for the next assault. 'And what of Torin? You must have been to see him by now?'

'Not yet. I haven't been here very long, remember?' Freya blushed nonetheless. Even the lightest of her mother's touches had always been able to make her feel guilty. 'But I'm planning a visit soon.'

'Well, I'm glad to hear it. Really, Freya, you can't closet yourself away up there.'

Now they were getting closer to it, to what she really wanted to say.

'So, darling, have you had any thoughts about when you are coming home?'

There it was. Clearly her parents had been hoping, ever since she arrived at Ailsa Cleit, that being there would prove too much and she would come straight back to London. But now she had been at the lighthouse nearly a week, they realised that this wasn't going to happen. 'I don't know, Mum.'

'What do you mean, you don't know?' Joan's incredulity was palpable – that there was no plan, no schedule.

'It means that I don't know,' Freya shot out. 'That I'll come back when I'm ready.' Then, regretting her snappiness, she added, 'Besides, Marta's here.'

'But your sister can't stay for ever.' Her mother's tone was forlorn.

'I know, Mum. But I just need to be here at the moment. I think it'll help me to come to terms with things.'

'But, darling,' her mother persisted, 'I don't see why you can't come to terms with things closer to home. Closer to us.'

Freya raised her eyes heavenwards and tried not to audibly tut. But she knew her mother only did it because she cared. 'I think a change of scene will be helpful to me.'

'But not one this radical. The doctor didn't think it would be, did he?'

Freya smiled. Round one to Joan. She knew there wasn't

much she could counter with when her own doctor had doubted that isolation would be beneficial. 'Even so, for now, especially with Marta here . . . '

Joan was silent on the other end and Freya could picture the pursed lips she always had when her daughter disagreed with her. It was usually around this time in their conversations that her mother admonished her for having inherited the stubbornness of her grandmother, Maggie. Yet it appeared to Freya that Joan had also inherited a healthy dose of stubbornness herself.

'Okay, Freya,' she said tartly, 'I'm going to put your father on. See if he can talk some sense into you.'

And before Freya could say anything else, the baton of the conversation was passed over. Her father chatted amiably enough and only once ventured into the territory his wife liked to plunder. 'Won't you come home, darling?'

She could hear the pleading in his tone. But the truth was that she was already home.

Freya handed the phone to Marta and moved into the sitting room, towards the bookshelves opposite the sofa, which were clustered, not just with books, but with photographs of her family. There were lots of her, Jack and Sam, as a family and individually. But these were not what she was looking for. Her mother had reminded her of something. Eventually she caught sight of it on the top shelf.

The photograph had been taken in autumn, a few weeks after Sam's birth, and in it Joan's mother, Maggie, was smiling broadly, clutching the bundle that was her grandson tightly to her. Maggie's once-auburn hair glowed white in the fading daylight and the scene seemed so close, so fresh, that Freya could almost hear her grandmother's laughter as it floated on the wind that day, as strong but as light as kittiwake wings.

As Freya looked at the image, the contours of the island visible in the background, the sea in the distance, she remembered her grandmother's stories of St Kilda, the tiny island on the very fringes of the Outer Hebrides, where Maggie had been born and that she had left in her youth. She never talked about why that was, but Freya thought she knew the reason. For a long time the newborns of St Kilda had been plagued with a mysterious sickness, killing many within days of their birth. Some said it was the islanders' dirty habits, their unventilated homes; others that it was the pink-tinged oil of the fulmar that they burned or the rich, bitter effect of the bird's fatty meat on the mothers' milk. Some said that it was all of these things; others that it was none and that the sole cause was that the midwife was a filthy wench. Her grandmother had never admitted that the sickness was the reason she had left her home, but Freya had always suspected that it was the case. She had seen a future for her children written in the graveyard and decided in that moment upon a different future for herself.

Freya looked at the photograph of Maggie holding Sam so closely to her, and her eyes filled with tears. If only she had followed in her grandmother's footsteps, had left behind the danger of this island, however difficult that was for her – perhaps she too would have had a different history to tell.

'Whatever she said, don't let it upset you.' Marta had

come up quietly behind Freya, her conversation with their parents over.

'She didn't say anything.' Freya managed a smile.

'Yeah, but sometimes she has a way of saying something without actually saying it.'

Freya nodded. She showed the picture to Marta.

'Ah, our beautiful Scottish grandmammy,' said Marta.

'Mum thinks I'm as stubborn as her. Perhaps I am.' Maybe more so, she thought, as she imagined Maggie, suitcase in hand, sailing away from dimly lit, smoky houses on an island far away.

'So what if you are?' Marta paused. 'It's not your fault, Freya. You have to accept that sometime.'

Freya nodded, blinking away tears.

'Now come and eat. And then you need to go to bed. You look exhausted.'

They sat down at the kitchen table and Marta dished out risotto and salad. For a while they ate in silence.

'Mum told me about the soldier's letters.'

'Oh yeah?'

'I'd like to see them if that's okay?'

'Sure.' Freya nodded. She was overcome with tiredness. Conversations with her mother always made her feel that way. 'We can read them together. But, for now, do you mind if I go to bed? I'm shattered.'

'Of course not. I'll see you in the morning.'

Freya woke suddenly out of sleep. The room was cold and dark and, even though she couldn't see, she knew that the sheets were soaking. She could feel them beneath her body. Her sleep had been filled with the sound of her grandmother's laughter, punctuated with the crying of babies, unable to feed, lingering painfully on the brink. Then there had been letters stained with salt, whether from tears or the sea she didn't know, ships and ship-wrecks. She sat upright and waited for the images from the dream to subside, then she threw off the duvet, lay back down and tried to think of something, anything else.

For a moment she concentrated on the sound of the sea. The rise and fall, the ebb and flow. The wind was up tonight. She could tell from the surf crashing against the beach. The waves out on the ocean would be high and rolling. As her mind strove to focus on this, driving away bleaker, blacker thoughts, she heard a plaintive, melancholy noise. After a moment it was gone, dissolved by the sea. But the next instant it came again. A haunting, almost human cry. What was it? Freya sat upright again and listened intently. Perhaps it was migrating whales? But surely it was a little early in the year for them. Besides, she had heard their noise before and she was sure it was different to this. She waited for the sound to return, half wanting it not to. It was eerie, hard on the heels of her dreams. But nothing more rose out of the blackness. Eventually, she got out of bed and made her way up the hallway to the guest bedroom. The door was ajar so she pushed it open. The room was dark and still.

'Marta?' she whispered.

Nothing came back to her but silence. Her sister was asleep, oblivious to what she had heard.

She closed the door and headed back down the hallway to the kitchen. At the threshold she paused again and listened. But she couldn't hear anything beyond the usual sounds of the night. She gazed into the dimness of the kitchen's interior, but it all looked the same as usual. As she turned around to go to bed, her hand glanced against the wooden doorway that none of them were allowed through. She ran her fingers slowly over the cool metal guarding the entrance to the lighthouse tower. Then her hand fell away and she walked on.

13

The day after the phone call with her parents, Freya made the journey to the tiny village in the south of Mull.

She knocked on the door and waited. Meanwhile, butterflies gathered in her stomach. It always took a while for him to answer, she knew. But she was surprised, after all this time, that she still felt the same way. Excitement mingled with a touch of anxiety at what exactly he might say. He had always provoked this response in her since she was a small child.

She shifted her weight from one foot to the other and looked at her watch. A minute passed and Freya began to think that she should have called ahead. But he had always seemed to know when she was coming. She was just raising her hand to knock again when the door opened silently and without warning. Instinctively she smiled. An old man stood in front of her, in a pair of faded beige cords and a shirt, of similar insipid colour, with flecks of red and green running through it. His face was brown and wrinkled, like a walnut, while his hair, in distinction, was a wiry eruption of white. For as long as she could remember, he had always looked like this; outside of time, he never seemed older or younger.

For a few moments neither of them said anything. Freya held her breath while the man stared out into the day with milky, unseeing eyes. Then, suddenly, he smiled. 'Freya. I was wondering when you would come. I've been expecting you.'

'Hello, Torin,' she said, and felt tears suddenly close. She hadn't appreciated until now just how much she had missed him.

'And Marta is staying with you, isn't she?'

'Yes. For the moment.'

'That's good.'

'She sends you her love and told me to tell you she'll come next time.'

Torin nodded. 'Of course. Come nearer,' he said softly.

She stepped forwards and his wizened hands reached for her face. He ran his fingers gently over her skin, tracing the indents of her eyes and the lines around them and on her forehead. So many more now than there had been when they last met over a year ago. His hands moved across her head, in the same light way as a priest during a blessing, and he murmured something to himself. Freya watched the movement of his thin, pale lips. It was as if he was incanting.

After a moment he spoke out loud again. 'You and I could almost be twins now.' He gave a lock of her hair a playful tug.

She nodded and her cheeks flushed. 'It's one of the many things I'm still not used to. I keep forgetting . . . ' and her voice petered out.

Torin stared at her for a moment and Freya felt herself becoming as transparent as a pane of glass. Then the old man's gaze dropped and he gestured to the house. 'Come in, my dear. So much to talk about. Did you make the frushie yourself?'

Freya paused. 'Yes,' she said, after a moment, looking down at the box of apple cake dangling from her fingers. 'Just how did you know about that?' she continued, shaking her head.

'It's a gift,' said the old man, and smiled again.

Torin had second sight. Or, at least, that's what half of the locals said about him. The others claimed it was nothing more than a fiction. There was nothing other-worldly about his blindness. They said he had lived peaceably with his wife on a livestock farm in Ireland until she had discovered his affair with her sister (or brother, depending on the source). The betrayal broke her heart and claimed her sanity, and just before she killed herself, she poisoned Torin with a concentrated dose of formic acid, a preservative she had used in the animal feed. The result was that he lost his sight and, along with it, his capacity to love again. Other stories were less ornate. Some claimed he was the son of a witch, others the offspring of a madman. But no one knew his true heritage. He never spoke of his family or where he originally came from. And he had lived on Mull for such a long time now that people almost treated him as one of their own. Those who did not simply ignored him.

Freya's Scottish grandmother, Maggie, had been Torin's

neighbour for most of her life. So Freya had seen him regularly over the years – on family trips to Scotland during the school holidays; on journeys she later made by herself to see her grandmother. She had heard all manner of stories about him. But she knew the truth of only one – that he could see things that other people could not. Over time she had learned to trust in him and his vision and she had grown to love him. Besides, he had another gift, one that she had adored from being a child. He was a great storyteller. Spinning the yarn, as he called it.

He was talking now, reminiscing, about when Sam was a baby. She and Jack had brought him to see Maggie. Torin had been keen to hold him. The little wriggler, he'd called him, as Sam squirmed right out of his arms and fell, head first, onto the tiled kitchen floor. Freya had turned cold, Maggie had gone crazy and Torin had been exiled from the house. He chuckled now in the remembrance of it – Jack, the calm one, bundling the whole family off to hospital, Maggie yelling from the departing car, why hadn't he seen it coming?

Freya smiled but she wasn't really listening. She heard the dulcet tone of his voice, the lilt of his words, but she couldn't focus on what he was saying. She found it painful. So instead she concentrated on the view from the window in front of her, taking in the lush expanse of Torin's garden and its subtle incline down to the water's edge. Loch Scridain glinted blue in the afternoon sunlight and the grey-green hills beyond it seemed to sprout right out of the water. An eagle, or a kestrel, she couldn't tell which from this distance, was circling high over the loch, and the sky was spattered with small white clouds. It was a beautiful place, but an isolated one for a blind man living alone. Freya's gaze shifted momentarily to her old friend and realised he had fallen silent.

She picked up the teapot from the table between them and poured them both another cup. Then she placed a second piece of cake on Torin's plate. 'It's funny,' she said at last, taking up the delicate thread of the conversation. 'But sometimes it doesn't feel as if they're gone at all. I keep expecting them to walk through the door, from work or school, from football practice or whatever. And then, eventually, there's a slow realisation, or a sudden recollection, I'm not sure which one is worse, that it isn't going to happen. They're gone. And I'm alone.' Freya stopped, took a breath and licked her lips. Should she tell Torin that sometimes the sense of loneliness was so acute that she could taste its bitterness in her throat, feel its touch and weight upon her? As if, heavy and oppressive, it was invading her body. And that, in her darkest moments, she imagined she could vanish beneath it. She took another breath. Perhaps, sometime, she would tell him all these things. But for now she said nothing.

Torin was nodding silently, his cloudy eyes staring ahead. Freya followed his gaze out over the water and wondered, not for the first time, if he could tell that there was sunlight and a dappled sky, or whether there was nothing there for him but darkness. She had asked him about it long ago and his answer had been vague. So she wasn't sure.

One thing she was sure of, however, was that Torin knew a thing or two about being alone.

'Yes, it's strange, isn't it?' he mused, and Freya wondered if he was talking about his blindness or solitariness, both or neither. Torin nodded again and his hand reached for the cake beside him. He broke off a corner and brought it slowly to his mouth. But he held it there, uneaten, for a moment, perhaps indulging a thought that had just come to mind. Freya both loved and hated this about him. He always took his time, in what he said and what he did.

'What you were saying reminds me of something, although the situations are different. Some said that was the work of loneliness. Perhaps it was, perhaps it wasn't. It may simply have been the result of being alone. People said a lot of things at the time. And later . . . ' Torin finally placed the cake in his mouth and began to chew, an inscrutable look on his face.

Freya waited patiently, imagining the narrative gathering pace within him.

'Have you heard of the old lighthouse keepers of the Flannan Islands?' he said at last.

'I remember something,' she said. 'But nothing clearly.'

'There are seven Flannan Islands, as you know. They lie just shy of twenty miles west of the isle of Lewis, at the very fringes of the Hebrides. They're also called the Seven Hunters, although I don't know why they are called that.' Torin paused for a moment, as if trying to remember if he had ever known. 'They have largely been uninhabited. Hebrideans, superstitious bunch that they are, were always fearful of the islands. Indeed, whenever they set foot upon their shores, they made a turn sunwise and removed their hat and other items of clothing. Such was their way.'

Freya's eye caught upon the eagle once more. She watched it floating upwards in the air thermals, wings outstretched. It reminded her of one of Torin's stories, gathering height and aspect, slowly, seemingly without effort.

'The lighthouse was built in 1899 on the largest of the islands, Eilean Mor, and in clear weather its light could be seen from twenty miles away. But more often than not, mist enshrouded the island and visibility was poor. A three-man crew maintained the lighthouse, and every fourteen days they would be replaced. No one wanted to remain on the Flannan Isles for long.'

Freya looked at the bird for a moment, still moving upwards, then closed her eyes. The Seven Hunters were mere pinpricks of land, bleak and isolated, encircled by a hostile, violent ocean. Eilean Mor had its lighthouse and the ruined chapel of St Flannan, and Eilean Taighe, also part of the northeast group, had a stone shelter. Further out in the western islands was Eilean a'Gobha (Isle of the Blacksmith). These brutal rocky outposts had been populated a long time ago. But they were not really a place for men. For some reason, Freya thought of Sam and the tale of the Green Island.

Torin cleared his throat and Freya sensed him drawing her back to him. She smiled and thought she caught the glimmer of a smile in return. 'Jack Ducat was principal keeper at the lighthouse and, on the seventh of December, 1900, he returned to duty. His usual first assistant, William Ross, had been taken ill, and had been replaced by local man, Donald MacArthur, an occasional keeper. The second assistant was Thomas Marshall, a regular member of the crew. For the two weeks following the men's return, a heavy fog hung over Eilean Mor and the lighthouse was not visible. The light, however, could still be seen from time to time. It was spotted on the evening of the seventh of December and then was obscured for the next four nights. It was seen again on the twelfth of December and after that was not visible again for over a fortnight.

'On the evening of the fiteenth of December, two ships passing in the vicinity of Eilean Mor reported that there was no light shining from the lighthouse. For some reason, no action was taken. The relief ship, the *Hesperus*, was due to sail to the Flannan Isles on the twenty-first of December. Perhaps that was why. But bad weather delayed the *Hesperus* and it didn't depart until Boxing Day.

'It was said that those on the relief boat were filled with a sense of dread and foreboding. They suspected something untoward – it was virtually unheard of for keepers to allow a light to go out. When they reached the shore their fears were compounded. A flag would usually be raised to show the relief vessel had been spotted. But the flag was down and there was no sign of the lighthouse crew who would usually assist the incoming men. When the siren was sounded, there was still no response.

'Third assistant keeper Joseph Moore and second mate McCormack of the *Hesperus* rowed ashore and Moore went to check on the station. He found the outer door locked. With his set of keys, he unlocked the building and went inside. But the place was deserted. The fire was unlit in the grate, the clock on the wall had stopped and the beds were unmade. Some versions of the tale say that an uneaten meal sat upon the table.'

Freya felt the hairs on her arms rise. 'Like the *Mary Celeste*.'

Torin nodded. 'Indeed. Moore returned to the launch and informed the relief that the crew were missing. Searches of the island were carried out but no one was found. It seemed that the crew had simply disappeared. The *Hesperus* returned to Lewis, while Moore and a team of others were left behind to man the lighthouse for the time being.'

So they relit the beacon, Freya thought. The light on the Flannan Islands flashed twice in rapid succession every thirty seconds. Freya had tried and failed, as Sam had enjoyed telling her, to memorise the distinctive qualities of each Scottish light. For some reason, however, she remembered this one.

'As they searched the building more thoroughly, they began to piece together bits of information. Everything appeared to have been running just as normal until the fourteenth of December. The keeper's log, always meticulously maintained, as you know from Pol, noted that there had been a storm on the fourteenth of December.

It had, however, blown over by the following day. But the jetty and railings had been badly damaged and while some ropes had been washed away, others had become entangled in a crane seventy feet above normal sea level. A stone, weighing over a tonne, had been tossed high up on the island. Quite a storm and no messing. There were a number of log entries noting the mood of the men during the storm. Ducat had been irritable while MacArthur had wept. Then Ducat had been quiet while MacArthur prayed. Then all three men had prayed together. Quite what had terrified them all, three seasoned veterans of storms, was puzzling.'

Torin paused for a moment, as if still trying to work it out. Then he carried on matter-of-factly. 'Two sets of the men's outdoor oilskins were missing. The one that remained at the lighthouse belonged to Donald MacArthur.

'Robert Muirhead, the superintendent of lighthouses for the Northern Lighthouse Board, made for Eilean Mor on the twenty-ninth of December and produced a report of his findings. Muirhead concluded that the three men had left the lighthouse to carry out repair work or secure stores against the storm and had either been blown off the edge of the rocks or washed away by a freak wave. The first theory was disproved as the wind had been blowing inland. And many disbelieved his second idea that a roller, as he called it, could have swept them out to sea.' Torin paused and closed his eyes for a moment. 'But we all know that freak waves have since been seen and proved.'

'So the sea took them,' said Freya.

'Perhaps,' said Torin. 'But a lot of people have said along the way that three lighthouse men would never leave the building all together, would never leave the lamp untended, no matter what. It is possible, I suppose, that Ducat and Marshall went out to patch things up after the storm and MacArthur stayed back. That would explain only two oilskins being missing. Perhaps MacArthur then caught sight of a freak wave approaching and ran out to warn the others without putting on his outdoor gear. Some accounts also have it that there was an upturned chair on the floor of the kitchen, as if someone had left in haste. So that is consistent with that theory. MacArthur might then have tried to raise the alarm, only for all three of the men to be swept out to sea.

'But,' continued Torin, drawing in his cheeks, 'you will remember that Moore found the outer lighthouse door locked. Why, if he was in a panic, would MacArthur have the presence of mind to secure the door after him? It makes no sense.'

'So what do you think happened?' Freya asked.

'I don't know what happened. It was a long time ago and the facts are hazy.' Torin frowned, scrunching up his eyes as if attempting to see something. 'But what I know is that the place was desolate and dangerous and three men were together there, stranded in close proximity. It can do strange things to a man.'

Torin's words triggered something in Freya's mind. It was what Pol had said to Sam when they went up the tower: 'It can do odd things to a man's head to be in a lighthouse alone at night, especially at night, looking out over the sea.' Loneliness and madness. Was this the moral of Torin's tale? 'So do you think MacArthur killed the other two? He was the outsider, after all, the irregular, if you like. Perhaps he killed them and then killed himself. Pushed their bodies off the high cliffs into the ocean and then jumped off too.'

'It is one possibility,' said Torin. 'One among many. One of the ships that passed the island while the lamp was unlit reported sighting a ghostly longboat close by on the water, crewed by three men with faces the colour of bone. The crew sounded the horn but there was no response from the boat, which later vanished. This fuelled the already-existing belief that the island was haunted, stalked by the Phantom of the Seven Hunters. Perhaps fear and madness, and subsequently murder, stemmed from that. Some said the keepers were taken by the Ceasg, Scottish mermaids; others were convinced it was the work of aliens.' Torin laughed and then was serious once more. 'Who knows where the truth lies. Some things in life are mysteries that cannot be solved, no matter how much we want them to be. We simply don't know what happened, and we have to accept that, no matter how much we don't want to. They are the disappeared.'

Freya stared at Torin. Now she thought she realised the purpose of the story. She had to accept that strange, horrible things happened all the time – things that cannot be explained, that make no sense. She had to stop wondering what had happened to her family. She had to stop asking questions that she would, perhaps, never find the answers to. And, most important of all, she had to stop living alone on an island. But what if she couldn't accept or stop all those things?

'You risk disappearing too,' Torin said, as if she had asked the question out loud. Then he paused. 'You need to be careful of the past.'

Freya looked at him. 'What do you mean?'

'You must take care.'

Freya didn't understand. 'What do you see?' she said, suddenly afraid.

But Torin simply shook his head. When he spoke there was real concern in his voice. 'I don't know. But perhaps this isn't the best place for you to be.'

Freya felt a flash of anger. Now he sounded like her mother and father. They were all worried about her it seemed, even Torin – out in the middle of the ocean, in a lighthouse, surrounded only by the sea and the disappeared. Suddenly, she heard her own words about the Flannan Isles. This was not a place for men. And yet she couldn't bear to think that they might have relevance for her. She thought of Ailsa and her gift, and was sure it could not be so. No. She wasn't ready to accept this just yet. She closed her eyes, to stop them filling with tears.

Torin reached for her hand and enclosed it within his own. 'Shhh,' he said. 'Calm yourself.' Then she heard him mutter something under his breath.

But she couldn't make out the words.

14

It was 3 a.m. and Freya's mind was dull, distracted. She was lying on the sofa drinking warm milk, having woken earlier from the familiar dream of her son ascending the lighthouse tower. Random thoughts slid slowly across her mind and then moved on. Marta, with a feather duster, laughing as they had cleaned and tidied the cottage that day. Eagles rising high in the air searching for prey, Torin's lilting voice accompanying their ascent. Freya smiled. Then, some of his words, spoken the day before, popped into her head.

'You risk disappearing too.'

Her smile faded. To distract herself she concentrated on the patterns of light dancing across the ceiling, intersecting the darkness, the bright flashes from the beam of the lighthouse and the paler threads of light from the moon. For a time she simply stared upwards, watching, unmoving, then suddenly she threw her legs off the sofa and headed into the kitchen. For a moment she stood over the pan of cooling milk and watched the soft curls of steam still rising from its surface. The subtle movement simultaneously gave her comfort and made her want to cry. A moment later, she grabbed the pan and poured its contents down the sink. Then she moved back towards her bedroom.

The corridor was in shadow but light spilled reassuringly from the open bedroom door. As Freya passed the locked door of the lighthouse tower in the hallway, her hand reached out once more and her fingers grazed the lock. The touch of cold metal sent a shiver through her, and with it came sudden flashes of the dream she had had. But now her recollection was sharp, crisp, the images in high definition. Sam was clambering up the stairs of the lighthouse tower, hotly pursuing Pol, turning and smiling at her periodically, the wide grin of one whose dreams were coming true right there and then. Her face in contrast had been pale and serious, her hand sweating, squeezing the metal banister tightly as she followed them in their dark, claustrophobic climb. They rose higher and higher. The voices of her son and Pol had pooled around her in the narrowing tower, the words indistinct, a cacophony of noise. And then suddenly there was relief as they reached the lamp room, with its glass and vistas and sense of light and space. She remembered Pol speaking about the lamp, the Fresnel lens, Sam standing beside him, mouth open a fraction, rapt.

After she and Sam had looked out over the sea and returned to the lamp room, she had been the first onto the staircase, eager to get back down the tower. She had turned momentarily at the top of the stairs to check that Sam was following behind her, and she had seen something,

something which, until now, she had forgotten. Pol handing the key to her son.

The recollection gave Freya a start and the images from the dream fell abruptly away. But the tingle in her fingers from the cold metal of the keyhole now journeyed up her spine. She wracked her brain but she couldn't remember, couldn't know for sure whether the giving of the key had actually happened, or was something she now misremembered or had simply dreamed. Besides, even if Pol had passed the key to her son, it was no doubt simply so he could lock up the tower when they had finished. It was highly unlikely he would have let Sam keep it. Yet something bothered her, nonetheless.

She remembered how her son had pestered and pestered her about the locked door, the lighthouse tower so tantalisingly close and yet out of bounds. She had had the same conversation with him over and over.

'If it was up to me, sweetheart, that doorway would be unlocked all the time. But you know it isn't up to me, don't you?'

'But why not?' Sam had wailed, at his most childlike and exasperating. It had always been one of the things he had wanted more than anything.

'Because when Grandma and Granddad bought the old keepers' cottage, that's exactly what they bought. The cottage, no more. It wasn't possible to buy the lighthouse. The Northern Lighthouse Board kept it and they maintain it so that it can still function as a beacon for ships. That's why Pol has to come back and service the light, check

that everything is working. You know all this, sweetheart.'
Her words were spoken low, calmly, hiding the deep irri-
tation she really felt.

Sam nodded, slowly. 'It just seems unfair that we have
to walk past this doorway every day and know that we
can't go inside. Even though it's the most exciting part of
the building.'

'I know. But there we are. Perhaps next time Pol comes,
you can ask him if he will show you the light.'

Such a thought had obviously never occurred to Sam
before and he could hardly contain his excitement. 'Do
you think Pol would?' he asked, suddenly jogging on the
spot.

'If you behave yourself and ask nicely.'

Shortly after this last exchange, Pol had taken them
both up the tower and Freya now recalled that Sam had
never mithered her again about the locked door. Perhaps
he was satisfied with this – a single journey up the narrow
lighthouse stairs. But knowing her son as she did, she
would have imagined that one visit would have pricked
his curiosity and his keenness to return more than ever.
Yet he had never mentioned it again.

Freya frowned now in the semi-darkness as her fingers
ran once more over the old metal housing of the lock. A
moment later she moved swiftly towards Sam's room, with
a sense of purpose that she had not felt for a year. She
switched on the overhead light, knelt beside her son's bed
and began pulling out the boxes she had meticulously
looked through over the past week. Before too long she

found what she was searching for – the old copper key. She turned it over in her hands: its three teeth, mouldering and green, the loops of metal at its end, bright in the sharp electric light.

She ran back to the tower door, trying to control the excitement she felt rising within her. Heart pounding, she placed the key in the lock and tried to turn it. There was a momentary sticking, metal against wood, and then, with a grating sound, the key moved. Freya stood still for a second then reached for the old doorknob. With a creak the door swung open. Freya froze, pupils dilated, knees suddenly weak. It was not the prospect of ascending the tower – for all the wonders that had held for her son. Rather it was being able to stand once more in a place that had brought him such joy. Perhaps it was even the prospect of discovering things that he had hidden in this secret playroom, a place he had kept from her.

The air was cold and musty with a winter that hadn't quite been shaken off. But despite the smell of stagnation, Freya stepped forwards. She looked upwards, could just make out the staircase curling like a snake around the edge of the tower wall, scaling up and up, disappearing into darkness. She ran her hands up and down the rough granite walls on either side of the door, searching for a light. But she couldn't find one. So be it. For now the journey would have to be made in the dark.

She felt almost delirious as she began to climb the stairs, the metal cold against her bare feet. She concentrated on putting one foot in front of the other, her hand on the supporting rail. In spite of the darkness, she felt less nervous than when she had last been here with Sam. Come on, Mum! She could almost hear the quivering urgency in his voice, a mix of delight and desperation to reach the top, not wanting to be held back by her.

She smiled and involuntarily picked up her pace a little. She passed through the first room, which was bare save for some unidentifiable shadowy items at its edges. She continued up and up the staircase, passing old storage rooms and the makeshift sitting room Pol had created, in spite of the fact that the tower didn't really need one, given the cottage below. Still, Pol had furnished it. Through the darkness she could just make out the shapes of the battered and tea-stained Parker Knoll armchairs, the tatty old rugs and the portable television set upon a chest of drawers. For the first time she wondered why the tower hadn't been cleared out when they automated the lamp. Perhaps to honour the wishes of a maintenance man who passed through now and again. At last she began to see why his visits to the tower made Pol so wistful.

The staircase did a final sweeping turn and Freya stood at the threshold of the lamp room. For a moment she simply looked at the light, revolving once every ten seconds, moving out over the Atlantic for three of those. It was so beautiful, the light sweeping out into the darkness. She walked to the long glass doors that opened onto the gallery and looked out over the waves. The sky was clear and she could tell with every revolution of the lamp that it was a quiet sea. She peered towards the horizon, mesmerised by the flash of the light. After a while, she sat down on the floor and stared out through the glass. She felt content watching the ocean, the wash of light over her – felt like she was sitting at the bottom of a well, the sun directly above her, bathing her in warmth and cleansing her soul.

15

The next morning, in spite of the sunshine, Marta was in a foul mood.

Whether this descended upon her after Freya produced the tower key and revealed she had ventured up into the lamp room alone, or whether it came from some other cause, Freya didn't know. But Marta reacted coldly to the news. She ate her breakfast in frosty silence and then curtly declared that she was going for a walk. By herself.

In Marta's absence, Freya prepared lunch. Perhaps a roast chicken would cheer her up. When it was ready, and her sister still hadn't returned, she crossed the garden to the edge of the enclosure. From here it was possible to see over most of the island. She could just make out Marta on the southwestern beach, furiously kicking pebbles around and then flinging them out to sea. She was angry, that much was apparent. Freya's actions alone couldn't have affected her this deeply.

Back in the kitchen, Freya saw Marta's phone lying on the table. There was so little service elsewhere on the island that it was pointless to take mobiles out of the cottage. Freya thought about it only for a moment before she picked it up and checked the history. Marta had had a call the night before from a Pete on a London number. Perhaps it was the married man. And perhaps that was what she was really upset about.

Freya took plates and cutlery up to the lamp room, laid a blanket on the floor, then made a second journey with the food and a bottle of wine. If her sister hadn't experienced the tower the night before, she would do so now, indulgently.

When Marta finally returned, and despite her protestations of indifference, Freya dragged her up the tower stairs and made her look out over the Western Isles. She never tired of the sweeping views and she could tell that her sister, for all her insouciance, was affected by them. By the time they had eaten, the worst of Marta's truculence had abated.

'So look at these,' said Freya, thrusting a bundle of papers towards her. 'They're the soldier's letters. I remembered you saying you wanted to have a look at them.'

'Oh, right,' said Marta, turning them over in her hands.

'Did Mum tell you they were found in a sealed Bellarmine jar?'

Marta nodded somewhat wearily.

'The jars were often used on ships to carry alcohol. That's probably how the soldier got his hands on it.' Freya paused, something suddenly occurring to her. 'But now I think of it, they were also used as "witch bottles".'

'Witch bottles?' Marta sneered. 'Really, Freya, where do you get all this stuff from?'

'Well, in case you'd forgotten, my son was obsessed with

shipwrecks and finds. I've been dragged around more museums on the subject than I care to remember.'

'Oh, yes, of course,' said Marta, more meekly. She lowered her head to read the first letter and muttered a small 'sorry'.

But Freya wasn't listening to her. She was trying to remember what she had read about the bottles. They'd be filled with objects considered to be of magical potency (pins, needles, nails, a written charm), sealed, and then buried or hidden. Their purpose was to deflect a witch's curse or to destroy the power of the magical being who had cast a spell upon the bottle's creator. Obviously this was not the purpose of the soldier's jar. But, even as she thought it, she remembered his persecuted soul. Perhaps the jar fulfilled a dual purpose.

'Hmm,' said Marta, turning back to her sister. 'Pretty interesting. Shall we continue with the second letter?'

'Absolutely,' said Freya.

8 September 1653
Speedwell

My dearest Josie,

Last night I tossed and turned, my sleep dark and disturbed with dreams.

This is what I remember from the first.

I was younger, back in Dublin aboard the *Swan*, manning guns in the King's service – the days when I still loved to fight. A lack of pay and food for many months had put mutinous thoughts in the men's minds. And so we surrendered our weapons and the *Swan*'s cannons and instead pledged loyalty to Cromwell.

I defected without a thought. I saw us sailing with the tide, our spirits high, my sword wielded freely and without remorse, while my hands grew ever more tainted with the blood of men I had once fought beside. I remember the sound of my laughter, the crack of broken, battered bones. It was all so lightly done. The betrayal, the killing.

Then I was no longer above the water but below it. I do not know whether this was still Dublin or somewhere else but the sea was dark and heavy, pressing against me. I saw ghostly reflections around me, dead men with pale faces, shimmering white bones. And beyond that horror there was something else in the distance. I could not see it but I knew it was there. And fear gripped my heart.

I awoke then, sweating in the darkness, with the rough scratch of the wooden deck against my body. But I fell back to sleep and dreamed again.

This time you were by my side, the softness of a mattress beneath us, the long red curl of your hair spread over the pillow. A candle flickered and the embers of a fire glowed in the grate. You asked me about my family. Family must have been on your mind.

I told you that I had no brothers or sisters and that my father I had never known. My mother rarely spoke of him, even though I asked her often, and now she was also gone.

So I was alone. But I thought, even as I said it, that I had always been alone.

You nodded, smiling at me in the half-light, as if my words explained everything. Then you said that perhaps my father was also from the north, like yours. You ran your fingers through my orange hair as you lay on my chest looking at me.

Perhaps, I thought. One of the few things that my mother had told me was that my father came from far away.

Suddenly a smile spread across your face and you said we should run away together. To the wildness of the north. You thought we would be happy there, away from all of this. You said that perhaps we could start a family.

You must have felt me flinch at your words, because suddenly you sat upright. I tried to pull you back to me but you resisted. I said I was sorry, that I didn't mean it.

But you shook your head and then stood up. A moment later you turned back to me and for the first time I saw hatred in your eyes. And then you told me you were with child.

That is all you said, knowing perhaps that was all that was needed. You must have watched the colour drain from my face. Then you told me that you didn't need me to respond. That you knew who I was, even if I did not. And that you knew that I would now go away again.

Your anger was calm and cold. Perhaps that was what was so shocking about it. Then you turned your back and waited for me to leave.

I awoke to the early morning light and chill of the *Speedwell*. The taste of you was in my mouth, the smell of you on my skin, the sweat on my brow a testament to your ire. As I lay on the floor of the ship, I remembered the day after this exchange between us.

My captain summoned me. There was an expedition to Scotland planned. I would not travel on my usual vessel, *Swan*, as he would prefer a good soldier like me aboard the *Speedwell*, a commandeered merchant ship which would accompany it. Its crew was inexperienced, not nearly as adept as the one on my craft. Those were exactly the words he spoke. He could use a good man like me. To help whip them into shape. They would sail the next day.

It would have been hard for me to resist the captain's request, but I did not even try. Instead I had smiled at him and shaken his hand, taken his words about me as a compliment. But I have been haunted by them since we departed. I am good at killing, Josie, and show no regret. That is what he meant for all his nicely chosen words. And I have no loyalty. But I think you knew that already.

I have been wracked with guilt since my departure and for not taking proper leave of you. I hope my note goodbye did not make you despise me. It cuts me to the quick to think upon it now and how I may have lost the most precious thing in my life.

I make my way onto deck. The sun is not yet risen but through the darkness I can see mist on the water. What will this day bring, I wonder, when the sun burns that away? Perhaps death. Perhaps that is what the other dreams signified. That I, cur that I am, will perish here. It never used to concern me which way. Yet now I am afraid. For death means that I shall never make it back to you and our child. And, I hope, to forgiveness.

For you have brought an end to my rootlessness.

You are my anchor, Josie.

And I am your
Edward

16

'What a selfish bastard,' Marta spat out. 'Long may his nightmares continue.'

Freya nodded, as if in agreement with her sister's sentiment. It was easier than contradicting Marta in her current mood. Besides, she felt her sister was only partly talking about Edward. The main thrust of her disdain seemed directed further afield, perhaps towards Pete, the married man, if that was indeed who he was. Freya longed to be told about the affair – whether Marta loved him, whether she wanted him to leave his wife or whether, as Freya suspected, she was actually relieved that he wouldn't. But as usual, whenever Freya pressed her, Marta refused to confide the details. Freya looked at her sister. It was a pattern that seemed to endlessly repeat. If a man wanted commitment from her, ultimately she fled in the opposite direction. She had more in common with Edward than perhaps she would care to admit.

Marta stood suddenly and walked to the gallery doors. The weather earlier had been beautiful: sunshine, endless blue sky, a light breeze. But now clouds hung dense and low, and the waves, ripped by a cold wind, were growing ever larger. Daylight was fading, and before long Freya knew fog and rain would move in and there would be no view to speak of.

'I wish you'd woken me last night,' Marta grumbled, turning to look at Freya over her shoulder. 'It must have been amazing to see the lamp, up here, at night, for the first time.'

So she was annoyed by being excluded from that. Freya shrugged, as if to signify that the whole experience had been underwhelming. But she still felt a tingle of excitement at the remembrance of it – the cloudless, star-filled night, the lamp ranging over a seemingly limitless ocean. She had considered waking her sister, but then had thought better of it, instead savouring the strange sensation of being cleansed with light, of being scrubbed clean. But she kept her silence on this now in case she too was declared a selfish bastard. Instead, all she said was, 'Well, you can see it tonight.'

'There won't be anything to see,' Marta whined. She stared out of the glass for a few more seconds, before turning abruptly and heading for the stairs. 'I'm going to have a cup of tea. Do you want one?'

Freya forced a smile. 'No, thanks. If you wait for a few more minutes, you'll see the lamp come on.'

But Marta shook her head obstinately and disappeared.

Freya sighed. Her sister could be so infuriating sometimes – worse than Sam on his most petulant days. She turned her attention back to the letter and read it again. But still she couldn't quite agree with Marta. She knew that

Edward's betrayal was callous, his abandonment cruel. But Freya was also touched by the acuteness of his regret – and his profound misery at having made a mistake that he knew he might not be able to put right. Adrift on the sea, he was plagued by dark dreams, images of loss and death, and though he was surrounded by other men, he felt entirely alone. Freya felt a certain kinship with him.

The lamp suddenly sprang into life and the foghorn sounded. Low, dull, penetrating. Freya put the letters on the floor and moved to the gallery doors. The fog was rolling in, and even with the sweep of the light, her gaze couldn't penetrate far. One moment the swell of the sea was visible, the next it was obscured by thin wisps of white. After a moment she realised she was searching, waiting to catch sight of a boat containing the figures of a man and a boy. She remembered Torin's words. You must be careful of the past. What had he meant by that?

She closed her eyes and tried to suppress the thought. As she stood in the darkness, the sporadic flash of light visible from behind her eyelids, she heard a sudden plaintive cry. Her eyes snapped open. It was the same almost human sound she had heard before. She peered into the night, trying to make out the surface of the water. But it was pointless. The fog continued to roll in. Still she looked, trying to search out the movement of whales, porpoises or other marine life. But these were hard enough to spot in the daylight. Now it was more than hopeless. She waited, and a moment later the baleful noise came again.

Something about it resonated with her. Freya narrowed her eyes and squinted. What was it? But the fog drew a pale white blanket over everything.

The telephone line crackled as Freya held the receiver to her ear. She had abandoned the lamp room and was now lying in bed, a mug of hot milk on the table beside her. It wasn't late but she felt exhausted. Marta had already gone sulkily to bed. The ringtone continued to sound, unanswered. Perhaps he wouldn't pick up after all. She was about to hang up when Torin's unmistakeable voice sounded on the other end of the line.

'Is everything all right?' he said, dispensing with introductions. It was usually the way he answered the phone, as if he knew who it was before they spoke.

Freya smiled. 'Yes, everything's fine. I'm not disturbing you, am I?'

'Not at all. What is it?'

The haunting sound she had heard in the lamp room was still on her mind and Torin was the person she wanted to talk to about it. When she had explained why she was calling, he was unusually quick to respond.

'Well, of course it could be whales.'

Freya nodded. She had thought the same thing.

'But it's early for the migration. That's all I would say.'

It was exactly what had gone through her mind.

'Did Marta hear it too?'

'No. She was in the kitchen with the radio on.'

'Hmm. Who knows what else it could be. Bird,

animal . . . practically anything . . . ' Torin's voice trailed away and Freya knew he was thinking of something else.

'What is it?' she asked.

'Oh. It reminds me of . . . But that's just myth.'

'Tell me,' said Freya, rearranging her head on the pillows piled beneath it. Then she pulled the duvet over the length of her body. She had hoped that he might tell her a story. Perhaps it would even make her sleep.

'Well, it's an old tale of the Scottish mermaid, the Ceasg. I mentioned them the other day when we spoke about the Flannan Islands' lighthouse. Some believed the Ceasg had spirited the keepers away. But you have to be of a certain . . . persuasion to believe that a possibility.'

Freya smiled. Torin could say what he liked, but she knew the things he did not believe in could be counted on one hand.

'Little is known about these creatures, for the Ceasg is mysterious – dangerous, some say. They are the sisters of the sirens of ancient Greece, with the bodies of women and the tails of fish. It is said that they possess great beauty and that, like the sirens, they too have haunting, bewitching voices, using them to entice sailors to them for sex.'

Freya closed her eyes, hearing the lap of waves against the shore. If she listened hard enough, would she also hear the plaintive song of the Ceasg, a hypnotic sound imbued with sadness?

'Sometimes the sailors might survive such an encounter,' Torin continued. 'But they were the lucky ones. Death often followed in the wake of pleasure. So the mariners learned to force abstinence and life upon themselves by blocking up their ears with wax.'

Freya remembered the books of her childhood, with their pictures of men aboard ship, driven half mad by the tantalising song of the mermaid. Some were melting down candles but others succumbed to the sound, diving overboard to satisfy their lust before surrendering to the deep and drowning. Life and death, the endless merry-go-round.

'It was said that if a person happened upon a Ceasg by chance and she was caught unawares, her wrath could be terrible. Death may indeed have followed swiftly. It was said that the best thing to do was leave quietly. Do not try to meet her eye and do not listen to her song. However, the lore has it that if the Ceasg came across a person who was blessed or otherwise captivated her, she may have granted them a wish.'

Freya saw herself, suddenly, swimming in a dark ocean, her white hair spread out around her, a presence somewhere in the blackness ahead of her. Was it the Ceasg and would it grant her a wish? Did it have the power to bring the dead back to life?

'It has been said that some Ceasg have had affairs with men and have even adopted human form and attempted to live a life on land. Perhaps they have even married and had children. But the call of the sea was always too strong and this life never lasted. The Ceasg always return to the ocean.'

'The sea took them,' Freya murmured, feeling the pull of sleep very close.

'Aye, the power of the sea always prevails.' Torin paused for a few moments then he went on. 'Which reminds me, you should hunker down. There's a storm coming.'

17

When she woke later, the first thing Freya heard was the rain lashing against the windows. She lay still for a few moments, listening, and then came the sound of the waves, heavy rollers pummelling the beach. She turned over, wondering if she would be able to go back to sleep. The small voice of experience inside her told her that would be unlikely. She turned on the lamp and looked at the clock. It was 11.30 p.m. Rising, she made her way to the sitting room. In spite of the rain flooding down the large windowpane, it still afforded a good view out over the ocean. The fog from earlier that evening had cleared and she could see, with every flash of the lamp, that the sea was broiling. It pounded against the shore and further out the waves cut across each other furiously. As she watched, she heard thunder sound in the distance, and a few seconds later lightning fractured the sky. A storm was in full swing. Torin had been right.

For a while, Freya sat on the sofa, watching. Sam had loved storms. He had always sat quietly, gazing out of the window, mesmerised by the onslaught of nature. Now, she wondered whether he had ever watched a storm from the top of the lighthouse. She doubted it. That he would have gone up alone in such circumstances. But she didn't know. Impulsively she rose and made her way to the door of the tower. She turned the handle, stepped forwards and instantly felt adrenalin pulse through her. The staircase was alive with noise. The wind howled as it circled around the tower and the rain drummed, amplified as it lashed the walls. As she put a foot on the stairs, Freya thought she felt them shake. She had heard of this before from keepers. How those stationed on rock lighthouses in the middle of the ocean tried to ignore the movement of the tower in heavy wind and simply prayed that the foundations had been laid well enough to withstand the weather. The wind must be gale force or thereabouts, she thought, feeling the reverberations of the building with each step she took.

By the time she reached the lamp room, the storm was almost overhead. Rain pounded against the glass doors of the gallery, the boom of thunder was louder and lightning forked ever closer. Dense black cloud hung low over a dark churning sea, both illuminated intermittently by the sweep of the lamp. Freya watched mesmerised, her eyes roving over the sky, the ocean and the land below her in succession. After a few moments, her gaze caught on something out at sea. She stared at it disbelieving. Then she looked down at her bare feet for a while before looking up again. Was it a boat? She really couldn't be certain that she wasn't simply imagining it. But looking out again, her eye stumbled upon the same object. She moved closer to the gallery doors. It was a boat, with a light upon its mast, she was sure of it. A boat not dissimilar from her own, perhaps bigger and sturdier. But, regardless of that, in this ocean it was in difficulty.

Freya's heart pounded. She ran to the tower staircase and yelled for Marta as loudly as she could, over and over. Then she moved back to the gallery doors and looked for the boat once more. She found it, lurching, tossed upwards, then pressed downwards by huge waves, heaved sideways by others. She watched the torrid rise and fall. It was in trouble, there was no doubt of that, and it was heading closer and closer towards her. Could that be right? She blinked hard, unsure. But the boat was moving, propelled by the turbulent sea, in the direction of the island. Before long it would hit the beach.

The realisation forced her gaze from the window and had her running down the stairs. The noise of the storm swirled around her in the tower as she descended. When she reached the bottom, she yelled to Marta again as she headed for the sitting-room window. She could now make out the boat from here, its light intermittently visible. Still she waited for the sweep of the lamp to be sure. She counted down the seconds and then followed its path. One, two, three. The boat was illuminated in the darkness. No doubt about it, it was heading this way.

'What is it? Is everything okay?' Marta stood behind her, eyes wide, worried.

'A boat. In trouble,' was all she said, pointing to the window.

As Marta looked, Freya picked up the phone. Then she put it down again, thinking better of it. The boat would have contacted the coastguard the moment it ran into trouble so they were no doubt already on their way. 'Get dressed. Quickly,' she said.

Moments later they were heading down the path to the beach, torches in hand. The boat was much closer now. For a moment Freya wondered whether it would be possible for it to moor alongside her boat. But then she caught sight of the *Valkyrie*, its rise and fall, and knew it was unlikely. The swell was simply too great.

She turned to Marta and pointed to her boat. 'Grab a life ring. Then meet me at the beach.'

Marta nodded and began to run.

As she approached the water's edge, Freya waved her torch, trying to signal her presence to whoever was on board and mark the edge of the beach. She could see the boat listing dangerously in the water, lurching nearer and nearer. Was it a man at the helm? She couldn't be sure. She tried to call out, but the howling gale swallowed up her voice entirely. Freya was conscious, for the first time in a long while, of her own insignificance in the face of nature.

She wasn't sure how much later it was, whether seconds or minutes, before there was a crunching sound, as the underside of the boat collided with something. As Marta joined her on the beach, there was a churning noise, as if air was escaping rapidly into water, and the boat began to overturn. It was now no more than thirty feet from where they stood. Freya frantically aimed her torch at the boat's captain – a man, she was now sure – and then downwards into the sea. She repeated the movement several times, trying to indicate to him what he should do. After a few moments, she saw a dark figure jump and she followed him with the beam of light.

Marta threw the ring towards the man and shouted out several times. Her voice was whipped away unheard. But the man seemed alert enough still to know what she had done. Freya illuminated the ring and she saw him try to catch hold of it. But the waves were strong and it eluded him. She took a couple of steps forwards into the water, wondering whether she could make it out to him. But Marta pulled her back, shaking her head. The waves were too forceful. Freya continued to shine the torch back and forth between the man and the life ring. She was just beginning to think that the struggle would prove too much for him when he made a final lunge and grabbed hold of it. She and Marta took up the slack on the rope and began to pull him, slowly and erratically, towards the shore.

'Are you all right?' Freya yelled when she was finally close enough to be heard. The cold water around her legs was making her breathless.

'Yes, I think so,' the man shouted back, as he moved in and out of the torchlight. She could see his ashen face and blood streaming down over one eye from a deep gash on his forehead.

The women pulled on the rope again and Freya gauged

that he was almost near enough for them to reach him. Then Marta took another step forward and grabbed for him, catching hold of his body. 'Can you stand?' she asked.

The man nodded, getting shakily to his feet.

'Is there anyone else aboard?'

'No,' he said, shaking his head, his blood dripping into the seawater.

Marta pulled him closer and both women took hold of him. His body was freezing. Moments later, stumbling, they made it onto the beach.

'Not much further,' yelled Freya. 'Put an arm over each of our shoulders. It's just up that hill. Come on, you can do it.'

The man looked at her and nodded. But she could see that his eyes were unfocused. He looked exhausted. Somehow they staggered back to the cottage. When they got inside and finally let go of him, he collapsed on the sofa and passed out.

For a second both women stared at him, bewildered. Then they sprang into action.

'You get towels and blankets from the bathroom cupboard,' Freya said to Marta. 'I'll get the first-aid kit.'

For several minutes there was a frenzy of movement and activity. Freya took the man's temperature. He was over 95 degrees Fahrenheit, so not hypothermic yet. But he needed to be warmed up. Marta returned and they stripped him of his sodden clothes. His body was icy and wet so they towelled him dry. Then they covered him tightly with blankets. While Marta boiled the kettle, Freya cleaned the wound on his head, bandaged it and then pulled a woollen hat on over the top. When Marta had prepared hot-water bottles, they placed them along his body – to avoid the shock of heating his extremities first. Then, finally, the women stood back.

'Jesus Christ,' said Marta, a small quiver in her voice.

'Yeah. Well done.' Freya hugged her sister and kissed her on the cheek. 'Now let's get out of these wet clothes.'

Outside the storm showed no sign of abating. Rain thrashed the cottage and lightning ruptured the sky. Freya took the man's temperature again. Higher this time. Exhausted, the sisters sat beside him, watching his breathing, still shallow, but not dangerous now. They looked at the man's face, watched the blue tinge of his lips slowly fade. Only when they were sure he was out of danger did they go to bed.

The following morning the weather had changed dramatically. The storm had blown itself out, the air was crisp and still and the sun was shining. Freya had risen early and had already been down to the beach to survey the damage by the time the man began to stir.

She was sitting in the armchair beside him when he opened his eyes and pushed himself up on his elbows. He looked around him, perplexed, without recognition, but when he caught sight of Freya, he seemed to remember and the tension went out of his body. 'Good morning,' he said, manoeuvring himself upright on the sofa. The blanket that Freya had covered him with the night before slid down, exposing his bare chest.

'Good morning,' she said and smiled.

'Good morning,' Marta called from the kitchen where she was making breakfast.

The man turned towards her but then winced and his hand moved to his head. He pulled off the woollen hat and touched the bandage on his forehead.

'Nasty wound. I dressed it,' Freya said. 'Other than that you're in pretty good shape. No hypothermia, you'll be glad to know. Just a few bumps and bruises. We had to take a look. I hope you don't mind.' She indicated his clothes on a chair next to the sofa.

The man seemed to notice his shirtless torso for the first time, but made no effort to pull the blanket up over himself. 'No, I don't mind,' he said. His clear blue eyes, as they flicked towards her, were flat, unreadable, but there seemed an absence of gratitude to his tone that made Freya wonder whether in fact he did. She felt a sudden flash of annoyance. Perhaps he would have preferred to be unexamined and die of internal bleeding or some other cause.

She assessed him for a moment: the dark, almost black, tousled hair, the pale skin, with stubble now sticking to the chin, the haunting eyes. He looked like he had been through the mill. But still.

'Yep – you had a lucky escape.' Marta made her way towards them with a pot of coffee. She paused on the threshold and smiled.

The man looked at her and nodded. In the movement, Freya thought again that she detected a hint of impatience, of resentment, perhaps, that he had to be thankful to them. He paused, and let out a quiet sigh. 'I might not have been so lucky but for you two.' And then, eventually, as if an afterthought, 'Thank you.' He paused again. 'I'm Daniel by the way. Sorry, I should have said that earlier. I'm not thinking straight and things are coming out in the wrong order.'

'I'm Freya.'

'And I'm Marta. Her sister. I'd offer you my hand but I feel we're beyond that somewhat.' She laughed. 'Strange to meet you.'

Daniel looked at her and smiled faintly. 'Yeah, you too.'

'Do you want some coffee?'

'Please.'

Marta put down the cafetiere and went back to the kitchen. Daniel's eyes followed her for a moment and then moved around the cottage.

'So do you two live out here?'

'I do. My sister's just visiting.'

Marta returned with mugs, milk and sugar. Then she poured them all a cup of coffee and moved back, leaning against the sitting-room wall. 'Help yourself.'

'Thanks.' As Daniel reached to pick up the milk jug, Freya noticed his hand was shaking slightly.

'Are you sure you're okay?' she asked.

'Yes, I'm fine.' He looked at her properly then for the first time, and in that moment there seemed to be a familiarity about him. At first Freya thought it was the eyes, their icy blueness, their hardness, so similar to Jack's. But it wasn't that. It was something else.

'So are you going to tell me what you were doing out in a storm like that? You don't look like a novice.'

Daniel smiled, but still it didn't touch his eyes. 'Thanks . . . I think. To be honest, I don't really know what happened. I'd been out in the boat all day and it kind of caught me unawares. I know that sounds ridiculous. I've been sailing here for years so I should have known better.'

'It came out of nowhere, I'll give you that. But didn't you follow the weather updates?'

He shrugged his shoulders but didn't answer.

'Or radio the coastguard?'

Again Daniel shrugged. Then he smiled almost apologetically. 'I thought I'd be okay.'

'I see,' Freya said. 'So what do you do around here when you're not being shipwrecked?' she asked. Her eyes flicked over to Marta, still leaning against the wall watching Daniel, and she wondered what her sister thought of him.

'I'm an archaeologist. I've lived on Barra on and off for the last ten years or so. But I'm not from there. I've been working with Sheffield University – finding and protecting sites, that sort of thing.'

Freya nodded. 'So where are you from originally?'

'Yorkshire,' Marta interjected. 'You still have the accent.'

Daniel smiled at her and for the first time his eyes smiled too. 'That I do. And what about you?'

'London,' Marta said.

'Hmm. They must love you here even more than they do me.'

Freya laughed. 'Some of them, perhaps.'

Daniel nodded. 'Even though I've done eight winters in Castlebay, I'm not truly accepted.'

'Of course not. You won't ever really belong, no matter how long you stay. So you took the boat from Barra yesterday?'

He nodded. 'I had some time off and it was a beautiful day. To start off with, at least. I sailed down to Vatersay, spent ages there, and then I got to thinking that I could make it over past Tiree to Mull and see some friends. But by the afternoon, when I was over halfway there, things on the sea were changing. By then it seemed as bad to turn back as to keep going, but I got blown seriously off course. Thank God for your little island.'

As Freya looked at him, she found herself wondering how old Daniel was. Perhaps thirty-five. He was younger than her by a few years – more Marta's age, she guessed. Again she had the feeling that there was something familiar about him. But she still couldn't put her finger on what it was. 'You'll have to get someone out here to take a look at your boat. It's damaged but reparable. Why don't we have some breakfast and then I can take you to Mull or Barra if you like?'

'That's kind of you, Freya. Thanks.' And, for the first time, she thought he meant it. That perhaps a little of his guard had come down.

'Yeah, she's all heart,' said Marta, winking at her sister. 'And fortunately for you, a much better sailor than you are.'

Daniel laughed.

'Why don't you get dressed and then come into the kitchen when you're ready,' Freya said.

'Thanks,' Daniel said. 'You've both been great.'

As the sisters left the sitting room, Marta turned to Freya and frowned slightly. Freya knew exactly what she meant. He was reserved, that was for sure, but he seemed to be opening up. She smiled. But then he had just spent the night on their sofa naked after battling through a pretty big storm. That was enough, perhaps, to throw quite a few men.

18

Two days had passed since the storm.

Freya stood on the lighthouse gallery looking west. The sky was bright and cloudless, and she thought that she could just make out the shadow of Dubh Artach in the distance. The lighthouse was a pale streak of pewter rising from the horizon, an insubstantial smudge that looked as if, in the blink of an eye, it could vanish beneath the waves. Besides that, there was nothing. The sea was empty.

She turned her attention northwards away from the distant lighthouse. Looking out over the ocean landscape she could see Coll and Tiree; beyond them, she knew, even though it was obscured, was Barra. It made her think of Daniel. The day before, someone had come out to the island to take his boat away for repair, but he had not come with them. No matter.

'He was a bit odd anyway,' was Marta's concise take on events. 'Dishy but somewhat aloof. I guess that might have had something to do with the near concussion and hypothermia. But whatever . . . '

Freya smiled and, releasing her grip on the iron railings, made her way back inside. As she closed the door behind her, she looked at the lamp, properly, perhaps for the first time. It was huge, with intersecting sections of glass which, she knew from Pol, were dust traps. She ran her fingers over one of them and surveyed the thick layer of grey dirt on her fingertips. Perhaps the coming and going in the tower, opening and closing the gallery door, was dirtying the lamp faster than usual. She couldn't bear the thought of that and, knowing that Pol would not be visiting for at least a couple more weeks, began to look around for the cleaning materials he used. She opened the cupboard doors below the lamp but there was nothing besides a few filthy old rags – no doubt abandoned by Pol at some point – which would dirty the lamp further.

She hunted around, on the shelves and floor nearby, but there was nothing. She was about to head down the stairs to the kitchen, when she spotted a tiny cupboard in a corner of the room. Looking inside, she could see nothing there but an old cardboard box. She opened the lid briefly but it looked to be filled with clutter, and there weren't any cloths, dusters or anything else useful nearby. Perhaps Pol brought all of that with him when he did his inspection. Freya let the lid fall shut once more and took a step back, about to close the cupboard door. Then, for the first time, she saw the faint scrawl on the side of the box. KEEP OUT. PRIVATE. Her heart leapt. It was Sam's writing. She knelt down and with shaking hands pulled the box out of the cupboard. Then she ran her fingers over the letters, written in faded red felt-tip pen. Yes, it had been written by Sam.

For a few moments she simply stared at the box in front of her. She couldn't quite believe it. After she had discovered the key to the lighthouse tower, she had spent time looking through its rooms in the hope of finding something, anything, that her son had left behind – hidden away from the prying eyes of his parents. But all she had discovered were the faded treasures of the keepers – books, maps, magazines, old notes; nothing that had belonged to her son. But now there was this. How had she overlooked this space before? She was terrified that the box would disappoint her. That it would turn out to be Pol's or someone else's after all. She ran her fingers once more over the lettering. KEEP OUT. PRIVATE. She smiled. It sounded so much like something Sam would write. And before she could change her mind, she pulled open the lid and started to delve through the contents.

Items flashed before her eyes. Shells and stones, sea-smoothed pieces of glass, a few coins, perhaps a Viking one amongst them, a small knife blade. They were beach-combing finds, no doubt. There was an intricate silver necklace, the metal tarnished but still surprisingly well preserved. Freya lifted it out of the box and examined it more closely. The silver curled round and round, one piece from beginning to end, that would presumably wind tightly around the throat of the person wearing it. The metal was thick, well made, its surface rough, striated, though the pattern it had once borne had been erased, perhaps by the sea. At its highest end, the silver shaped itself into the tail of a serpent. It was a stunning piece, Freya thought, replacing it in the box and continuing her search through it. There were some pens and pencils and an exercise pad, with writing across it – Sam's diary, it said, in hesitant red felt pen. Freya gasped, felt the hot rush of tears to her eyes, the quick flow of them down her cheeks. For a moment she struggled to breathe, then she grabbed the diary and flicked through its pages. A familiar scrawl of red letters flashed into and out of view, page after page, interspersed with scribbles and drawings. She closed her eyes, hardly able to believe it. She had found something new, something else to hold on to. Something that had belonged to her son.

19

'Marta!'

Freya shouted loudly down the tower. She tried to keep the tremor out of her voice but her hand, holding the diary, was shaking uncontrollably. She listened and was about to shout again, when she heard Marta's footsteps running up the stairs. A moment later, her sister appeared, panting.

'What is it?' Marta's eyes were wide, panicked. 'Are you all right?'

'Yes, sorry. It's just . . . I found this.' She thrust the diary at her sister. It was easier than trying to explain everything she was feeling.

Marta took it and read the writing across the front. 'Oh, I see,' she said, smiling. 'How amazing. Where did you find it?'

Freya pointed to the cupboard. Suddenly, her mouth felt as dry as a desert.

Marta flicked through the pages, scanning the writing. 'Have you read any yet?'

Freya shook her head. 'My first instinct was to read the whole lot. I desperately wanted to hear his voice again.'

She took a deep breath. 'But then, when I sat down to begin, I couldn't do it. I found it hard enough to read the first line.'

'Oh, I see,' Marta said again, taking hold of Freya's hand.

'I think I need to pace myself. Read a little bit of it now and again.'

Marta nodded. 'Why don't you start with the first entry? See how you go?'

'Yes, that's what I thought.'

Marta turned to leave her but Freya held on to her hand.

'Do you want me to stay?'

Freya nodded.

'Are you sure you don't want to read it alone?'

'Yes.' Freya gave a small, slight smile. In truth, she was a little afraid of what the diary might say.

'Okay then,' said Marta, handing it to Freya. 'Let's start at page one.'

18 April 2014

It is now five days since Mum went to France to work. It is the first time that she has been away from us for so long. I miss her and I told Dad. He said that I should write a diary. When I asked him why, he said so I could write about my feelings. So I am writing this diary. And in red pen as I miss Mum so much. Even though she phones it is not the same.

Anyway, the weather was good today. Dad said that to take my mind off it we would go out in the boat to Fingal's Cave. I had wanted to go there for ages but with one thing and another it had never been the right time. I think Mum said that once. So we sailed up from our island between Mull and Iona and after what felt like ages arrived at Staffa. But it was excellent and worth the wait. The sea cave is brilliant with columns of lava and you can hear the echoes of the waves inside it. It's like a natural cathedral, Dad said. He also said it was named after Finn MacCool, a great clan leader. Afterwards we walked over the island which is very flat. I didn't think it was as good as our island because we have a lighthouse and hills.

Dad told me about a man, whose name I can't remember, who visited Staffa a long time ago and caught lice during his stay. But he still had a good time and enjoyed the cave. I have had lice and I couldn't imagine that was right – even though the cave was good. But I didn't say anything.

Then we bumped into Callum. He said he would take me to the Treshnish Isles and we could see some birds and visit the castle. I said that sounded brilliant. I like Callum. Dad agrees. He said he is a really good guy.

On the way back home the sun came out and it was nice. Dad told me the story of the Land under Waves. He said that when no wind is blowing and the surface of the sea is still and really clear if you're lucky you can see the Land under Waves. He said you can see deep forests and green valleys with streams running through them and if you look really closely the pebbles in the beds of the streams. He said the rocks are made of gold and the sand is silver dust. There was then a lot of stuff about a princess who was ill and a man, Jeermit, who had to go to the Land under Waves and give the princess water in a special cup from a magic well. After he had done that she got better, so he could return to his family, who included Finn MacCool. But he had been gone for seven years by the time he got back even though it didn't feel long to him.

That was basically it. To be honest, it sounded much more like a story Mum would have told and it made me think that Dad was missing her too. He wouldn't normally tell a story like that. The interesting bit was that the entrance to the Land under Waves was through a sea cave and I wondered if that was meant to be the one we had just been to on Staffa – especially because the cave was named after Finn MacCool and he was also in the story. Dad said it's possible. That's what he always says when he doesn't know. I wish Mum was here. She would give me a better answer. I thought about Jeermit then, being gone for seven years with no one knowing whether he would come back. He must've missed his family a lot – and they must have missed him too.

Silence sat heavily in the lamp room after the sisters had finished reading.

Freya, silent tears flowing down her cheeks, finally spoke. 'I wish we'd taken him to Staffa earlier.'

'Don't be silly,' said Marta, pulling Freya to her. 'He

went there with his father. And he had a wonderful time. You can hear it in his voice.' She took a deep breath, to stop herself from crying.

Freya nodded and closed her eyes, trying to picture her son running wild over Staffa's empty green wilderness, laughing and shouting to his father. She tried to see him in the cave, listening to the rise and fall of the water, astounded by the strangely shaped columns of rock. She squeezed her eyes tightly shut, but she couldn't see any of these things. They were obscured by a veil of guilt and sadness. She remembered the last line of the entry, its haunting irony, and her tears fell even faster.

'Hey. You know what we should do?' Marta said.

'What?'

'We should go to Staffa. We should retrace their steps. You never know, it might help.'

Freya thought about it. Not a bad idea. But the more she considered it, the more she knew it was more than that. They could take the boat out over the ocean, stand in the cave where her son had stood, his words fresh in their minds.

'That's a great idea,' she said, turning to face her sister.

And she knew in that moment that if the diary told of other places Sam and Jack had been to, she would follow. She would conduct a pilgrimage, and at the end of it perhaps she would be offered redemption.

20

'Remind me again why we had to come out here.'

It was the day after they had read the diary entry, and Freya was manoeuvring the boat into position at the landing place near Clamshell Cave. Even though it was low tide and the sea calm, she knew that Marta would be suffering. She was not a good sailor. 'Hop out and rope up the boat,' she called to her sister. 'You'll feel better as soon as you're on land. I promise.'

A few minutes later, the boat secure, the sisters walked southwards, towards Fingal's Cave, picking their way over the misshapen stones underfoot. On one side, basalt cliffs towered above them; on the other the ocean, less than ten feet away, lapped against the rocky shoreline. Mull loomed large in the east, Ben More towering in the distance, and closer to them was the tiny island of Ulva.

Freya looked at a nearby cluster of rock columns descending diagonally into the sea and felt a pang of guilt. 'I can't believe we never came to Staffa,' she muttered.

'What did I tell you before about that?' her sister admonished.

Freya looked at Marta and smiled. 'Okay, okay.'

'Besides, really, what's the big deal?' Marta gestured around her, attempting nonchalance and failing.

Fulmars circled overhead in the clear blue sky and puffins dive-bombed from the top of the cliffs and headed out to sea. Freya could hear the distinctive call of kittiwakes and the high whistle of guillemots. Even though the mating season was barely under way, the island was already full of birds, alive with their noise. As they rounded the southern tip of the island, Fingal's Cave came into view.

'I really don't want to count my chickens, but there doesn't seem to be anyone here,' Marta said, a tinge of excitement in her voice.

Freya nodded. 'It's still a little early for tourists. With a bit of luck we'll have it to ourselves.'

They skirted the narrow ledge that led into the cave, holding on to the rail to guide them. Once inside, Freya saw that it was much higher and deeper than she had imagined, the basalt columns rising upwards on both sides to form an almost perfect arch. In the sunshine of the day, the water at the bottom of the cave seemed luminous, a fluorescent aquamarine, and it threw dappled patterns up into the darkness overhead. The effect was magical. But perhaps the most arresting thing about the cave was the unearthly sound that echoed through it. It was the pressing and lapping of water against rock, Freya knew. But it sounded like something else entirely.

She sat down and closed her eyes, listening to the noises, deep and churning, sometimes otherworldly, at other times guttural, almost human. She remembered that Sam had wondered whether the cave could have been the entrance to the Land under Waves. Now she was here, she almost believed it was possible. She opened her eyes and looked down into the clear water, watched its hypnotic rise and fall. Could she make out rocks of gold below the surface and sand of silver dust? Perhaps the shadows of a boy and his father, separated from their family, unaware of time, thinking they had been gone only for an instant?

'It's unbelievable.' Marta was standing at the back of the cave, beside what looked like an altar of stone. 'It really is like a natural cathedral.'

Freya nodded. Then she turned and looked back through the cave's mouth. In the distance, perhaps six miles away, was the island of Iona, a splash of green against the blue of the sea. Freya knew what she could see was the machair, stretching down the north coast to the ocean. And although she couldn't see them from here, Freya could imagine the wild white beauty of Iona's west coast beaches. From their fringes there was nothing else for thousands of miles but ocean. And it was there that Jack's boat had washed ashore, devastated, its passengers nowhere to be found. There was just a white carcass, flaking paint, battered wood and broken glass. It was on Iona's green isle that her life had started to unravel.

'Are you okay?' Marta had made her way back through the cave and sat down next to her sister. 'Does it bring back too many thoughts?' she said, following Freya's line of sight.

'No. Actually it feels good to be here. They feel close.'

Freya looked back down into the water, and tried to focus on its melody. A sudden surge of seawater into the cave produced a long sad noise, and Freya was reminded of the sound she had heard from the lighthouse gallery, and once before that, when she had woken from dreams. Her eyes searched beneath the surface of the waves but there was nothing there.

'These noises are bizarre,' Marta said. 'I've never heard anything like it.'

Freya paused, wondering whether she should share Torin's stories of the Ceasg. But she knew her sister would in all likelihood make light of it.

After a moment, Marta rose. 'Are you ready?' she said.

Freya nodded. 'Yes, I think so. Thanks for coming with me.'

'No problem. It's amazing. As Sam said, even the guy who got nits still enjoyed the visit. So it says a lot for the cave.'

21

Freya, sitting at the back of the boat, looked out over the ocean. The sky was darkening and the wind was getting up. A storm was brewing. She turned back to see Sam sitting on the bottom of the boat. He was looking down at a map arranged in front of him.

'I think it could be there, Mum.' Sam pointed to a speck in the middle of a vast expanse of blue.

'Why do you think that?' Freya asked, moving to kneel beside him.

The map ranged from the western islands of Scotland across the Atlantic to North America.

'Because it's so far away, it's practically halfway to Greenland. So, the way I see it, it could be the Green Island.'

Freya smiled. There was a certain beautiful logic to what he said, and part of her didn't want to disillusion him. 'But I thought the Green Island never stayed in one place. That it moved around, floating over the sea, never still for very long, never really wanting to be found.'

Sam was quiet for a while, deep in thought. 'That's true,' he said at last and removed his finger. 'So it can't be the Green Island. It wouldn't be on a map.'

'I think that's right,' Freya murmured, stroking his head. 'Perhaps it's out there in the vast ocean somewhere,' she circled the Atlantic with the index finger of her free hand, 'waiting for someone to stumble upon it accidentally.'

'Hmm,' said Sam, wrinkling his nose and then pointing to the island again. 'What is that place then?'

'It's St Kilda,' said Freya, taking in the expanse of water between it and the coast of Scotland. 'Almost the westernmost point of the United Kingdom.' And with Sam's finger hovering over it, that was just what it looked like – a point, a dot on a map almost submerged by sea, a mere hint of an existence.

Sam was still frowning. 'Is that where my great-grandmammy was from?'

Freya paused, surprised he remembered. He had been just a baby when she passed. 'Yes,' she replied. 'It is.'

Sam nodded. 'I thought so. That place is filled with death.'

Freya started. It was. She knew that from her grandmother. But how did Sam know? 'Where did you hear that, darling?'

'It doesn't matter. The point is that these islands are dangerous. Death is everywhere.' His finger moved northwards over the Flannan Islands, then circled around over Lewis, Harris, Barra, and back to the islands nearest to Ailsa Cleit. 'And you,' he said, looking at his mother for the first time, 'have to be careful.'

'What?' said Freya, a dull sensation of fear rising in her stomach. She felt sweat sting her armpits. Her son didn't sound at all like her son. 'What are you talking about, Sam?'

'Here,' he said, his finger now circling a stretch of water closer to home. 'You must be careful. Especially here.' Freya looked towards where he was pointing, but she didn't understand what he was talking about. She began to feel very afraid. 'Mum, do you understand? You must avoid this place. You must be very careful. There is danger for you here.' Then Sam looked her directly in the eye. His intensity frightened her.

At that moment, Jack appeared from the cabin. He fixed her with an icy stare. 'Do you hear him, Freya? Be careful.'

'Do you hear us, Mum?'

'Yes,' she said, softly, closing her eyes to avoid their gazes. 'I hear you.'

Freya sat upright, abruptly, startled out of sleep. As she remembered the dream, she felt a sudden biting fear and the chill of the room. The hairs on the backs of her arms were standing on end and there was a cool slick of sweat across her chest. She tried to move her legs, to get out of bed, but she was frozen to the spot. Moonlight flooded the bedroom, rays of lilac and pale blue, hazy around the edges, and she heard the soft breaths of the waves through the open window. Then she thought she heard something else.

'Sam?' she whispered, so quietly she almost couldn't make out her own voice.

The air of the room seemed to crystallise and come into sharp focus. She could see the wardrobe door slightly ajar, the dresser with stones and shells across its top. In the hallway beyond the half-open door, shadows lurked. She fixed her eyes upon them. The smell of night jasmine flooded her nostrils.

'Sam?' she said again, louder this time.

She thought she saw a quiver of movement followed by the soft sound of footfalls along the hallway. She listened hard but she was distracted by the loud thump of her heart in her chest. Then the room fell into darkness, the moon suddenly eclipsed by cloud.

'Freya.'

She took a sharp intake of breath and flicked on her bedside lamp. Then she turned back towards the doorway. She saw Marta standing there.

'Jesus. You gave me a fright.'

'Sorry.' Her sister took a few steps into the room. 'Are you okay? I heard you calling out.'

'Bad dream,' said Freya. She looked around the room again and breathed deeply. It was the same as usual.

Marta made her way over to the bed and climbed in beside Freya. 'Do you want to tell me about it?'

Freya nodded and recounted the dream. 'I don't under-stand it. So far since their deaths, everything I've dreamed about Sam and Jack has been a memory – with the one exception of the nightmare of Sam drowning. But this was not a memory. We looked at maps together, plotted boat trips and journeys to islands. But we never talked like this, about dangerous places close to home. And Jack never spoke to me in such a way.'

No, this was a new kind of nightmare. She closed her eyes and tried to think. But the sweat now pooling at the base of her spine was distracting. She shivered.

'It's just a dream, Freya. It was probably brought on by being out on the sea, by our trip to Staffa yesterday. By finding the diary and hearing Sam's voice again.'

Freya nodded. That made sense, whereas the dream made no sense at all.

'Shall I make you a hot drink?'

'No. You go back to bed. I'll get up. Do you want anything?'

Marta shook her head and rose to leave. 'Are you sure you're okay?'

Freya nodded.

'I'm sure it's nothing, you know. Just emotions.'

Freya nodded again. 'I'm sure you're right. Good night, sis.'

'Good night.'

Freya closed her eyes and ran her fingers over her face. But in that moment of darkness behind her eyelids, she saw again the intensity of both Sam and Jack's stare, their message for her, their words of warning. You must be very careful. There is danger for you here.

Hours later, the words, so like Torin's, still fluttered fretfully around Freya's head as she sat at the kitchen table. What did they mean? Not only Torin's words, but now Sam's and Jack's as well.

She inhaled deeply, tried to breathe out the sick, agitated

feeling she hadn't been able to shed, and looked down at the map resting on the kitchen table. Her finger lightly touched the tiny island where she was now. The place they had all called home. Then it moved in a sweeping arc directly northwards over Coll and Tiree and then clockwise over Mull, Luing and Scarba, southwest over Jura and beyond it to Islay. Then it circled out into the Atlantic before moving northwards again. Further afield, to the north and west, were the outer isles of Barra, South and North Uist, Lewis and Harris. Freya's finger strayed westwards, past the Flannan Islands, hesitating over St Kilda for a second, and then moved back to the waters nearest the lighthouse.

She leaned closer into the map but she struggled to remember now exactly where Sam's finger had been pointing in the dream. Had he been intending to single out particular islands, or simply the watery expanse around them? How far afield had he been signalling? Freya looked over the area directly east of the lighthouse. She knew that there were hundreds of rocky islets in this area, but nothing stood out – from her map at least. She reached for her tablets and took two of them with a large sip of steaming tea from the mug next to her. It was so hot it burnt her tongue. But she didn't react. She still felt the chill of Sam's words deep in her body. There is danger for you here.

22

The next day, Freya stood at the kitchen sink, her eyes closed, the warmth of sunlight upon her body. She relished it, surrendered to it, and for a brief moment was present only in its touch. She smiled, suspended in light. Its caress was soft, teasing, like the hand of a playful lover. It could almost have been Jack.

For a second she hovered on the brink of remembrance, then her eyes snapped open. As the room came back into focus, goose bumps pricked her skin. She was in front of the kitchen window, her hands immersed in soapy water, on this tiny island, alone. She looked into the messy garden, saw the dead flowers on the bushes, the stark brightness of the enclosure wall. Gulls screeched overhead, winged flashes of white against a cobalt sky. Everything was the same and yet everything was different.

Freya stood still for a minute, waiting for the sensation to pass. Then she dried her hands and filled the kettle. It was helpful, the doctor had told her, to do small things at times like this, indulge in distracting routines to keep panic at bay. Make a cup of tea, run a bath. Perhaps she would do both, she thought, as she went into the sitting room. She wanted to talk to Marta, but she had gone to Iona for the day to see a friend. So instead perhaps she would go for a walk. Make the most of the sunshine.

As she looked out of the window to the blurred line of the horizon, there was a sharp knock on the cottage door. Freya jumped. She wasn't expecting anyone and she wasn't sure she would be able to sustain chitchat for very long. Reluctantly she moved back into the kitchen, wondering whether, if she left it long enough, whoever it was would just go away. She waited for a few moments and the knock came again. A hard rap – that of a man, she was sure of it. She took a deep breath and opened the door.

Daniel stood before her. He was taller than she remembered, his hair darker, longer.

'Hi,' he said, when it became clear that Freya would not speak first. 'I hope you don't mind me barging in on you like this . . . but if it's not convenient . . . ' His words faded out awkwardly as if he sensed her mood.

She tried to rearrange her face into a smile. But she couldn't quite manage it. 'No, it's fine,' she said eventually, hoping her tone didn't sound too insincere. 'I wasn't doing anything. Please, come in.'

She moved back into the kitchen and instinctively went to fill the kettle with water, realising as she picked it up that it was already full. She put it down again, feeling her nerves jangle.

Daniel, next to her, surveyed the quiet interior of the cottage. 'Is your sister here?'

'No. She's out.' After she'd said it, Freya was aware that

the remark might have sounded a little abrupt. She added, 'She went to visit a friend.'

'Ah, I see,' said Daniel.

Again Freya thought he was difficult to read. His eyes remained as inscrutable as they had the last time they'd met: distant, as if shutters had been pulled down behind them. And from his tone she couldn't tell if he was disappointed or indifferent about this news. Not that it really mattered either way. She turned away from him and occupied herself with making coffee. The process soothed her. While she did this, Daniel spoke intermittently – about his boat, now fixed, the repri-mands he had received from his family after the accident. It was small talk that she barely listened to, yet somehow it was comforting.

Finally, they made their way into the sitting room. 'I don't remember much of this at all from the last time,' Daniel said, smiling awkwardly. 'Other than that it was weird to be here.'

Freya nodded, sitting down and putting the cafetiere, milk and cups down on the table. 'It was quite odd.'

'Right,' said Daniel. 'I mean, I've been there once before.' He pointed to the sofa. 'Flat out and naked. As I said, weird.'

Freya laughed. Yes, it was. She had undressed him and thought nothing of it at the time. Suddenly she felt strangely self-conscious. To give herself something else to concentrate on, she poured the coffee.

'Anyway,' said Daniel, breaking the silence. 'I just

wanted to say thank you. To you and Marta. I don't think I said it properly before.'

'It was no problem. Really. We're just glad you're okay.'

Daniel smiled. 'So how've you been?'

'Fine,' said Freya, noncommittally. She stirred milk into their coffee. 'You?'

'Yeah. Busy. But no storms, no catastrophes.'

Freya nodded, noticing that he was looking at the book-shelves along the wall opposite the sofa. They were floor to ceiling, books sandwiched spine to spine, a real reader's set of shelves. Jack had built them for her out of a beau-tiful rich walnut and she had loved to simply look at them, feel the warmth of the wood beneath her fingertips as she took her time selecting her next book. And yet, she thought, with a touch of sadness, she hadn't read in such a long time.

'Is that you and your family?' Daniel's question seemed to come from a long way away. 'If you don't mind me asking?' he added.

Freya finally registered him pointing to a photograph and nodded. 'Yes, that's me with my husband and son.' She closed her eyes, anticipating his next questions and the awkwardness that would follow. So she decided she would save him from it.

'There's a lovely one, up there, of my son, Sam, running along the beach. He was five then.' He was laughing, almost doubled over, one of his eyes obscured by his thick blond hair, the other glinting with delight. He had been running towards her and Jack when she had taken the picture. But what had he been laughing at? She couldn't remember now. No doubt it had been something silly, inconsequential. But she knew he had that broad smile of total mirth on his face. 'And I think there's one of my husband, Jack, quite close to it. He was always slightly awkward when he was having his photo taken. God knows why. So photogenic.' Freya paused and took a breath. 'They died, last year, in a boating accident not far from here, although no one's too sure where it happened. A freak storm, or something else untoward. Again, no one's quite sure. The boat was found but the bodies never were . . . ' Freya's voice ground to a halt and an uneasy silence settled over the room.

Daniel moved back towards the sofa and sat beside Freya. He looked as if he couldn't quite believe it. Then he shook his head.

'God, Freya, I'm sorry. I'm so very, very sorry.'

'Thanks,' she said.

'The pictures are beautiful. You look like you were happy.'

'Yes, we were. Very happy.'

'Well that must bring you some comfort.' Daniel paused and then went on quietly, 'And probably your fair share of despair.'

Freya nodded, surprised. It was not what most people said aloud to the bereaved. Yet he was exactly right. She had been blessed to have experienced such happiness. Some people never did. Yet at the same time it cut her deep that she had lost it. That wound was so rough and jagged that she thought it incapable of ever being healed. It was constantly reopened by memory: bitter, gushing, bloody and painful. And by her dreams. She blinked away an image of Sam, staring at her with big warning eyes, and tried to change the subject.

'Are you married?' Freya asked.

Daniel paused for a moment before answering. 'No,' he said.

'Girlfriend?'

'No.' He shook his head softly.

'So you live alone too.'

He nodded, glanced at her briefly and looked out of the window.

Freya followed his gaze out to the ocean, its untameable force subdued in this moment, in the calmness of the day. She didn't understand how she could bear to be here, surrounded by the thing that had stripped her of everything she loved. But perhaps that was the point. It was both the rub and the salve. It had taken everything from her and it was only that which could give something back, could give her peace. Until that time, she would remain, tossed back and forth on capricious waves, flotsam bobbing on a tide of grief.

She turned back to find Daniel scrutinising her. 'I imagine it's hard not knowing what happened to them.'

She nodded. 'I think it's part of why I came back – to try to understand that. Quite why I thought I could uncover something, when investigators and police and God knows who else haven't been able to, I don't know.

But perhaps it's what I thought I needed for closure, for finality.' For peace and reconciliation, she thought, turning her gaze once more to the waves breaking across the shore. They were flinty, cold in spite of the sunshine. 'Now I'm here, I understand that I will probably never get it. In all likelihood, I will never know what happened to them. Or what they were doing when they disappeared. But the remaining is important. Does that make sense?'

Daniel nodded. 'Perfectly.'

She stood up, made her way to the bookshelves, singled out the picture of Sam on the beach. 'And I am finding out some things.' Freya drew her finger over the image of the laughing boy. 'Something amazing happened the other day. I found another box of his things hidden in the lighthouse tower – a secret hideaway, perhaps for his most secret possessions.'

'Really?' Daniel smiled. 'What did you find?'

'Things washed up by the ocean, I think. Shells, an old knife blade, some jewellery.' For a moment she contemplated showing Daniel the necklace and other items and then she changed her mind. Maybe later. 'Sam was obsessed with beachcombing. You won't believe what he's found over the years on rocks and beaches. We've got boxes and boxes of it. The sea is rich with pickings.' She paused a moment, breathless, as she realised what she'd said. Then she continued. 'There was a diary. That was the best of the haul. Marta and I have read a little. It was like hearing his voice, fresh, alive, having him speak to me again after all this time.' Freya paused, her throat dry. 'The first diary entry was about a trip Sam took to Staffa with his father. After we read it, Marta and I decided to go there, retrace their steps.'

Daniel nodded, looking at her. 'And did it help?'

'I'm not sure. Fingal's Cave was beautiful.' Freya laughed as she looked back to the photos on the shelves. One of her and Jack, mounted in an antique silver frame, caught her eye. Their faces were in profile to the camera, their foreheads closely locked together, and they were laughing. Again she couldn't remember why. Jack's grey hair was pale against the shock of hers – long, black and wild. The light and the dark. If it was taken now, Freya would be the palest, the one who looked like a ghost.

Her face blanched at the irony of it. She turned back to Daniel to find him still watching her. 'Before it happened, you know, my hair was black.'

He nodded, an almost imperceptible tilt of the head. He had seen the photographs after all.

'The day after I heard the news, it was white. It turned overnight . . . ' she said before her words evaporated once more. It was traumatic for her to think and speak about it even now.

For a moment Daniel was quiet. Then he smiled and said, 'Like Finn.'

Finn MacCool, the great mythical hunter, whose hair had also turned white prematurely. Perhaps even over-night. She thought of her son again, and of the diary and her trip to Fingal's Cave. 'Yes, Finn,' she said. 'I love the story of the Land under Waves. Do you know it?'

Daniel nodded. 'I do. You can't live here all this time and not buy into that stuff just a little.'

Freya smiled. 'That's what I've always thought.'

23

After Daniel had gone, Freya retrieved the necklace from Sam's box and held it up to the light. She watched the late afternoon sunshine dance across it, and wondered, not for the first time, where it had come from, who it had once belonged to. It was beautiful, unique. Still, she thought, it could look better.

Moving to the kitchen, she mixed baking soda with a little water in a bowl. When it had formed a paste, she dipped a damp sponge into it and rubbed it into the silver – it was an old trick of her mother's and apparently worked wonders. After a few minutes she rinsed off the paste and held the necklace up to the light again.

'Well, what do you know?' Freya murmured to herself. The silver had regained a soft sheen.

She dried the necklace with a clean tea towel and then put it on, taking care not to break it. Then she studied it in the hallway mirror. It was striking against the pale thinness of her neck. She took a step closer to the mirror, running her fingers over the silver loops. Then she went into her bedroom to lie down and read the second entry in Sam's diary.

What a brilliant day.

I don't remember what time it was when Dad came into my room to get me up but I had already been awake for ages. We had our breakfast quickly and then got in the boat and raced to Mull. That was what it felt like anyway. Racing along. The wind and the tide were both with us Dad said.

When we got to Fionnphort, Callum was already waiting. He was taking me to the Treshnish Isles where I'd never been before. I was so excited I could hardly wait. Callum said it was a good day for it – fine with a light breeze.

After we waved goodbye to Dad and set off, Callum told me a bit about the isles. This is what I can remember:

1. He said that there were 8 in total (as well as a few very small ones which didn't really count as they were more like rocks),
2. They are very remote and have been uninhabited for a long time, although they still have the remains of houses and a castle on them.

The first one we came to was Bac Beag (which was very flat) but right next to it was Bac Mor, which means Dutchman's cap because it looks like one.

Lunga was the next one along. It was the biggest with a mountain, Cruachan, at the northern end. Callum told me that Lunga means 'longship' in Old Norse, the language of the Vikings. I asked if it was because its shape was a bit like a Viking longboat. Callum said that he thought it probably was that – but he said it in that tone that Dad sometimes has when he doesn't really know. So I'm not sure that that really is the reason.

Anyway, even if he didn't know that, he knows most things and is an excellent sailor. It's hard to land on Lunga as there's no jetty. Callum had to attach the boat to what he called a 'pontoon' which floats. He then drove it onto the rocks. I jumped onto the pontoon thing and ran onto the rocky beach while Callum slipped the boat back into the bay and dropped anchor. Then he jumped off in all his wet gear and marched through the shallows to meet me. He's so cool.

For a while we looked for fossils among the rocks. Callum knows that I love that stuff so he helped me. I didn't really find anything other than a few nice fossil shells but then I came across what looked at first like an old piece of coral. I showed it to Callum and he said it was a blade, a rough-fashioned knife made from basalt, for killing fish. Then he looked me in the eye and told me it probably belonged to a mermaid – that they hunted with such objects tied to wooden spears. I waited for him to pull a face or smile to show me that he was joking. But he didn't. He just kept nodding his head and his face was so serious that I think perhaps he even believed what he was saying. He then told me a few other mermaid 'facts' – which was a bit odd as I knew they couldn't be facts.

After all everyone knows mermaids don't actually exist. Except Mum perhaps. And now, I think, maybe Callum.

Anyway, there were some grey seals on the low rocks and wildflowers near where we had come ashore. There were lots of what Callum told me was sea campion, something weird called birdsfoot trefoil, tormentil and thrift. Callum wrote down all the names for me. I told him I was writing the diary while Mum was away and I think he guessed how much I was missing her. He suggested that we pick a few flowers which I could put in my diary and show her when she got back. I thought that was a good idea.

Then we set off to see the birds. We went to Harp Rock which is a stack separated from Lunga by the sea. We saw black and white razorbills, diving down and catching fish in their beaks. They were nesting and breeding on the stack. We also saw fulmars, which are grey and white like seagulls, and guillemots, which look a bit like small penguins. There were loads of puffins wandering around where we were standing. They are so tame, Callum said, because there are no predators on the isles and they are not used to seeing humans. One came up really close and Callum took a photograph of it right next to me. It was very funny and we sent it to Mum. He also told me that there would be over 2,000 pairs of puffins on the island before the end of summer. That's a lot!

After we had had enough of watching the birds we went off to climb the mountain. From the top we could see the ruined village in the northeast of Lunga where there are still the remains of black houses. We also had great views over the sea and Callum pointed out the other isles that we would sail to later and stop at if we had time. Fladda was the next big flat one we could see and then beyond that were Cairn na Burgh Mor and Cairn na Burgh Beag where there are the ruins of the castle of Cairnburgh. I didn't say it to Callum but I really hoped we did moor there so we could climb over the castle remains and I could think about the Macleans. Mum had told me that they once ruled over the Treshnish Isles and that they probably hid out on these faraway islands when they got into trouble with the local clans and the English.

We had our lunch at the top of Cruachan – tuna and sweetcorn sandwiches which Callum had made because he knows that they are my favourite. We also had crisps and apples, which I also really like. As I said, Callum is a great guy.

By the time we got back to the boat, the sky was clouding over and the weather was becoming 'changeable' Callum said. We passed Fladda and did make it to the castle ruins, but we didn't get to anchor and explore. I begged Callum to let us and he said that he would have if he could. But we really needed to be getting back just in case the weather turned. I bet Dad would have let us moor and have a look around.

I was a bit gutted but as we were getting close to Mull the sky got really dark and the waves started getting high and rough. So he had been right about the weather. When we docked it was great to see Dad who said he didn't want to take the boat back to our island in this weather. So we would visit Torin and spend the night there instead. Hurray. What a brilliant way to round off a brilliant day. Sailing with Callum then stories with Torin.

All it needed to have been perfect was Mum. I miss her.

24

Freya sat on the edge of her bed, motionless. Rain had begun to lash against the window but she didn't turn to look at it. Her mind was elsewhere, repeatedly stumbling upon a sentence in Sam's diary. She had faltered over it when she first read the entry, but had put it to the back of her mind. *I bet Dad would have let us moor and have a look around.*

She turned the words over again and then said them out loud, as if trying them out. They curdled instantly on her tongue. She closed her eyes and remembered a time when she and Jack had been out on the boat, the weather turning. He was smiling at her, a mischievous glint in his eye. Persuading her to stay out longer, go farther than he knew they should. She had always been the disciplined one; he the one who lacked such will. But when Sam came along she had noticed a change in him. He had curbed that side of his nature, hadn't he? Or had he simply hidden it from her more effectively?

Panic seared through her. It had been a constant nagging doubt. But the diary entry proved it, didn't it? Sam could persuade his father to do things he shouldn't, to take risks and gamble with the weather and their lives.

Freya leapt to her feet and began pacing the room. Her face was hot and she felt uncontrollable tears welling inside her. She had left her only child, her son, alone with Jack and he had killed them both. How could she have left Sam with such a man? What kind of woman was she?

Freya sat down heavily on the corner of the bed as her tears fell. Her breath was thick and laboured and she felt dizzy. She knew that if she continued down this path, these scorching thoughts would burn her. She had to stop herself, stop her mind from growing ever wilder, more extreme.

She took a deep breath and looked up, catching sight of herself in the mirror beside the wardrobe. The sight made her start. Her face was pale, her tired eyes dark and lined and her hair stood out in a white mess from her head. Her cheeks were hollow, she had lost weight. She looked entirely unlike herself: unearthly; a banshee bewailing those who were already gone. Freya stood and moved towards the mirror, repulsed and mesmerised at the same time. It was hard to comprehend, looking at herself now, just how much she had changed. And with the thought something popped in her head.

Her lips curled into a snarl and she screamed. She grabbed the wardrobe door and yanked it open with such force that it came off its hinges.

'You stupid, selfish bastard,' she yelled, pulling Jack's shirts off their hangers and flinging them to the ground. 'How dare you be so reckless?' She kicked the shirts across the floor then reached for a pile of jumpers on a shelf.

'How could you be so careless with the most precious thing we had?' She reached for T-shirts, trousers, a suit, a winter coat, anything she could get her hands on, throwing it all to the floor; raging, shouting and stomping, ripping and grappling.

'Freya!'

It took a while for her to register the voice behind her.

'Freya!'

She turned to see Marta standing in the doorway, still wearing her outdoor coat, her hair wet and windswept, a horrified look on her face.

'What are you doing?'

Freya followed Marta's gaze to the floor. At the sight of Jack's clothes, randomly scattered about, she felt the rage surge within her again. 'Selfish bastard,' she spat out, picking up a T-shirt from the floor and then flinging it back down.

Marta stepped forward and put her hand on Freya's arm. 'It's okay,' she murmured quietly, trying to calm her.

But Freya flinched and spun away from her. 'Get off me. It's not okay. It's *not* okay. You have no idea what it's like. No fucking idea what it means to love someone, really love someone, more than yourself, and then have them gone. Vanished. Disappeared. Not *you* walking away from it. Not your choice.' She jabbed her finger at Marta, feeling pressure rise inside her head, the rapid beat of her pulse against her temples. 'You've never had a real relationship in your life. Something you didn't have some sort of distance from. Never, ever. So don't *ever* tell me it's okay.

Don't you *ever*.' She stopped talking and took a deep, ragged breath.

Stunned, Marta stood frozen to the spot, and for a few moments she simply stared at Freya. Then she looked away and walked silently out of the room.

The rain had stopped and the light had gone out of the sky. The bedroom was in shadow. Freya lay across the pile of clothes scattered on the floor. How long she had been like this she didn't know, but still she lay, her body unmoving. Her mind was empty and she wallowed in the absence of feeling. Her fingers stroked the soft cotton of a shirt, moving backwards and forwards over it. The rhythm soothed her. Eventually she brought the shirt to her chest and hugged it to her, inhaling the woody scent, sandalwood and musk, that reminded her so much of Jack. His smell was still so fresh, as if he had just peeled off the shirt, thrown it to the floor and walked into the next room. Sometimes she thought she heard him, the smack of his feet against the stone floor of the kitchen, the sound ominous and reassuring at the same time. But now there was only silence. She closed her eyes and let the scent envelop her. In this space, this quiet, she remembered another part of Sam's diary. *When we docked it was great to see Dad who said he didn't want to take the boat back to our island in this weather.*

Tears pricked her eyes so Freya kept them clamped shut. This time she needed to keep control of herself.

'I'm sorry,' she said, and sat upright.

She surveyed the carnage of the bedroom.

'I'm so sorry. I didn't mean it. Please forgive me.'

For a moment she sat in silence, as if waiting for a reply. Then she stood, began to pick up the clothes and fold them. The slow process, the habit of it soothed her. By the time she had finished, and Jack's clothes were neatly stacked in the wardrobe once more, the bedroom was in darkness.

She stood in front of the mirror, hardly able to see her own reflection this time. She ran her fingers through her hair, straightened her clothes.

'Please forgive me,' she said again, as much to herself as Jack.

Then she went to find her sister.

25

Marta was standing at the kitchen stove, stirring a pan. She seemed immersed in the task, but Freya knew that she wasn't concentrating on it. Instead her brain would be turning over and over the horrible things Freya had said to her. She felt the sharp sting of guilt, so familiar now.

'Marta.'

When Marta didn't move, Freya stepped closer towards her.

'I'm so sorry, sis. Please forgive me. I don't know what came over me.' She paused as Marta remained facing the wall. 'You have every right to be furious,' she persisted. 'I said terrible things and I didn't mean them. Of course I didn't. I'm so sorry,' she said again.

Finally Marta turned. Her face was pale and she looked as though she'd been crying.

'Oh, Marta.' Freya moved towards her and hugged her hard.

'It's okay. I forgive you.'

Freya pulled away from her and ran her fingers gently over Marta's eyes. I'm sorry, she mouthed again. I didn't mean it.

'Yes, you did. But never mind.'

Freya opened her mouth to speak but Marta put a finger over her lips and made a shushing noise.

'So what brought it on?'

Freya sighed. 'I read the next entry in Sam's diary and thought Jack had taken a risk with their safety. That got me into all kinds of thoughts. I'm sorry you got caught up in it.'

Marta smiled. 'Is Jack forgiven too?'

Freya nodded.

'Good. Okay then.' She paused, looking at Freya's throat. 'Is that the necklace Sam found beachcombing?'

'It is.'

'It's stunning. And fits you perfectly.' Marta reached out and momentarily touched its silver. 'Lindsay says hi, by the way.'

Freya nodded. Lindsay was the old university friend Marta had visited that day. She had moved with her husband and two children to Iona a couple of years before. 'How is she?'

'Oh, she's fine,' Marta said. 'I think they found the winter hard.'

No doubt. Freya tried not to think about what she would have given to have had winter at the lighthouse with her family.

'I got a call while I was with her. From the office. Something urgent has come up. I have to go back to London.'

'Oh.' Freya felt the almost physical punch in her stomach. 'Is it him?'

Marta shook her head. 'It's just work. I said I needed to talk to you first.'

Freya nodded. But she realised that, for all Marta's reassurances, she probably had no choice but to go. And even now, moments after an argument, she realised just how much she wanted her to stay. 'Well, of course you must go. I'll be fine.' Freya said it with a conviction she didn't by any means feel.

Marta frowned. 'Will you? I'm not so sure after today.'

Freya shrugged. 'Of course. Look, I'm okay now. It was just a momentary thing. And I'm bound to have those from time to time. You know that.'

Marta nodded but still looked unconvinced. 'Why don't you come with me? Just for a few weeks until I've worked out my notice. Then we can come back together for a while before I start a new job.'

But Freya shook her head. She knew with total certainty that she didn't want to go to London. She wanted to go to the Treshnish Isles, the second destination of her pilgrimage. 'Really I'm fine. I can't leave. When do you need to go?'

'Tomorrow.'

'Oh,' she said again.

'What about Mum and Dad coming to stay?'

'No.' Freya said it with fervour. 'Seriously. I'll be okay on my own. Besides, Torin's nearby, and Callum.'

'Ah, Callum. Of course.' Marta smiled at Freya and winked.

Freya ignored her. 'And there's Daniel too.'

'Daniel?' Marta raised her eyebrows.

'He dropped by today.'

'Really? What did he want?'

'He came to thank us for our help on the night of the storm. We talked a bit. I told him about Jack and Sam. It was okay.'

Marta nodded. 'I see. So you've made a new friend.'

Freya shrugged and laughed. 'I wouldn't say that. He doesn't give a lot away about himself. In fact, thinking about it, I'm surprised you haven't bonded with him yet.'

'Hey, watch it.' But Marta was smiling.

Freya hugged her again. 'Really, it's fine for you to go.'

'Really?'

'Yes, really. Now can you tell me what it is you're stirring?'

'To be honest I don't know,' Marta said, eyeing the thick greenish liquid at the bottom of the pan. 'It came out of a tin but I wasn't paying attention to what it was.' She looked at it again and laughed. 'As penance, you know you're going to have to eat it.'

26

After Marta had gone to bed, Freya paced around the cottage. She sat at the kitchen table playing with the post. She climbed the tower staircase but came straight back down again. Whatever she did, wherever she went, she couldn't settle. She poured herself another glass of wine and drank it down. But it didn't calm her. Instead her breath grew shallow. Her nerves were tight, overstretched, and nausea lurked at the base of her throat, waiting to take a stranglehold. Soon she would be alone again. The thought flashed through her huge and terrifying. Her skull began to pound, her body felt as if it was upon a shifting sea. Freya opened the kitchen door, took a deep breath and tried to centre herself.

A damp chill loitered on the air from the late afternoon rainstorm and thick clouds hung low in the sky. Crossing the garden, Freya felt the wet ooze of grass beneath her feet, as if her own wretchedness was seeping from her with each step. She grasped the enclosure wall, to dispel the fear that she would topple and fall, and looked down over the island. But there was no salvation there. It was barren and bare, the sea beyond it monstrous and black.

She watched the blink of distant lights on a cargo ship. It crept slowly towards the horizon until eventually it disappeared. Where were those sailors going? she wondered. And what had brought them so far from home to this pitiless place on the fringes of the world? As she stared into the night, she remembered Edward, the soldier, isolated far from the warmth and comfort of Josie. And something about the thought made her feel less alone.

As she walked back to the cottage, her disequilibrium began to disperse. She closed the door, tidied the kitchen and finally turned out the lights. By the time she headed to bed, she felt steadier. And Edward's letters were in her hands.

9 September 1653
Speedwell

My dearest Josie,

Today I am simply looking about me. The weather yesterday became poor and I had to work hard to prevent another dark humour from taking over me. But today could not have been more different. A clear sky and a light wind made my spirits rise. And at sunset, the hills behind the castle glowed as if on fire. There is a clarity to the light here, which, of course, also endures far longer than in the south. Tonight, as I walked alone in the area surrounding the castle, I watched the moon rise in a still-bright sky. There are a few kinds of houses in these parts, most built sturdily from the nearby rock, and which shelter local fishermen, crofters and their families. There was also an inn, built in the same manner, that appeared to beckon to me, Josie, as well you can imagine.

I entered cautiously, unsure of the welcome I would receive, but there were already a few of our party within, tolerated – by which I mean ignored – by the locals. I took my ale, with a civil nod to the barman, to a seat by a fireside table quite removed from my countrymen. Then I looked about me.

In spite of the basic nature of the accommodation, the place was homely enough, flames dancing in the peaty grate, and at the table beside me a family, I supposed, speaking together and laughing. I noticed that an elderly man was talking, the grandfather, perhaps, in quiet but engaging tones that seemed to mesmerise the younger children, of which there were three below the age of about seven. He spoke in an accented voice, harsh and soft at the same time, and something about it caused me to listen in. As I became accustomed to his manner of speaking, I realised he was telling stories. I smiled at the crackling voice, the rise and fall of the words pulling at me, their melody drawing me in. He was a good storyteller the old man, I would give him that. I ventured another quick look at him before returning my gaze to the fire and thought he must be one of those oral storytellers that were famed from these parts, as I could not see him referring to any book.

And so it was that I found myself listening when he began another story – one, he said, from long ago, when he was just a boy.

Perhaps one hundred years then, I thought to myself smiling, if Duncan's stories were to be believed. To stop myself from laughing, I looked out of the nearby window and up into the sky. It had grown somewhat darker and was beginning to twinkle with stars. The witching hour. And I smiled to myself again.

This story, the old man said, took place nearby, one scorching day in summer. A young man had taken out a fishing boat, without permission. And he hadn't taken it to fish. He had taken it to go swimming. The old man chuckled then, recounting what his father had said about the young man. Nothing but a blaggard and a rogue, a lazy rascal. The old man chuckled some more, took a mouthful of ale and continued.

The boy rowed and rowed, far out into the ocean, away from the village and everything that he knew. Eventually, he moored off some rocks and plunged into the water. So cool, so refreshing in the soaring heat of the day. When he had finished his swim he climbed up onto the rocks and lay in the sun, idling. After a time he dozed off but awakened, or thought he awakened, to hear the sweetest sound of singing. A more beautiful sound than he had ever heard. For a long while the boy lay there, unable to imagine where the sound was coming from. After all, this boy was far from shore, alone in the middle of the ocean. Perhaps he was still dreaming, but he remembered the daylight, the sun beating down, felt the tingle of saltwater on his skin. And the sound of the singing made him shiver even more in the heat, made his throat feel tight and parched.

Well, this boy stood and clambered over the rocks but could see no one. Neither could he see any boat upon the waves nearby. But as he continued to look, his eye caught upon something below the surface of the sea. He thought it was a beautiful maiden swimming there, her long flowing hair gliding upwards in the current. Like liquid gold. The boy watched the maiden beneath the waves, saw her skin, also like gold, glisten in the sunlight, heard her haunting, mysterious voice all around him. For it was her voice that he heard, he was sure of it. And the boy couldn't stop watching her. She was mesmerising, the sound of her song hypnotic. Then, as if she realised someone had seen her, had stolen a glance of her perhaps, she turned from beneath the water and looked up at him. Her face was so beautiful the boy gasped, felt almost as if he was drowning. But he wasn't even in the water. For a long, long moment the boy stared at the woman – at her piercing blue eyes, her pink lips, her glistening, beautiful golden hair and skin. Then it was as if the sea and the sky darkened and her face distorted from beauty into a ferocious terror; her lips snarled, her hair spread out in fiery points. In the next instant she was gone.

The boy waited until nightfall before he dared row back to shore, more afraid of the sea and what lurked within it than the beating he would get when he returned home.

And he never sailed upon the ocean again, knowing in his heart that if the maiden found him once more she would lure him to his death. He knew that it had been both a blessing and a curse to see her, to hear her song, and that he had been lucky – without a token to give to her in exchange for his life – to have escaped.

At this point I could not help but look directly at the old man, so intrigued was I by his dark tale. But as I peered at him, more brazenly no doubt than I ought, he turned and looked at me. For a moment I feared my eavesdropping was discovered. But then, to my relief, I saw that his eyes were pale and cloudy and I realised that he was blind. I breathed more easily. But as I continued to look, the old man's unseeing eyes upon me, I felt a chill to my core and the sensation that, no matter how ridiculous it sounds, he saw deep inside me. That he could see into my soul and its secrets.

The little girl asked the old man over and over if the story was true. To my relief she drew the eyes of her grandfather away from me. I waited for him to say that it was a fable, just a tale. After all, not all stories are to be believed. But instead the old man smiled, stroked her hair and nodded his head. Just because a strange thing happens, he said, it doesn't mean it cannot be true. Strange things happen every day, peculiar things, odd coincidences, events that come to pass that perhaps we have dreamt about. We have more difficulty accepting these things as real. But it does not mean they are not so, that they have strayed from history into myth.

Then the youngest boy asked him if he was the boy in the tale. The old man chuckled. That, he said, is a secret. But I have to admit, Josie, that I had wondered the same thing.

As they stood and gathered themselves, the eldest boy asked if they could return the following day and hear more stories.

The old man's answer surprised me. It will depend when the storm arrives, he said. All the children then asked in unison how he knew a storm was coming.

The smell and sound of the sea, the old man replied. The feel of it upon my skin. Changes in the light and air. I do not need to be able to see it. I sense it. I have not been out on the ocean for over eighty years, and yet I understand its rhythms perfectly. And they are changing.

He glanced swiftly at me then, nothing more than a passing look, but in that moment I knew it for certain. He was the boy from the tale – the one who had never ventured onto the water again after he caught sight of the mermaid, for fear of retribution and death. And yet precisely because of its curse, he understood the sea as well as any seafaring man. A storm was coming.

As he and his grandchildren passed by me and disappeared into the crowd, I heard him whisper beneath his breath. Now more than ever is not a time to be at sea. And then he was gone.

I did not even know the old man's name and yet for some reason his words filled me with dread. I did not want to be caught in this wild place of possibilities when truly inclement weather struck. For something told me that we would not survive it. I rose then from my seat and headed for the door, coldness in my heart. I told myself it was nothing, that it was nonsense. That I was becoming as superstitious as these simple folk I had been thrown among. But I could not shake the feeling, the grip of fear deep inside me, until I had returned to the ship, taken a tankard of beer and written this letter to you.

Forgive me, dearest Josie, for my lack of words the last time we were together, the lack of comfort I gave you. You bring me happiness beyond measure. God speed my journey home to you and our babe from this desolate land.

Until then
I am your
Edward

27

Freya stood on the deck of her boat, the rise and fall of the waves echoing in the pit of her stomach. She felt both sad and sick. She had dropped Marta at the ferry terminal on Mull, then taken the boat straight out again. It wasn't the best day to be on the sea, but if she wasn't mistaken the weather wouldn't turn truly bad. The worst she could expect was a downpour and a growing swell.

She stared west, over the restless grey of the sea. Coll and Tiree were close now, flat and windswept, and she thought she could perhaps just make out Barra or maybe the Uists, through the gap between the two islands, rimy sea-stained blurs on the horizon. But perhaps it was simply the sky reflecting the dull water beneath it.

Freya turned and looked over the craggy landscape of Lunga. It rose behind her, ancient and rocky, cloaked in greenery. There was something special about it, about its wild, remote beauty. Birds were already nesting on the stack and seals were also in evidence, their lithe grey bodies twisting and turning in the shallow waters, dancing around the contours of the boat. Freya stared captivated and the movement triggered a thought of Edward, and the letter that she had read the night before. It was incredible, unbelievable. And yet, as she watched, she half expected one of the creatures to spin around below the surface, more woman than fish, and fix her with a fiery stare.

Freya blinked hard and looked up. The rocking of the boat was nauseating in spite of her good sea legs. But then she had drunk glass after glass of wine the night before and was paying for it now. She thought again of her sister, plagued by a nagging doubt that Marta was going because of her. Because of her hurtful words. No, it wasn't that, she told herself sternly. She was tired and irrational. But she had slept fitfully after all, and at the edges of her sleep had heard the haunting call of mermaids.

Freya was roused by the sound of an engine and voices upon the air. She turned to see Callum's boat approaching, bringing a party of tourists to the isles. As he drew closer, he waved at her, a black woollen hat pulled down low over his brow. She waved back, pleased to see him. He made a circular gesture with his hand which meant, she supposed, that he was going to drop off his passengers and then make his way back to her. She nodded and waited.

'Now you're the last person I was expecting to see here,' Callum shouted over the noise of his boat as he drew alongside the *Valkyrie*. Wafts of diesel fumes rose towards Freya, intensifying her nausea.

A moment later Callum cut the engine; the silence that flowed back in its wake was a relief. 'Yes, I haven't been out here for ages,' she said, watching him deftly tether the two boats, the rope moving easily in his hands.

'Well, you could have picked a better day for it,' said Callum, grimacing at the sky. 'It's going to rain for sure later. Let's hope I get this lot back in time before the heavens open.'

Freya let out a small, fleeting laugh. He was always so obsessed with the weather. Her eyes filled with sudden tears at the thought of it.

'Are you okay?' Callum's look of concern dissolved the last remnants of Freya's resolve and the hot heavy drops spilled from her eyes.

'I'm sorry,' she said, quickly wiping them away.

For a few moments they stood in silence while Freya tried to gather herself. She began to apologise once more, but Callum simply brushed her words away. When she had composed herself, he spoke again.

'You look tired, Freya. Everything all right?'

She nodded. 'I always have trouble sleeping,' she said, seeing herself suddenly as if from the outside. Her skin pale, with an unhealthy tinge, the bags under her eyes dark with lack of sleep. 'And I'm missing Marta already. She had to go back to London.'

'Ah, that's a shame. But she'll be back before you know it.' Callum smiled, then looked out over the watery landscape. 'So what brings you out here?'

'I found a diary of Sam's,' she said, after a moment. 'It had an entry from when he came here with you last Easter.' Her eyes filled with tears again.

'Ah, I see.' Callum looked at her for a moment before shifting his gaze to the island. 'Aye, we came here. A lot of noise from the birds and seals as I remember. We climbed the mountain, ate a picnic, had a great day.' Callum paused as he thought back. 'He picked you flowers, I think.'

Freya nodded and smiled. 'Yes. I found them in the diary.' She thought of the yellow, pink and purple of the tormentil and thrift sandwiched between the white pages. They still looked so colourful, so vibrant and alive. 'And I still have the photo in my phone that you took of Sam with the puffin.' She stifled another sob. 'I'm sorry, Callum.'

'Don't be silly, Freya.' His grey eyes looked at her kindly, steadily.

She took a deep breath and, to change the subject, pointed to the beach on Lunga. 'I read that you found a mermaid blade here.'

Callum's face broke into a reminiscent smile. 'Aye, that's right, now that you mention it. We did.'

'Although I'm not sure that Sam bought that it was anything other than a blade carved out of basalt.'

'No. A sceptic, that one. Even when I recited my failsafe history of mermaid sightings. The one I reel out for the tourists.' And he leaned in towards her conspiratorially with a nod of his head towards the party he had seemingly abandoned on Lunga. 'I told him Columbus had spotted three back in 1493 and documented it. And do you know what he said to that?'

Freya shook her head.

'He insisted that it was more likely he had seen manatees.'

Freya heard the rational voice of her father-in-law at work on her son. Alister always doused everything in a splash of fine, cold rationality, consigning the miraculous to the unbelievable.

'So then I tried the encounter of the schoolteacher from Thurso in 1797. He was so sure, as he ambled along the beach one day, that he had seen a mermaid out on a rock in the Pentland Firth, that he risked ridicule and infamy by writing to *The Times* about it.'

Freya nodded. She knew this tale.

'And even though the rock was cut off from land and surrounded by a deep gully of pounding surf, hard for any human to swim out to, Sam remained unconvinced. He said that the man was looking from a distance, didn't see the tail clearly and was largely reluctant to believe it to be just a woman because the rock upon which she sat seemed to him difficult to get to. But that was no reason why, if she was a good swimmer, she couldn't have reached there. He mentioned you as proof of this.'

Callum chuckled, obviously entertained by what he remembered.

'Then I tried a further sighting by an old Scottish fisherman in 1947. Now he was my great-great-grandfather, teetotal and a Presbyterian. He claims he saw a mermaid in the waters off the Isle of Muck, twenty yards from shore, sitting on a floating lobster box, combing her hair. When she caught sight of him watching she disappeared under the water. Now he was eighty years old at the time, but he still had his eyesight and all his marbles. Not to mention that by all accounts he was the most reliable and honest man you could ever hope to meet.'

'I didn't know that.' Freya was taken aback and, secretly, not a little delighted.

'Aye, that's what he said he saw. And he maintained it was the truth until his death.' Callum nodded pensively. 'But still Sam would not be swayed from what he thought was a fiction. Even my favourite story was met with resistance.'

'Benbecula?'

'Aye. You know it?'

'Of course. Everyone around here does.' Freya had told it to Sam and she couldn't help smiling at his likely reaction if Callum had tried to tell it as truth.

'Well, I said the mermaid's body washed up on the shore of the island after a great storm in 1830 – the long, dark hair, the soft white skin of the upper body, the lower part like a salmon. I told him of the villagers burying it in a coffin.' Callum paused and shook his head. 'And Sam said to me that if the body was truly as the villagers claimed, surely they would have exhumed it later for it to be examined properly and scientifically. Never have I encountered such a young dissenter.' Freya laughed. 'I suggested that perhaps the clergy would not allow for the removal of the body after burial – that it was the church rather than the villagers. But he was having none of that.' Callum nodded soberly. 'The only time Sam even wavered was when I told him how fishermen out in deep, open ocean, miles from here, have caught fish in their nets with blades, like the one we found, already piercing their bodies. Finally, he looked a little less sure of himself.' Callum smiled, obviously pleased to have unsettled the doubter.

Freya frowned. 'Is that true?'

'Aye, it's true. Fishermen from these parts have come across it. Not often, but it has happened. They've photographed it even, as it was such a strange thing to see.'

Freya was surprised. 'I've never seen those pictures. Never even heard of them.' Over the years, she had come across many tales of mermaids from these parts and beyond to Norway and Greenland. But never this.

Callum shrugged. 'Well I don't know what it means. But I know what the fishermen think it means.'

Freya was silent for a moment. Just as she imagined her son had been. Stumped, perhaps, that he couldn't immediately think of an explanation for such a thing. Jack would have called it superstitious nonsense. They'll have been sure to have doctored the photographs. Who's to say such things were ever found in the body of fish? She remembered how his upper lip would curl slightly in derision, and even now something about it made her angry. She was glad that her son had spent the day with Callum, with someone for whom the inexplicable wasn't simply laughable. Suddenly she found herself telling him about Edward, his letters; the one about the old man and the mermaid.

'Well, that just goes to show the miraculous does happen

around here. And I don't mean simply the recovery of those letters.' Callum winked. 'I'd like to see those sometime.'

'You're welcome whenever. You know that, I hope.' Freya smiled as she looked at Callum, and then her eyes moved beyond him to the increasingly darkening sky. She needed to be heading back soon.

'I heard that you and Marta helped out Daniel Jefferies the other day,' said Callum, changing the direction of the conversation.

Freya looked at him blankly.

'During the storm, I mean.'

'Oh. Of course.' Freya hadn't remembered Daniel's surname. 'We only did what anyone would have done.'

'I doubt that,' said Callum, smiling. 'I heard he was in big trouble. Hard to imagine how he got himself into that situation.' He shook his head. 'Could have been another tragedy for his family.'

'What?' said Freya. She was only half listening, but she didn't understand.

Callum looked at her. 'I mean with his wife and everything.'

Freya raised an eyebrow questioningly. Daniel had told her that he didn't have a wife.

'Ah. I assumed that he would have said, with . . . you know . . . you helping him and . . . ' Callum's awkwardness was immediate and obvious.

Slowly it began to dawn on her. She remembered Daniel's eyes – their haunted quality, their hollowness.

She had always wondered what it was that hid behind them. Now she thought she began to understand.

'What happened?' Freya asked.

Callum took a breath. 'His wife drowned. Like you, she liked to swim. But one day she went out and never came back.'

Freya stared at him, shocked. For a moment her mind went blank. Then it began to race. It made perfect sense. His initial distance, his awkwardness – she had taken that to be somehow connected to his accident. But it was connected to another accident altogether. As was the sense of something familiar about him which she hadn't been able to place. It was so obvious now. It was grief.

'He took it very hard by all accounts. Doesn't talk about it much.' This last comment was clearly for her benefit.

She nodded, wondering why he hadn't told her. He had had the perfect opportunity the last time they met. But perhaps he simply hadn't wanted to speak about it – she understood that all too well. Or perhaps he had wanted to allow her the space to talk. Whatever the reason, she felt her heart break for him.

Callum was shifting from foot to foot looking uncomfortable. 'I'm sorry, Freya. I shouldn't have mentioned it. It probably brings back all kinds of bad thoughts. I just assumed he would have said something.'

'It's okay, Callum. Don't worry yourself. I get it.' Freya reached out and touched his shoulder to indicate that there was nothing for him to be sorry for. But she became suddenly conscious again of how very tired and sick she felt. She looked at the blackening horizon. It was time to make a move for home. The sea was getting choppier, the rocking of the boat more insistent.

'Sam had a wonderful day with you, you know. Thank you so much for that.' And she leaned in and hugged him. He smelled of salt and soap and reassurance.

'It was my pleasure,' he said. His voice sounded as awkward as his body felt.

As Freya pulled away she noticed a mark left on his shoulder by her tears. She ran her fingers over it gently. A dark, salty stain that would remain until it was washed away.

28

The next day, Freya's thoughts kept returning to what Callum had told her, out on the sea at Lunga, his stories of the mermaid.

She had just recounted them to Torin, who was sitting beside her, then turned her head lazily away from him, feeling dullness in her brain. She had started taking more of her pills since Marta left – only a small increase in her dose, but it somehow managed to take the edge off.

She stared out of Torin's sitting-room window and could just make out two eagles as they circled higher and higher over the loch. They were calling to each other noisily and she was surprised, as always, that they didn't sound more dignified, more in keeping with the way they looked. Instead, rather like gulls, their call was high-pitched, shrill and slightly raucous.

'Are you all right, Freya? You don't seem quite yourself.'

She turned back to Torin, then reached across the table between them and took his hand. 'I'm okay,' she said. Lying had become a way of life. 'Do you want some more cake?' She had bought it this time, instead of making it, and wondered if he had noticed. But if he had, he kept it to himself.

'No, my dear, I'm fine, thank you. I'll take a drop more tea, though.'

Freya poured them both another cup, then sat right back in her seat. She followed the undulating line of the garden down to the loch's edge. The water looked molten in the thickening evening light, the heavy orange-red of sunset settling upon it. She looked up into the sky once more but the eagles had already gone.

'Well, I don't need second sight to pick up on your mood.'

In spite of herself, Freya smiled. He was an old devil, she thought, who it was impossible to keep things from. He seemed to know so much, even unspoken private things. The next moment she found herself telling him about the discovery of Sam's secret box; the diary and the entries that she had read.

'It made me so happy to hear his voice again. And so sad and guilty that he had missed me so much. That I wasn't there for him in those last weeks.'

Torin nodded gravely. 'I can imagine. But his father was,' he added, matter-of-factly. Then he took a sip of his tea.

'Yes, that's true.' Still, it was not the same as her being there. She knew that from what Sam had written. 'But it got me into that spiral again. Would it have been different if I had been around the day they disappeared? Would they have even done what they did? Would they be alive now?' She shuddered, wracked with doubt.

Torin put down his teacup slowly and leaned in towards her. 'Look, my dear. You have to forgive yourself. Everything would have been the same, even if you had been here.'

'But how can you be sure of that?'

'I'm sure,' said the old man, and reached across to her. She grasped his hand again. 'You need to accept that. Or, perhaps, things would have been even worse. Perhaps you would be gone too.'

'But I'm not gone,' Freya said despondently. Torin's words had tapped into something she had long felt. 'I survived and they didn't.'

Torin nodded. 'Aye. But how would it be better if you too had gone, Freya? Really, deep down, you must know this.'

She nodded. 'I do. But the guilt I feel is so huge sometimes, suffocating. I feel I'll never be able to forgive myself, to move on.'

'You must learn to let it go. There is nothing to forgive.'

Even if she didn't feel his words were true, it was good to hear them. And, besides, one day, maybe, she would actually believe them. For a few moments they sat in silence, Torin holding her hand. Then he tried to move the conversation on.

'So,' he said. 'What else did you discover in Sam's box of goodies?'

'Why don't you tell me?' said Freya, looking at him.

'Hmm,' said Torin. 'I must admit I do not know.'

'So there *are* limits. I did wonder.' Freya laughed. 'There were lots of other beach finds. And, best of all, there was this.'

She leaned forwards, guiding Torin's hand to the necklace at her throat. His fingers moved over the bands of silver which twisted around Freya's neck. She had taken to wearing it. She wondered now, as Torin's fingers touched its surface, if he could sense its beauty.

'Is it one piece?' he said at last.

'Yes,' said Freya. 'Amazing, isn't it? I've done some research since I found it and I think it's a Permian ring – a neck ring made by the Russian Vikings out of twisted silver. It's stunning, Torin.'

'Hmm. They were used as currency, you know. Vikings carried their wealth in their jewellery and then chopped it up when they needed money. Hack silver, they called it. Rather appropriate, given their way of life, wouldn't you say?' Torin's fingers moved over the necklace inch by inch, slowly. 'I think part of it is missing. Broken off.' Then he frowned. 'Hmm. I see something – a boat and the ocean, maybe.'

Was it Jack and Sam out on the sea? Freya wondered. She looked out of the window and down to the loch. The last wisps of coloured evening light were thinning and receding, absorbed by the spread of deep inky blue. Before long the sky would transform itself again. And another black night would begin. Freya shivered even though it wasn't cold.

'No, perhaps it isn't the ocean. Although I'm not sure. There is also something underground. A grave, I think.'

Freya had wondered about the history of the necklace and what, if anything, Torin would see. But now she wondered whether in fact she wanted to hear it.

'Ah,' said Torin. 'I think I understand. Vikings were often buried in their ships, with many worldly possessions beside them. I can see fragments of the scene – a red wool dress, a tunic made of silk, a white linen veil. A rich site and grave goods. A wealthy woman was buried in this necklace.'

Freya touched the rough surface of the silver once again. She had imagined it once adorning the neck of a woman, someone from the distant past. But she hadn't thought of it being entombed with the dead who had once worn it.

For a moment Torin was silent, as if gathering his thoughts. Then he spoke. 'I would like to beg your indulgence, Freya. I know you will think me a silly, superstitious old man. No doubt you think that anyway.' Torin smiled. 'But perhaps you will humour me nonetheless. Please don't wear the necklace any more.'

Freya was taken aback by the sudden and unexpected nature of the request. 'Really?'

'There is a darkness, a heaviness around it. It may simply be from its heritage, but I think it is more than that. There is sadness around it too, more recent. I feel it. But I cannot see more than this.' He paused. 'I think it would be better if you put it back where you found it.'

Freya raised her hand instinctively to the silver at her neck.

'Please, Freya. Can you do this for me?' Torin's voice was tight, strained.

'Of course,' she said. 'If it means so much to you, of course.' She reached for his hand once more to reassure him. 'Now, let's have some more tea and talk about something else.'

29

Freya had wondered whether, given her reaction the last time, it was wise to continue reading the diary. She had weighed both sides as carefully as she could: her pleasure in hearing her son's voice whispering to her anew, against the potential of what he told her to fuel her rage and her sadness, to disrupt her already precarious equilibrium. Perhaps there had never really been a contest to speak of, but she had decided to keep reading. Besides, she had been so disciplined, savouring these last moments, rationing herself to just one entry at a time, that she felt, no matter the consequences, she couldn't deny herself this. So the day after visiting Torin, Freya had read another entry.

22 April 2014

Today the weather was brilliant. The sun shone all day and it was really warm. So Dad said that we would take the boat to Tiree. I was really excited as there are great beaches there and fantastic beachcombing.

We sailed to Balevullin Bay on the northwest of the island and Dad let me steer nearly all the way there. Last time we went there Granddad came with us and I found an old pipe. I remember Granddad saying that lots of things get washed up on beaches because of the sea currents. He then told me a story about the people who lived on St Kilda who used to put letters in wooden boxes that they sealed up and attached to an animal stomach, or something like that, filled with air. Then they floated them to Lewis, Harris and Skye on the tides. It was the only way of getting their news regularly to the mainland, he said. I thought this was cool even though it sounded like it was made up. But then it was Granddad saying it. Mum says that Granddad always tells the bald truth – meaning he never tells lies or stories. And it did seem possible. It would be very annoying though and also a bit sad if the letters got lost or didn't make it to the people they were written to.

When we got to Tiree Dad and I went swimming. Then we had our lunch. The sea was too flat for any good surfing so we spent time hunting for stuff on the beach. Granddad bought me a mini metal detector for Christmas and I had been dying to try it out. It didn't have very good range so I had to walk very slowly along the beach. After a long time finding nothing, Dad had a go. He seemed to take AGES even though he found nothing either. Then, when I took over again, covering a different patch of sand, the beeper finally went off. That was really exciting. Dad helped me dig with my spade and it turned out that we found the most amazing necklace. It was a big loop of silver and Dad said it was probably meant to wind round and round a woman's neck. He said it looked really old but amazingly well preserved considering it'd probably been washed up by the sea. He said it was a specktacular find. I said straight away that we should give it to Mum as a surprise. Dad smiled and said it would look lovely on her. We then did more hunting for treasure and found a few old coins but by then the whole day had practically gone and we had to go. I didn't want to. I could have carried on treasure hunting for ever. And who knows what else we might have found.

I sailed the boat back to our island. The sea was very flat and the sky had loads of little clouds in it like tiny candyfloss. What a great day. I love being on the boat. In fact I think that heaven would be sailing on a nice day. And maybe finding the Green Island.

After she had read the entry, Freya had headed directly for Tiree. Now, standing on the edge of the boat, the sun beating down on her bare skin, she rejoiced in her decision to keep reading. Balevullin Bay was behind her, and in front the wide-open ocean. She took a deep lungful of air and dived into the water. The icy coldness was shocking but also thrilling. She surfaced, took another breath and began a fast front crawl, ploughing away from the boat. At first she concentrated on her direction. The water was calm but still she picked the line of least resistance – swimming at an angle to the path of the waves. Then she set her rhythm, a swift pace but one she knew she could sustain. She had not swum once in the open ocean since she had returned to the lighthouse, and only now did she realise how much she had missed it. She would head southwest out to the *Cairnsmuir* wreck, circling back through Hough skerries. But then, as she calculated the distance, she thought better of it. It was a round trip of about ten miles. That would be optimistic on a first outing, even for her. Maybe next time. For now she would content herself with Hough skerries and back. And if she was tired she could break up the journey by resting on the rocks there.

As she settled into a pattern, inhaling the clear salty air, exhaling it into the deep blue of the sea, she thought of the *Cairnsmuir* out on Bo Mor reef. The last time they had taken the boat out there, Jack had told Sam about the shipwreck and the subsequent whisky highjacking.

'The *Cairnsmuir* was a thousand-ton steamer on its way from Hamburg to Glasgow. It had already sailed past the Orkneys along the Pentland Firth and was now making its way down through the Hebrides. On Monday the sixth of July, 1885, approaching Tiree, she ran into dense fog. At a quarter to three in the morning, she ran aground, here, on this reef.'

Freya remembered that all three of them had looked over the side of the boat, trying to make out the wreck underwater. At low tide and in good weather it was possible to see it. But that day had been cloudy and the sea had followed suit. It revealed nothing but a pale reflective surface.

'Her captain was John Georgie,' Jack continued, as Sam

stared down into the depths. 'He tried to rescue the *Cairnsmuir* by reversing off the rocks, but seawater gushed into the engine room and flooded her. As the weather worsened to a gale, the crew grabbed the lifeboats and made for shore.

'Now these shipmen, perhaps glad to have survived the storm and been met with hospitality by the locals, told the islanders that among the ship's cargo were spirits and wine. So when the Customs men arrived, they found gangs of local men looting the beaches. They tried to chase them off but were heartily abused instead.'

Both Jack and Sam, she remembered, had started giggling at this point. Two peas in a pod. She had started laughing too, but less about the story.

'Highly enterprising as were these men of Tiree,' Jack continued, 'they set up watchmen to keep an eye on anything that washed up. As soon as it was seen, they transferred it to more reliable containers and buried it beneath the sand to be retrieved later. Away from spying eyes, if you know what I mean.'

Jack winked at Sam and they both laughed again.

'When a case of liquor was spotted floating on the water, a man named Kennedy stripped naked and dived into the sea, wrestling the case through the waves and onto the beach. The officials tried to take it from him but his friends turned out in support and they eventually backed down.

'At an inquiry into the accident, Captain Georgie was found guilty of careless navigation. But his reputation was restored on appeal. What was never restored was the booty from the ship's cargo, the sea's quarry – the islanders never revealed where they had concealed it.'

'Perhaps it's still there, buried under the sand,' said Sam, looking back to shore.

'Perhaps it is,' said Jack in his most mysterious tone. 'We'll hunt for it sometime. But for now let's check out if there's anything left of this wreck.' And suddenly Jack had stripped off all his clothes and, with a cry of, 'Come along, Kennedy,' jumped overboard. Sam had dissolved into laughter, followed suit and dived naked into the sea. Suddenly Freya was alone on the boat, laughter ringing in her ears. She had thrown their snorkels overboard and left them to it. Then she had dived in and begun to swim back to the mainland. She heard the voice of her son, muffled but audible, as she glided away. 'See you later. Swim hard, Mum. The shore will be in front of you before you know it.'

As she lay on a rock among Hough skerries, Freya thought back once again to that day at the *Cairnsmuir*. And she remembered Daniel's words when he came to the cottage. You look like you were happy, he had said. We were, she had replied. And she had meant it. She thought of Daniel's wife, also a keen swimmer, and realised just how precarious happiness was. You had to be vigilant. Death stalked these waters and sailed in on a change of tide. He'd take offerings like wine and whisky, but only in the short term. Everyone knew what he really wanted. And what he took when you least expected it.

Freya rolled onto her front. She had found this rock the last time she had come here. It was perfect: flat and smooth like an altar, perching just inches above sea level. As she lay in the searing heat, the place deserted and silent, snippets of Callum's tales of the mermaid floated through her mind again. The schoolteacher, so sure of what he'd seen that he had risked everything to write about it. And Callum's great-great-grandfather, convinced that the woman he saw, combing her hair on fishing baskets, was a magical being. It was incredible to imagine.

She thought of Edward's letter and the old man chancing upon a mermaid on his rock far out at sea. Freya smiled and looked down into the water, trying to see the bottom of the ocean floor. Perhaps if she looked hard enough she would be able to see the flash of a mermaid's tail below the surface. She stared hard for a while, but the only movement she saw, an occasional flicker at the edge of her vision, was the breaking of waves over the skerries. There was nothing else there. Freya sat upright and let her hands drop into the ocean. Then she washed water over her face and head. A baptism of sorts, she thought, as she made a silent prayer to the mermaid, if such things indeed existed. Protect me, and my family, if they are with you. Watch over us.

Then she stood, dived off the rock and headed back to her boat.

30

Later that day, sitting on the lamp-room floor, bathed in the warm late-evening light, Freya felt the love of her family wrapped close about her. Spring was melting into summer, the nights were growing longer, and rose and red hues spattered the cloud-speckled sky. She knew the contentment she felt was fleeting, that it wouldn't last, but for the moment she could hold it, tentatively, in the palm of her hand. She stroked the silver coiled around her neck, sitting so comfortably against her skin, and remembered what Torin had told her and what he had asked of her. Then she thought of the diary and that her son's first thought on finding the necklace was that she should have it. So it felt as though it was destined for her. What would it hurt if she wore it at home?

She picked up the phone and dialled Alister's number. She'd promised her mother some time ago that she would call, and somehow this evening seemed like a good time. It took a while to connect and then the ringtone came, faint and with an echo. Even Edinburgh was a long way away. Finally, someone picked up.

'Hello.' Her father-in-law's voice had always been hard and abrupt. Yet now it was softer.

'Hi, Alister. It's Freya.'

'Ah, lassie. It's good to hear your voice. How are you?'

His tone was so different from how she remembered it that Freya let go of the breath she hadn't even realised she was holding. 'I'm okay, thanks. And you?'

'Ach, well. It's difficult. But I don't need to tell you that now, do I?'

Freya, surprised by his honesty, shook her head. He had always been so gruff and practical, never permitting of weakness. She tried and failed to think of something to say. Silence, heavy with their mutual sadness, hung on the line.

'Are you still in London?' Alister asked after a few moments.

'No. I'm on Ailsa Cleit. Have been for a couple of weeks now.'

'Aye? And how is it to be back?'

Freya knew that Alister meant how was it to be back without Jack and Sam.

'There are lots of memories. And that can be hard. But on the whole it's been good.' And then, quite why she wasn't sure, perhaps because he seemed different, Freya told him something she hadn't told anyone else. That in her grief, London had grown too big for her. It had crept up on her, slowly, but she had seen it with clarity as she walked down the street one day. As she looked at the people all around, anonymous and jostling for space, it occurred to her that they had no knowledge of her husband or her son and now they never would. They would never know what they looked like, the sound of their laughter, the joy they had brought and the sheer magnitude of the space that their passing had left behind. They would never know what had caused a black hole to form inside her, one that had collapsed her world and sucked all her pleasure into it. It was then that she had decided to leave. She needed a small, familiar place where the people around her had known Jack and Sam, knew that they had existed in the universe, and how dreadful it was that they were gone.

'Aye. I can understand that.' Alister exhaled slowly down the line. 'And Ailsa always said that your place was on the island. She saw something in you.'

Even though Freya had always felt this, she was surprised he was the one to tell her.

'But she saw a lot of things no one else did. You know how she was.' And Alister chuckled lightly at the end of the phone.

Freya wondered if he was nodding his head. It had been a reflex with him – a swift, reinforcing nod after he had declared something. And yet now she couldn't imagine him doing it. Perhaps he had even begun to buy into Ailsa's mysticism. It became apparent to her then that grief had hit them all hard, jumbled them up and put them back together somewhat differently. She felt a sudden and unexpected fondness for him.

'You know I found letters here when I came back.' She paused and let her hand rest beside her, on the copies that she had brought up to the lamp room. 'Transcripts of the ones the National Museum of Edinburgh recovered from the Bellarmine jar. It was good of you to send it off.'

'Aye, well. I thought if anything inside it could be salvaged then it should be.'

Freya smiled. 'Have you read them?'

'Aye. MacCallister sent me copies too. Quite astonishing they could recover so much. It's a pity Sam won't see them.'

'Yes, he would have loved a soldier's tale of battle and shipwreck.' Less so one of lost love and mermaids, but Freya kept this to herself. In that respect he was probably like his grandfather and she didn't want Alister pouring cold water over it right now.

'I went swimming today,' she said to change the subject. 'Hough skerries and back.'

'That's good, Freya,' he said. He had always been a fan of her swimming and yet she detected hesitancy in his voice. 'Be careful, though. And make sure to pace yourself. Don't push yourself too much in the open water in the beginning.'

'I won't. I couldn't have done much more. But as we get into summer and I build my stamina, I'll be back to swimming the big ones.' She smiled and hoped Alister was smiling down the phone too. It wouldn't do for them all to grow too cautious in their grief.

'That's good, Freya,' he said again. 'Perhaps Ailsa was right and you are exactly where you should be.'

Freya wondered. She thought of the pills, the alcohol

she needed more often than not to prop her up. It didn't take much to knock her off any kind of even keel. But it had taken less in London. She shivered at the remembrance of it. Things were better here, she thought, even if she still felt her grief, acute and disabling sometimes. She thought of Torin's warning, the nightmares, Sam's face looking up at her, sharply, his clear voice warning her of danger. That too, she kept to herself. 'I think so,' was all she said in response. Then, again to change the subject, she told Alister about Sam's diary and the necklace he had discovered on Tiree.

'I can just picture the wee bairn,' Alister said. 'All smiles and excitement.' He liked the tale, no doubt the symmetry and order of tracking and unearthing something, and while he talked for a while about the merits of this or that metal detector, Freya's mind strayed to the story he had told Sam about letters from St Kilda floated in wooden boxes on the tides. It was miraculous that they could circle the landmass of Lewis and Harris and make it to Skye on dependable currents. But then there were lots of miraculous things, it seemed, if you simply accepted they were possible. She stroked the silver at her throat and watched the sun creep below the sea, her mind filled with thoughts of Edward's letters, buried for so long beneath the waves.

31

11 September 1653
Speedwell

My dearest Josie,

Today we went after the Macleans. Pursuit – that is what our Colonel called it, although I could not believe it to be so when we knew so little about the destination of our enemies and therefore had so little hope of finding them. What did he have in mind, I wonder, upon our reaching Tiree? The Macleans would hardly be sitting aboard their ships, at anchor in some convenient harbour, awaiting our arrival. Were we to make an entire sweep of the island when we had no idea where the deserters might be hiding out and no idea of the terrain upon which we would find ourselves? In short, Josie, I found it an ill-advised venture.

Four ships set out northwards, circling round the coast of Mull until Coll, the island adjacent to Tiree, appeared. We were fortunate in that both the wind and tide seemed to be with us and we moved swiftly. In short time, we dropped anchor in Tiree's southern harbour of Scarinish and a small party was put ashore to try and gather information. Needless to say they returned with nothing useful. Some locals said the Macleans had headed inland, others that they had set sail westwards to the outer isles, others that they journeyed northwards to Skye. So it was decided that on the morrow, a number of small scouting forces would be despatched to search the land while the ships sailed around the island. All forces were to meet back at Scarinish Bay. I am among those who are to remain a-ship. The better of two evils I suppose. Although I suspect the Macleans have already moved on or gone to ground and I do not believe that we will find them.

This night we all sleep aboard, there being too much uncertainty to camp on land. So we are packed in and there is a deal of snoring and sound to aggravate me. Perhaps because of the noise and the stink, I was unable to sleep. I rose and went onto the deck. Before long I noticed that Duncan had followed me. He could not sleep either and was not in his usual humour, that is for sure. I asked him what the matter was and for a long moment he simply looked at me. Then he whispered that there are some in these parts that have second sight. His voice was quiet, conspiratorial even. No doubt he didn't want the others on board to hear him. He asked me if I knew what that was. I nodded my head, wishing that I had not asked what was bothering him. Feeling myself a little out of sorts, I was not in the humour for tales of witchcraft or other magic. But he went on to tell me that there have been too many instances of visions and the coming to pass of seen events for people not to believe it. He paused and I felt his eyes upon me again, even though I was looking out to sea.

His father had the sight, he said, and had predicted many things which came to pass in time. The woman a man would marry, for instance. And death. There was always death. He grew more and more agitated and told me that there were signs to show when death was at hand – sometimes the seer would hear a cry that no one else heard. And, at others, a shroud would be perceived around a person. That was a sure sign.

I nodded. I thought I sensed where this tale was taking us and I asked him if he too had the sight.

He smiled thinly and nodded. He saw things, he said, and often didn't realise until afterwards that it was a vision.

I asked him what it was he had seen now, feeling the sense of unease in my stomach grow.

He told me he had seen shrouds about the men on the *Speedwell* and at other times covering those on other ships among our party. Not all the men. But some.

I paused before I asked him when death would come.

Duncan shrugged. I cannot be exact, he said.

Of course not, I wanted to shout at him then. It is all hocus-pocus and nonsense. I wanted to grab him by the shoulders and shake some sense into him. But I held my tongue and kept my body in check.

It is said, he continued, that the height of the shroud about a person is a signifier. If it is not seen above the middle, death is not to be expected for a year, perhaps longer. But the higher it ascends towards the head, the closer death is perceived to be.

And you have seen these shrouds high about these men? I asked.

Duncan nodded and then answered the question that I did not want to ask again. Death will likely come within a few days, he said.

I nodded, more to myself than him. It was a nod aimed to dismiss, to dispel from my mind this work of fiction I had just heard. For it was ridiculous, was it not, to give any credence to such a flight of fancy? And yet I could not shake his words from my mind. I was not, *am not* – as well you know, Josie – a superstitious man. But, as I stood there on the deck of the *Speedwell*, with the late gloaming light of the north upon me and Duncan, with the certainty of his visions, by my side; as I stared out into the vast ocean to the west and felt my own isolation, my smallness in the face of nature, in spite of myself, of my love of the harsh, dull realities of life, I began to wonder whether death would come soon and whether it would be by land, or by sea, in a fight against the Macleans or in some other guise.

For some reason my thoughts returned to the old man from the tavern, who had told the story of the mermaid. And I saw again in my mind's eye the way he had looked at me. For, doubtless, in spite of his milky eyes and his lack of sight, he had seen me and, more than that, perhaps, had seen into me. And he had felt a kind of pity or sympathy. I had seen it in his face at the time and it had made my blood run cold. And then I began to wonder whether he, like Duncan and his father before him, had seen something that had not yet come to pass. Perhaps he too was one of these seers of the north and had caught a vision of me, perhaps foreseen my death. For even though I did not ask Duncan, clearly it had been on my mind: whether he had seen a shroud about my own shoulders.

I shivered then, even though the air was mild, as if someone had walked over my grave. Duncan was still beside me but silent now, wrapped up in his own black thoughts as he stared out to sea. In the gathering darkness of the night, the stars grew in strength and cast a faint flickering glimmer upon the surface of the ocean. I looked down into the water, lapping quietly against the side of the *Speedwell*, and tried to see past its surface into the shadowy depths beyond. What lurked there in the darkness? For a long time I stared into the quietness of the night, for the men were asleep or, for once, speaking to one another in hushed rather than raucous tones. And I prayed to the mermaid, if she existed, that she spirit me back to you, and the life now growing inside you, on subtle winds and calm seas. That she let me escape this strange kingdom with my life.

Having read once more these words I have written to you, you will no doubt think me fast becoming a heathen. Much of my disquiet arises, I am sure, from the fact that it is night and we may well face a battle on the morrow. And that I am tired yet sleep evades me. But my thoughts, as well as my dreams, come back to you often and give me some comfort.

I pray for life so that I may see you again. If you receive another letter from me then you will know that I have survived tomorrow – both Duncan's curse and that of the wild Macleans.

Until then
I am your
Edward

32

A few days later, Freya was sitting in the window of Ena Maclean's tea shop in Craignure, a pot of tea growing cold on the table in front of her. Outside the sky was overcast and the day was frigid, like winter. From time to time, Freya looked at the smattering of windswept customers inside the shop then bent her head back down to the book resting on her lap. But her show of reading was pretence. She simply didn't want to talk to anybody.

She heard the sound of the shop door opening and the tinkle of the bell. A moment later she felt the presence of someone beside her and heard a male voice speak her name.

She raised her eyes to see Daniel standing beside her. 'Hi,' she said, surprised. She closed her book and laid it on the table. 'What brings you here?'

'Visiting friends. And now taking the ferry to Oban. I'm on my way to Glasgow.' He looked around, at the dim interior of the tea shop, the plastic covers on the small round tables, the gaggle of middle-aged women bunched around Ena at the till, catching up on the day's gossip. 'Can't say I expected to find you here.'

Freya smiled. 'I needed to pick up some supplies. And Ena's Victoria sponge is the best on the island,' she added, pushing out the chair in front of her to indicate he should join her.

He nodded, sitting down. His face looked a little strained.

'How are you?' Freya tried to keep her tone light but couldn't help thinking of the recent conversation she had had with Callum.

His response was sure, automatic, as always. 'I'm fine, thanks.'

Freya studied him, the cold blue of his eyes, the hard set of his mouth, and wondered whether in fact he was.

'And you?' he asked her.

She smiled and looked down into her lap. 'Oh. I guess I'm all right.' As the lie slid easily out of her mouth, she knew it wasn't strange at all that Daniel hadn't talked about his wife. She could see how he was still so affected by his loss and that he had perhaps simply wanted to keep it to himself.

Ena silently set a fresh pot of tea down on the table.

'Thanks,' Freya said, smiling at her.

'Nay bother,' Ena replied, giving Freya a quick smile before doing an about turn and leaving them to it.

Freya watched her return to the till to a flurry of raised eyebrows and hushed voices. No doubt she and Daniel were the subject of the conversation. Turning her attention back to him, she caught him looking at her.

'You're a little . . . pale, Freya.'

She smiled at the euphemism. She knew she didn't look well. But she didn't want to talk about her dreams or her anxiety, the pills she was taking and the wine she knew she shouldn't be drinking on top of them. Somehow, it was easier not to mention any of it. 'Marta's gone back to London and I just haven't been sleeping all that well,' she said.

'Nightmares?' His tone was hushed, empathetic.

'Yeah. New but unimproved.' She had had the dream again – Sam, Jack and their warnings, only this time she had been wearing the necklace in it. 'They just seem to get worse not better,' she continued. 'And I'm not sure why that is.'

Daniel nodded, knowingly. Or perhaps Freya was just imagining that, given what she now knew. She poured them both a cup of tea and then sat back in her chair. She had determined that she wouldn't ask him about his wife. She knew how intrusive it could be from the wrong person. 'So you're going to Glasgow?' she said at last, into the quiet that had fallen between them. 'What's happening there?'

'Oh, it's just work. A meeting of some of our funders. We need to talk about strategy, allocation of money, that kind of stuff.' For a few minutes Daniel expanded on it and then they fell silent once again.

'So, Freya. I'm glad I ran into you . . . ' he began and then halted. He opened his mouth, closed it again, and then ran a hand through his hair. He looked awkward. 'I wanted to tell you something,' he managed to get out at last.

'Okay,' Freya said.

'Last time I saw you, when you told me about Jack and Sam, there was something I wanted to tell you too. I wanted to but I couldn't.'

'Okay,' Freya said again.

'I said that I didn't have a wife. I did once though. But she died.'

Even though she was expecting it, Freya still felt the shock of his words. Her reaction was heartfelt. 'Oh, Daniel. I'm so sorry.'

He gave her a slight nod of acknowledgement. 'I just couldn't explain.'

Freya waved her hand in a dismissive gesture. 'It's fine. You don't have to justify yourself. Least of all to me.'

'Thanks.' Daniel gave her a quick smile.

'And you don't have to talk about it now if you don't want to.'

Daniel nodded, but there was obviously something he wanted to say. 'Strangely she died at sea too. I've been thinking about it a lot since I last saw you. It's a strange coincidence, don't you think?'

Perhaps. Freya wasn't sure. But she nodded anyway.

'Her name was Annalise. She was Norwegian. Long blonde hair, honeyed skin. She was beautiful. We met in Barra when she was travelling and we fell in love. And out here, with the landscape, the mountains and the water, she always felt this place was like home. So she stayed and we got married.' Daniel took a sip of his tea. 'She was an amazing swimmer. Used to take part in loads of competitions. She was really fast and strong. She'd swim all the time, good weather and bad. I used to call her my mermaid. The sea seemed so much more her home than the land. Anyway, one day she went out and never came back. Spring tides, they said afterwards. The strength and unpredictability at the turn of the season. They never found her body, though, so I don't know how they could say this. Truth is, they have no idea what really happened.'

Daniel paused and looked away for a moment. Then he turned back to Freya. 'So I know a little of what you're feeling.'

Freya nodded. 'When did it happen?'

'Three years ago. But it feels like yesterday. I still get confused. Forget sometimes. I don't think my mind can accept it, even now. And sometimes, I still think she's going to come back. Come walking through the door.' Daniel looked away again, down at his hands on the table, interlocked and squeezing each other tightly. Then he spoke so quietly that Freya wasn't sure she even heard correctly. 'I struggle sometimes. I really struggle.'

Freya put her hand over his and let it rest there. She heard the room grow instantly quieter and, even though she didn't see it, she felt the women's eyes upon her. After a moment she removed her hand. 'You didn't have any children?'

'No. A blessing perhaps.'

Perhaps, thought Freya. She wasn't sure.

'Do you want to see a photograph of Annalise?'

'Of course,' Freya said, smiling.

Daniel reached into his pocket for his wallet, pulled a picture from it and passed it to her. It was crumpled and well thumbed around the edges, the colour faded. But Freya could still see the young woman at its centre. The image was shot closely, only the head visible, long hair, straight and white blonde, framing an oval face. Annalise had bright blue eyes like Daniel's, but they had a warmth and depth to them that his had perhaps once had but had now lost. Her lips were full and a deep pink, pouting into the camera, emphasising her cheekbones. She was beautiful, the mood of the photo light and vivacious. Full of life. Freya felt her stomach contract.

'She's lovely, isn't she?' Daniel said.

'Yes, she is,' said Freya, looking closely over the image. Annalise was also wearing a silver necklace that curled around the neck in much the same way as the one Sam had recovered from the beach. Freya looked again. It could almost have been the same one, except that this had an extra section beyond the serpent's tail. She suddenly remembered Torin's words that a piece of her necklace might have broken off. She reached for her teacup, her throat parched.

'Are you looking at the necklace?' Daniel asked. His eyes seemed to bore into hers.

She nodded, unable to reply.

'Beautiful, isn't it? It's Viking. I think she must have been wearing it that last time she went swimming. I've hunted everywhere in the house and can't find it. And she was pretty inseparable from it.'

Freya blanched and felt her stomach twist. Could it be the same necklace, the upper section ripped off by the tide? No, surely, it was too unlikely.

'Are you okay?' said Daniel, taking the photo from her and putting it back into his wallet.

She nodded and took another large gulp of tea. But it didn't warm her. 'Next time you're near the island, drop in and see me. I have something I'd like to give you.'

'Yeah? What is it?'

For a moment Freya hesitated. She wanted, more than anything, to do the right thing. But then she thought of Sam and his first thoughts on finding the necklace. 'Well,' she coughed, her throat dry and itchy. 'It looks like some kind of ancient knife or dagger blade. But I have it on good authority that it belonged to a mermaid.'

'Get out of here.' But Daniel smiled broadly. 'Who told you that?'

'A friend.' She saw him raise his eyebrows. 'I know, I know. However, these blades have apparently been found in the bodies of fish out in the deep open ocean.'

'That can't be true, can it?'

Freya shrugged. 'Perhaps you can tell me when you see it. You're the archaeologist after all. But it makes for a nice story. I just thought you might like it. Given what you just told me about your nickname for your wife.'

Daniel looked at Freya and for the first time that day his eyes were animated. 'Thank you. I'll come round and pick it up as soon as I'm back from Glasgow.'

'Good.' Freya held his gaze for a moment while guilt

bloomed in her stomach. Then she looked out of the window. She could see the Oban ferry about to dock, the terminal busy now with cars, lorries and coaches, people milling around. 'I guess you have to get going. They'll be boarding soon.'

Daniel nodded, finished the tea in his cup and reached for his wallet.

Freya raised a hand. 'Don't worry about it. I've got this.'

'Are you sure?'

'Positive.'

'Okay then.' Daniel stood up and touched her hand lightly. 'I'll see you soon.'

Freya nodded. 'Have a safe journey.'

The next moment he was walking away, hand raised in goodbye. Freya watched him go, moving across the car park to the ticket office, head down, shoulders slumped, pace slow. It might just be mistaken for his body's defence against the weather. It was a miserable grey day, after all. But Freya knew that it was something more than that – like Duncan's doomed sailors with their shrouds, the afflictions of his life hung about him like a pall. She felt a stab of remorse. She had let him go and failed to mention that she may have found his lost treasure. But, she rationalised, even if it was the same necklace, it would make little difference. As Freya watched him depart she became more convinced than ever that on the night of the storm, when his boat tumbled upon the waves and washed up on her shore, it had been no accident that had found him in that predicament. He had surrendered to the overwhelming melancholy he felt.

And, perhaps to his dismay, death had spared him.

33

Freya felt the wind in her hair. It tugged softly at her but it was growing in strength. She stood steadily on the light-house gallery, her body at some distance from the railing. But her hands around it were nervous, slick with sweat.

Over the ocean, she could make out Iona, small and flat, and just beyond it Mull, the dark brown of the burgh jutting into the sky. It made her think of Daniel, their recent encounter, and her despondency intensified. She shifted her gaze. But the islands lying further afield had already disappeared from view. The forecast was for rain, and dense, low cloud was already moving in.

She sighed. Before long she would have to retreat inside. Or that is what the small voice inside her said. The other, louder voice told her to stay where she was, even if the wind grew strong and dangerous and threatened to blow her off the gallery. She heard that voice more insistently now, even though she tried to suppress it, to sedate it into nonexistence. But it would not be silenced. From time to time, she thought she felt the tower shift, move sideways in the wind. The voice told her body to follow the move-ment, to surrender to the urge to fall.

Gulls soared overhead, shrieking mercilessly, and gannets dropped from great heights down into the sea. As Freya watched, the still of the ocean dissolved, transformed into something harder. The waves, whipped by the wind, grew larger. Edges of white foam appeared above the grey, sea horses chomping at the bit, racing towards the land and oblivion. Freya felt the push of wind, more insistent now, and the enticing tilt of the tower. Her feet moved closer to the railing. She looked down, saw the waves crashing against the rocks below and for some reason thought of the Flannan Islands' keepers. It would not, after all, be such a great leap to take, to become one of the disappeared. She focused on the rocks, the brittle sound of the waves crashing against them. The smell of the sea enclosed her, wrapping her in a salty embrace. She closed her eyes and stepped forwards again.

Then she heard it – the sound of a horn, loud, with a familiar melody. She opened her eyes and looked out over the growing tumult of the sea. It took a moment for her to find it – the small boat, still at some distance, but heading in the direction of the island. She gripped the railing harder as she watched its solitary progress. It was Pol. He always announced his return in this way. She felt the instant rise of resentment. He was supposed to give her notice of his visits, check that it was convenient. But then he had never done that before, never taken notice of whether his timings suited or not. So why should he do it now?

Jolted into action, Freya moved back from the railing.

She wondered if Pol had seen her. It was likely. He took pride in watching the lighthouse as it grew ever nearer on his approach. She stepped into the lamp room and bolted the gallery door. Then she moved quickly down the staircase. At the bottom of the tower, she locked the door, then looked at the tarnished key, given to her son by the old keeper, and wondered what, if anything, he would say to her about it.

Freya watched Pol as he talked, seated at the kitchen table, drinking tea and eating digestives. They were his favourite biscuit and he was lucky, she thought somewhat irritably, that she had found a packet at the back of a kitchen cupboard. God knew how long they had been there – a year at least. They were doubtless a little stale but he didn't seem to mind. He munched away uncomplainingly as he talked.

Freya found his manner markedly different to the previous times he had been there. Perhaps it was simply that he found her so much changed that the shock of it forced a change in him. But it seemed more than that. Unless she was mistaken, he had lost his hostility towards her.

He offered heartfelt condolences. A grand little chap. A fine man. That was it. He didn't linger. He then moved on to talk of other things. Other lighthouses he had visited, tales from the NLB, fears of further contraction of the workforce and other small bits of news. News that he had always shared with her before, but which, she had always thought, contained an undertone of blame. That had gone, vanished along with her husband and son. Perhaps she had imagined it before and only now, when she was beyond caring, had the clarity to hear what was really there. But she didn't think she was wrong. And so far he hadn't mentioned spotting her on the gallery. As a result she had held her tongue and refrained from asking why he had given her son access to the lighthouse. What did it matter now, after all?

She drifted in and out of the conversation, paying only scant attention, thinking about Sam and the key. How many times, she wondered, had he ventured up the tower, when she, close by or far away, was oblivious to his comings and goings? Why hadn't he told her about it? But that of course was obvious. She would have stopped his visits, alone at least. She liked to think that she would not; that her heart, now eaten up with pain and regret, would have been bountiful and allowed it. But she knew that she wouldn't have. She looked at Pol again and realised what a gift he had given her son. And she felt something unprecedented towards him. Gratitude.

She made an effort to pay attention and follow the thread of his words. He was back on his favourite subject: lighthouses.

'Keepers. They always tended to fall into two camps. Those that loved the life and those that didn't.' He took a loud slurp of his tea. 'Some keepers I know started out the first way and grew to resent it only later on – the isolation, the separation from family and friends. And then it seemed so close to retirement that they didn't want to sacrifice their pension. So they kept at it. Others who became keepers you always thought were running away from something: the booze, the law, hotfooting it to an isolated life they thought might be better, that might heal them. And for some that worked, for others it didn't. Others just made a mistake – thought the life would suit them. And it's a lonely life for sure. You're kidding yourself if you don't see that. Here you are, miles from anywhere, alone. It isn't for everyone. Drive you mad, you know.'

Pol paused and stared at Freya. It was another new thing she had noticed: before he had largely avoided eye contact with her.

'I've known keepers wanted to throw themselves into the sea and swim home so unhappy they was. Out at Dubh Artach, for instance. Others wanted to throw themselves clear off the gallery.'

Pol gave Freya another look at this point, but she couldn't decipher its meaning. She wondered again if he had seen her at the top of the tower. More than likely. She would never actually have done it, she wanted to say out loud. Instead she broke his gaze and shifted in her seat.

'And what about you, Pol? You always loved the life of a keeper, didn't you?'

'Mostly,' he said. 'Not always.'

Freya was surprised by the admission. She reached for a digestive and bit into it. It was soft with a slightly mouldering taste. She took a large gulp of tea to wash it down.

'Sometimes there were moments when even I wished I was elsewhere.' Pol paused, a reminiscent look in his eye. 'Aye, it had never really occurred to me at the start that there would be times I would be afraid.' He nodded sombrely. 'And it wasn't the wind that I was scared of, even though that could be bad enough. No. Not a gale or even a bunch of them back to back.' Pol nodded.

Freya remembered the first time she had gone up the tower and felt the power of the wind against it, shaking its foundations.

'It was what followed after, the heavy ground sea they call it – thousands of miles of ocean all stirred up, moving great boulders along the sea bed as if they were pebbles. Towers were the worst of course, perched out on a tiny bit of rock in the middle of the ocean. Aye, those boulders would be flung against the base of the lighthouse making the whole place shake and sound with the boom boom boom of the collision. But any lighthouse in such a storm was bad enough. You'd sit in the lamp room of a night, lit up in that terrifying darkness, wondering if the tower was strong enough to take it – or whether the whole thing would come crashing down with you in it.' Pol was silent for a moment, pale faced, as he remembered. 'Aye, face to face with the strength of the sea, unable to escape it, it can rock a man to the core. But I overcame the fear. Or perhaps a better way of putting it is that I got used to being afraid. Aye, the sea can be beautiful but it can also be frightening.'

Freya had never heard Pol talk like this. She imagined the terror of such a sea, whipped up by a powerful storm, and her son and husband lost within it. She closed her eyes and tried to put it out of her mind.

'Even when it isn't at its worst we must always be wary, always on guard. Aye, there was this one keeper. He was brought in to replace an assistant keeper who was ill. Anyway, one calm day when the sea was flat, he decides he wants to do a spot of fishing. Now, on a tower lighthouse, there's only one place you can fish from – the entrance doorway. This doorway is pretty high above the sea – about thirty feet – and, as I said, there was not much swell on the water. So the principal keeper lets him go ahead and they all go about their business as usual. Trouble is that, a little while later, when the other assistant keeper goes to see if he wants a cup of tea, he's not there. He searches the whole lighthouse from the top down and still can't find him. So he tells the principal and they both search again from top to bottom and then back up to the top again. No sign of him.'

The sea took him, Freya thought. But she remained silent.

'The principal radioed out a message that a keeper was overboard. And local ships came to help search. But by the time they all arrived it was getting dark, and the sea was getting up. His body was never found.'

They were both silent for a few minutes. Freya thought of the Flannan Islands' keepers again.

'What do you think happened to him, Pol?'

'Hard to say. There was no water on the floor of the doorway, so the sea hadn't come up suddenly and washed him out. But the iron bar that should have been across the entrance wasn't there. So maybe he'd fallen out or . . . ' Pol paused and shook his head.

'Did you know him?'

'No. But I almost feel like I did. It's the same sort of stories all over the place. Most keepers have had a near miss.' Pol chewed on his digestive meditatively. 'Anyway, my point, if there was one to this story,' and he paused and looked at Freya, 'was that you have to move beyond the fear and the loneliness and the other hardships that anyone inhabiting a lighthouse has to face. Or you'll never survive. And there are those who can move beyond those things. For whom this will be a symbol of light, a marker.'

A form of redemption, Freya thought.

'One keeper I know built a house for himself on the top of a cliff. From his sitting-room window he had a view over the sweeping ocean and he could see the rock light upon which he had worked for much of his life.' Pol looked at her and winked. 'He could check every morning and every evening that she was lit and be satisfied that however hard the wind blasted or how wild the sea grew she was still there, a beacon in the darkness.'

'Oh Pol, really?'

Pol nodded, and then did a peculiar thing that Freya had never seen him do before. He smiled at her. A warm, open smile. 'Aye, my girl. A lighthouse, like the sea itself perhaps, can be life and it can be death. Perhaps for a time it can feel like both. But in the end you have to choose. I hope that one day, my dear, this lighthouse will come to mean to you what it has meant to me.'

And suddenly Freya saw, as if laid out before her, the years of hardship Pol had suffered, alone, moving from lighthouse to lighthouse, his own burdens moving with him. She knew that he had had a wife but that she had died a long time ago and that he had never remarried. In some sense she knew that this lighthouse had been his salvation in a simple, spartan life of trials. And then automation had come and stripped him once more of everything he loved. For the first time she felt ashamed that she had not felt as much sympathy for Pol as perhaps she should have.

He picked up another biscuit from the plate and Freya was filled with a sudden rush of affection for him. 'Don't eat that, Pol. I was going to bake some fresh ones,' she lied. 'They'll be waiting for you when you've finished your tests on the light.'

He looked at her a moment, confused. 'Only if you're sure. There's really nothing wrong with these.'

'I'm sure,' she said.

'Well, I'll get to it then. See how the old girl's doing.' Pol nodded at Freya, then rose from the table, picked up the box of cleaning materials he had brought with him, and made his way towards the tower door. After a moment he turned back to her. 'Thought for a second that I'd forgotten my key,' he said, taking it from his pocket, waving it at her and smiling broadly.

She smiled back, knowingly, then watched him turn and walk away. She wasn't sure but she thought she detected a new lightness in his step.

34

Later that afternoon, while the biscuits were cooling on a rack, and Pol was still busy in the tower, Freya took Sam's cardboard box into the sitting room and sat down on the sofa. She opened the lid and rifled through its contents once again. For some reason she tended to keep them together.

She flicked through the diary, staggered once more by the strength of her own will, and that she had stuck to her policy of rationing and reading only one entry at a time. As compensation she had read and reread the entries she had allowed herself and now knew them almost by heart. As she was thinking about reading on, there was a knock at the kitchen door.

'Who is it?' she shouted.

'Daniel,' came the reply.

'Come on in,' she said, getting up and heading into the kitchen. 'The door's never locked. No need.'

He came in, smiling, looking more relaxed than when she had seen him before. 'Hope it's not inconvenient. I saw another boat moored and wondered if you had company.'

'No. It's fine. Pol, from the Northern Lighthouse Board, is testing the light, that's all. It's actually good timing on your part – I've made biscuits.' She pointed to them on the kitchen table as he closed the door behind him and put his rucksack on the floor.

'Wow. They smell good,' he said. 'The weather's roughing up so I won't stay long. But I thought I'd pick up the mermaid blade on my way home. If that's okay?'

'Of course,' Freya said, putting the kettle on and then moving back into the sitting room. 'It's in this box.'

Daniel followed her and sat down on the sofa. 'Is that Sam's box of tricks?' he asked.

'Uh-huh,' she nodded, rifling through it. As she did so, her eye caught upon the necklace and she felt her heart flutter. She wished she'd known he was coming, then she could have hidden it somewhere else. She looked at Daniel, unsuspecting on the sofa, then down again at the contents of the box. Her hand hovered over the necklace for a moment but then she grasped the blade with her fingertips. As she offered it to him she felt another stab of remorse. It felt inappropriate, childish even, in light of his grief.

But he reached to take the object eagerly, turning the sharp piece of rock over in his hands. 'Basalt chiselled to make a primitive blade.'

Freya nodded. 'It's a fairly crude design,' she said, lowering the box lid.

He ran his hands over the blade, pressed his index finger to the point. 'It's different to the knives and other objects coming out of this area. This gully at the base of the blade was obviously made so it would fit over a piece of wood or another kind of handle. It was probably tied to it. So it makes sense that it was some type of hunting or fishing spear. Do you believe that it once belonged to a mermaid?'

Freya shrugged. 'I don't know. But I think Callum believes it. He's the one who found it with Sam. And he said there are photographs that show fish pierced by the blades. That's a bit hard to explain away.'

'Yes. If it's true,' Daniel said. 'But a picture doesn't mean the fish came out of the water looking like that.'

Now he sounded like Jack. Freya felt a rush of guilt. She'd dragged him out here to pick up a fake mermaid blade when she really could have given him something worthwhile. 'Perhaps you can carry out some tests on it,' she muttered. 'Maybe that will tell you something.'

'I'm sure it would. Still, I don't really care about that. Thanks for thinking of me.'

She flooded with shame and to deflect it she said, 'I didn't tell you that Jack and Sam found a Bellarmine jar – amazingly well preserved – which actually contained letters. They've been salvaged. Would you like to see them?'

'Sure.'

Freya ran to her bedroom where she had left them, then strode briskly back to the sitting room. 'There are tales of mermaids in here too,' she said, lightly. 'I haven't finished reading them yet, but have a look while I make some coffee.'

229

Freya moved back into the kitchen, and, so Daniel could read, took her time. Then she made her way back into the sitting room with a tray of coffee and biscuits. As she approached, she noticed that Daniel was standing, letters in hand, staring into the open cardboard box.

Freya's heart sank. At the same time, she felt a flash of anger. What was he doing nosing through her son's things? She put the tray down on the table and turned towards him. Only then did she notice the sudden pallor of his face. Hers, in distinction, flushed.

'Daniel. Are you okay?'

He jumped and turned towards her.

'Are you okay?' she repeated, startled by his sudden movement.

He looked back at the box. Then he nodded. 'I'm sorry. It's nothing. I just . . . I don't know what really.' He paused. 'I didn't open this, by the way. The lid fell open by itself.'

She nodded, even though she wasn't sure she believed him. Then she decided to bite the bullet. She reached for the necklace and lifted it out of the box. She might as well find out the truth. 'It's a Permian ring. Sam found it washed up on a beach in Tiree.'

Daniel nodded, his eyes moving over the surface of the silver, its thick, uneven texture, its partially erased pattern. 'Jormungand,' he muttered.

'What?' said Freya.

'Jormungand,' he said again, louder this time. He pointed to the tail of the snake at the end of the ring. 'It was the serpent child of Loki, cast into the great ocean by Odin. It grew so large that it completely encircled the whole of earth and could grasp its own tail in its mouth.' He pointed to the area beyond the tail. 'Here there would have been a head, a mouth, which interlinked with the tail. Then the silver would have continued to wind round and finally taper off. The piece containing the head has obviously broken away.' Daniel faltered. 'In legend, when Jormungand lets go of its tail, the end of the world will come.' Daniel shook his head, looking visibly upset, and for a moment Freya wondered if he would cry. 'It reminds me of a necklace I uncovered at a burial ground in Ardnamurchan not that long ago.'

Freya leapt upon this. Perhaps it wasn't his wife's after all. Perhaps it simply reminded him of death, of a site he had once worked on. Torin had implied much the same thing. 'Daniel, why don't you give this to me? Have some coffee and a biscuit.'

'No, I'm okay,' he said, and tried to pull the necklace away from her.

But Freya didn't let go. Unless she knew for certain that it was his wife's, all she could think was that Sam had thought of her when he'd found it, had wanted her to have it. And she wanted it back. She tried to wrest it from Daniel's grasp but his grip remained firm. 'Please give me the necklace,' she said.

'I just want to look at it, to be sure.'

But Freya felt anger rising inside, hot, quick and uncontrollable. She stood up, pulling the necklace with her. But instead of letting go, Daniel rose too. They stood side by side, each holding one half.

'Let go of it,' she said, louder than she'd intended, almost spitting the words out.

Daniel didn't reply but his eyes moved from the necklace to meet Freya's. She saw defiance there.

'Let go,' she said again.

Then a small voice floated into the sitting room.

'Is everything okay?'

Both Daniel and Freya turned towards it. It was Pol, a dirtied yellow duster in his hand, smudges of dust and grime on his face. 'I heard raised voices. Is everything okay?' he said again.

Daniel's hand immediately fell away from the necklace and Freya felt the tension drop out of the situation. 'Yes, Pol,' she said. 'Everything's fine. Just a misunderstanding.' She placed the necklace back in the box and closed the lid. 'In fact you're just in time for coffee. Shall I pour you a cup?'

'That'd be lovely,' said Pol, looking from one to the other and then, satisfied that the situation was defused, he made his way to the kitchen table and sat down.

Freya felt embarrassed by her own behaviour. She shouldn't have been so aggressive. She should have let Daniel take a look. But she was worried about what he might have discovered. She shot a look at him, still standing in the sitting room, as she took the tray of coffee and biscuits back to the kitchen table. He seemed to have recovered himself a little but he still looked upset.

Finally he followed her into the kitchen. 'I'm sorry, Freya.'

'Don't worry,' she said. 'I'm sorry too. I shouldn't have raised my voice.'

He shrugged.

'Do you want some coffee?' she asked.

'Thanks, but I should probably go.'

'Okay,' said Freya. She wanted to say something else but couldn't think what.

'Thanks for the mermaid blade,' he said and, picking up his rucksack by the door, left the house with a quick wave goodbye to Pol.

'Who was that?' Pol asked after a moment, picking up a biscuit from the plate.

Freya came to sit beside him. 'That's Daniel.' She sighed. 'And it's a bit of a long story. His wife died a while ago.'

'Ah,' said Pol. 'That why he was upset?'

'I'm guessing so,' said Freya, but then felt a deep, curdling sense of shame.

'Are you okay?' Pol asked.

'Yes, I'm fine. But thanks for coming down.'

He smiled. 'I was always the one in the lighthouse smoothing over a situation, deflating tempers.' He nodded, then turned to face Freya again. 'But are you sure you're okay on your own out here? No one to help you if you need it.'

His words reminded her so much of everyone around her. Torin, Callum, her mother and father, Marta. Her dead husband and son. They all said the same thing. And she had wilfully defied them all and stayed on at Ailsa Cleit, so sure that this place would make her feel better. Now she wasn't sure. But she still wasn't ready to leave.

Freya looked at Pol, at the concern in his eyes, and all she could do was nod. The words just wouldn't come.

35

Today was a beautiful day. The sky was really blue with practically no clouds and the sea was still. We have had a lot of great weather while Mum has been away. Dad says we have been very lucky. I know what he means but I think we would have been much luckier if Mum had been here. Anyway, she is back in a few days so that will be great.

To make the most of the day Dad and I went to the Torran Rocks. I don't remember ever having been there before but they are really cool. People call them the dragon's teeth as they are so sharp and dangerous in bad weather. Dad says they have caused many shipwrecks and he told me two very interesting and big statisticks which I had to write down.

1. Between 1800 and 1854 there were 30 wrecks on the rocks and 50 lives were lost.
2. In 1865 during a single storm 24 vessels were lost.

I asked Dad why people who die at sea are called 'lost'.

Because they aren't lost really – or not like someone who might get lost in a supermarket or at the aquarium like happened to me. To say that someone is lost makes it sound like they might be found again. But if they're gone at sea, they're dead and they aren't coming back. Dad agreed with me that it didn't make much sense.

Anyway, after we set off from our island, we reached the west reef of the rocks first. They are really small and so we didn't stop there. We kept going until we reached a clump of the bigger ones which also sit much higher out of the water. I said to Dad that it was very hard to imagine how this place could be dangerous because it was so lovely when the water was still. But Dad said that when the wind and the tide were up it would be treacherous here, huge waves smashing the rocks, rushing between them, cross currents or something like that. I tried to imagine it with the wind howling and blowing everything to bits. But it was very difficult.

We anchored the boat and went swimming which was fun. Then we climbed up on some of the rocks and dived in – but Dad made me be very careful as there are lots of rocks below the surface of the water. We had taken our snorkelling gear and after lunch we swam around looking for things. I found an old silver coin under the water. But Dad found something so much more brilliant – a stone flagon – that's what he called it – wedged into a crevice lined with seaweed high in the rock above the tide line. Basically it was a jug with a man's head engraved on it. Dad said it looked in really great condition – it was even sealed – and it was amazing given the number of rocks in this area that it hadn't been broken into bits. Anyway, Dad said it looked really old and that we should package it carefully and send it to Granddad. He would know who to give it to to see if there was anything inside. Mum says that Granddad has been to the museum in Edinburgh so many times that he thinks he knows everyone there and also that he knows as much as them. But I didn't say this. I just thought it to myself and told Dad that it was a great idea.

I shook the bottle but I couldn't hear anything move inside. Dad said it wasn't good to do that – much better to keep it still in case whatever was inside was delicate as it was so old. But he said if I kept it safe I could look after it until we sent it to Granddad.

After that we went to Dubh Artach – the black rock – to see the lighthouse built on it by Thomas Stevenson. I remembered from when we came here the last time with Mum that she had said it was built to light not just the black rock but also to mark the Torran Rocks beyond it.

I stared up at the lighthouse – it is really big – 145 feet tall, Dad said. It has a red band around the middle to make it look different from Skerryvore lighthouse which is not far from here. Even though Dubh Artach sits out in the middle of nowhere, today it wasn't scary. But Dad said that when the weather was bad the seas could be very frightening here. That is because the black rock is at the end of an underwater valley which stretches out 80 miles into the Atlantic. This acts like a funnel and makes the seas in this area big and dangerous, drawing everything from the bottom to the top. I looked down into the water then and it was dark and even though there was no wind the sea was still churning and sploshing around the rock. And it made me a little bit afraid. I was glad when Dad said let's go.

When we got home Dad and I put the flagon in bubble wrap ready for posting and I put the coin in a box where I am keeping everything I have found beachcombing or in the sea. I am keeping everything safe.

Freya raised her eyes to the sky. It was clear and unthreatening, the day sunny and still; a similar day, perhaps, to when Sam and Jack were there. Yet, even in such weather, there was something foreboding about this place, and Freya kept the boat at a distance from the black rock. That's how they said Dubh Artach translated from the Gaelic. Although Freya had once heard that the root from old Irish meant death – the black, deadly one. And looking at the rock today, looming 35 dark feet above the sea, she preferred this translation. The water growled around the outer reef, even though otherwise it was flat, barely shifting, and she felt goose bumps rise on her skin even though the temperature was mild.

Her eyes crept up the lighthouse tower until they reached the lamp room and gallery lookout. She was reminded of Pol's tale from a few days earlier – the old keeper who had tried to throw himself from the lighthouse and swim back to shore. So many stories. There had also been a keeper who, despite the inhospitable conditions here, had kept the lighthouse for eleven years. Still, she felt it clearly. Disquiet lurking inside her. She raised her eyes upwards to the sky again, then over the sea into the distance. But there was nothing to be afraid of. The weather was with her. Just as it had been at the Torran Rocks. There the islands and skerries had been idyllic, scattered haphazardly within the water. She had navigated easily around the granite below the surface, watched the seaweed floating in the water, shaping and shifting in a timeless dance. And she had imagined her husband and her son, swimming and diving down into the green, enticing water, its movement soft upon the rocks, whispering upon the breeze. She had pictured Jack finding the Bellarmine jar sandwiched in a rocky crevice, cushioned by kelp, heard Sam's whoops of delight as he dive-bombed into the water. And it had made her happy.

But here, just like her son, she felt differently. She wondered whether she was simply mirroring the feelings of disquiet that she had read about in his diary. But she didn't think so. She shivered and looked at the black rock again, the ghostly lighthouse sitting upon it, long abandoned to automation. She listened to the ocean churning upon the reef, haunting and angry. Then she stared over the side of the boat into the deep, impenetrable blue. She thought of Sam, doing the same thing, face to face with the darkness of the sea and feeling afraid. Her heart crumpled at the idea of it, folded itself into tiny pieces. And she wanted it to keep on collapsing until it vanished entirely and she couldn't feel anything any more. For the thought of her son's fear was perhaps worse than anything else in the world. And on the day he disappeared, his fear would have been much greater.

She took a hard breath inwards, and imagined the dark, submarine valley stretching out into the wilds of the ocean. She felt an urgent pull to follow its deep track and lose herself there. Yes, she too could join the lost, the dead, the gone. Whatever her darling boy wanted to call them. As she stared into the darkness, she thought of her nightmare, of her son being taken by the sea, of her waiting on the threshold of life and death. Then his small clear voice brought her back to herself. *You must be very careful. There is danger for you here. Do you hear us, Mum?*

She looked up suddenly and turned round, half expecting to see him standing at the back of the boat, frowning at her. But there was no one. Nothing. Of course. It was all in her head. But the words pricked at her memory and she heard her son's voice. Death is everywhere, he said, pointing to the sea.

Freya shivered. Anxiety, that's all it was; her doctor had said so, many times. Anxiety, pure and simple. And she had believed him. Then she heard Torin's voice whispering to her. You risk disappearing too. You need to be careful of the past.

Freya looked down into the water once more. Perhaps the dreams and warnings were connected somehow? Did they come together to form a coherent narrative, or was it madness even to think such a thing, to try to make truth of dreams?

She felt suddenly out of breath and gulped greedily at the air. Her throat was parched, salty and dry, as if it recalled the taste of seawater. She needed to calm down, get back home, take some of her pills and wash them down with lots of cool water. Her hand reached instinctively for the necklace at her throat. But it wasn't there. It was in the box at home where she had left it. She looked around her once more. But there was nothing to be afraid of. The sea was calm, deserted but for a few boats in the distance, too far away for her to make out clearly. She tried to see her own lighthouse, a tiny marker, a beacon to guide her home. And after a while of searching, she thought she found it on the horizon, suspended somewhere between sky and sea.

Her breathing stilled. It was time for her to go. As she started the engine and began to manoeuvre the boat towards home, she tried to ignore the persistent tug of memory, that in the darkness of the ocean of her dreams, there was something hovering there, unseen, watching her, waiting.

36

Freya was washing the deck of the *Valkyrie*, throwing buckets of water over it and brushing it down. She had already polished the wood of the cabin, cleaned the glass of the windows, the brass of the portholes, tidied the interior. The work was therapeutic and absorbing. So much so that it was not until the boat was close that she became aware of it. She watched it approach and, even though it was still some distance away, she recognised it as Callum's.

The sea was choppy, whipped by the wind; it was an entirely different day to the one before when she had visited Dubh Artach and the Torran Rocks. Yet Callum handled the boat skilfully, avoiding the bigger waves, riding the smaller ones. As the boat came into the bay, he raised a hand in greeting to her. She waved back and climbed down onto the jetty to wait for him.

'Doing a bit of spring cleaning?' he said as his boat glided next to the *Valkyrie* and he roped them together.

'I was. But I'm delighted to have the interruption. Do you fancy some tea?'

'Sounds great,' he said, jumping down to join her.

As they began to climb up the steep pathway to the lighthouse, Freya turned to look at him. 'How's things?'

'Oh, I can't complain. Business is good. I've taken three tours to the Treshnish Isles already this week and I imagine it'll keep on getting better as we get properly into summer.' His grey eyes were soft as he looked at her. 'And you? How are you feeling?'

'I'm okay,' she said, but dropped her gaze from his as she answered. He would notice, no doubt. In fact, it was probably why, in part, he was out here. Dropping by to read Edward's letters, but also checking up on her after their recent meeting at Lunga. But instead of feeling annoyed about it, as she did with so many others, she realised that with Callum she didn't mind.

Half an hour later, they were sitting next to one another at the kitchen table, a pot of tea and some cake in front of them. Callum was reading the bundle of letters from the *Speedwell*. Freya, waiting for him to catch up to where she'd got to, peered over his shoulder intermittently.

From time to time, Callum would shake his head, murmur or tut. But mostly he read in silence. When he got to the final letter, he looked up and smiled at Freya.

'It should become less incredible the more I read of these. But instead I can't help but feel it's astonishing. Your son was obsessed with shipwrecks, particularly the one that sank out in the Sound of Mull . . .'

'The *Swan*,' said Freya, thinking of Sam looking out

towards the wreck the last time they had been to Duart Castle, reciting the excavation finds by heart.

'Aye, *Swan*. And then it turns out that he and Jack find this jar, from another ship in the same flotilla, and it contains these letters which we are reading now. It's amazing.' Callum smiled. 'And Sam's grandfather knew who to send them to for restoration.' Callum shook his head again. 'There feels like something of destiny about it, don't you think?'

Freya reached out and touched the letters, even though the pages weren't the originals. 'I know what you mean,' she said. Then she thought of Sam uncovering buried treasure in another place and the strange and unlikely providence of that find. Her hand rose involuntarily to her neck. But it was bare. Nonetheless, she felt a tremor of disquiet within her. Perhaps, she told herself again, the necklace hadn't belonged to Daniel's wife.

'Shall we read the final letter then?' she said to distract herself.

'Yes, I'd like to.' Callum picked up the teapot and poured them both another cup of tea. 'I want to know what happens to him.'

37

13 September 1653
Speedwell

My dearest Josie,

We are returned from Tiree, the Macleans nowhere to be found. So that is the smallest of mercies – no bloody skirmish or loss of life. But since we are back at Mull, the wind has been up.

For fourteen hours it has churned the sea and *Speedwell* rolls from side to side, creaking and groaning like an old man in his death throes. We are consigned to ship by the orders of the Colonel and will ride out this storm on board he says. So all six vessels are anchored in Duart Bay and lurch against the waves, straining and sick. The cloud is thick and black as tar in parts, the rain batters down upon the deck and thunder grumbles low in the distance. My thoughts are dark, returning often to the words of the blind old man. His storm has come.

Below deck the stench of seasickness is overwhelming and enough to turn even my hardened stomach. The men are ill and – much worse – are losing hope. Even Duncan is preoccupied, his face beset with frowns. When he speaks, he talks of his mother, and he was but small when she died. He recalls the shadow that her form cast over him in his crib, the sweetness of her smell. He feels these things close about him now, and from this, I know, he thinks death is near. I try to cheer him and myself besides. Then I remember his words of shrouds hanging about men's shoulders and my spirits fall. And I fight the urge to ask whether he sees such a thing about me, whether I too am condemned.

A sound of ripping and grating, the ship lurching sharply sideways before righting itself once more.

Duncan and I stagger upwards to the deck. Only there is the true horror of our situation revealed. The force of the wind has grown so strong that the ship has torn free of its anchor and is being blown out into the Sound. *Martha and Margaret* and *Swan* are in the same predicament, unanchored and at the mercy of the waves.

Our captain is shouting, his voice blown unheeded, into nothingness. Men are scrambling on deck trying to regain control. And all the while the tempest rages wild and wilful about us. Just outside Duart Bay, the *Swan* flounders, caught perhaps upon some rocks. I watch the fray and clamour, think I catch the echoes of men's screams on the air. Some plunge into the churning sea seeking to evade death, others cling to the ship for dear life. Most, I fear, will perish.

It is all coming to pass as the old man and Duncan have said. My heart grows cold and I remember the *Florencia*, sunk in Tobermory harbour, all disappeared in the mud and silt of the sea bottom. Will that be our epitaph? Our Cromwellian force wrecked off the coast of Mull, no bodies ever found to stand testament to the lives of the men. Will we disappear, covered by shadowy waves, and ultimately be forgotten?

[*missing text*]

I feel it in my heart, my love. This is my last letter.

We have been dragged south towards Jura, battered by the wind. The helmsman tried to steer a straight course, but the ship was pounded by surf and tide and blown about like a child's toy. Finally we heard a horrible splintering sound and then came the terrible pitching of the ship. We had run aground at the edge of the Corry Vreckan.

Above the noise of the gale I could hear it. A sound of great grumbling and thrashing. And all about us were waves at least 20 feet high, rising and falling, even greater in the gulf, with the swirl of the whirlpool, black and devilish in the growing darkness of the evening.

I have seen many a storm in my time, but nothing to compare with this. The unholy shrieking of men crashes upon us with each burst of the wind. The ship, crushed by colossal waves, raised high by the swell and then dashed back down upon the rocks, is slowly being stripped down to nothing. The *Martha and Margaret* has disappeared.

We are doomed, I feel it.

[*missing text*]

I see men trying to make it to land. But all too many are smashed against the rocks, or dragged under by the waves; worst of all, I think, sucked into the awful blackness of that whirlpool.

Then I hear another noise. A wild wailing erupting from the maelstrom. Whether from the whirlpool, the press of water, rock and wind, or whether from an animal I cannot say. But it is high-pitched, plaintive even, almost like a battle cry. And I feel, even though I do not understand it, as though something has been declared.

I turn to Duncan, my ears overwhelmed, but in the paleness of his face, I know I am not mistaken. I see now the cause of my vision, he says. This is what will kill us. Although you, he says, studying my body and my face closely, I think will escape with your life.

And all the time he speaks, in the back of my head I hear this relentless, almost human cry.

Do not listen to it, says Duncan. Block it out. And he reaches into his pocket and hands me a stick of wax. Stopper up your ears against the sound. And may your God help you.

I think I see something dart below the surface of the waves. Out of the darkness and then back down into the depths. Pale, quick, shimmering and vanished in a second. And once it is gone I question whether I have seen anything at all. But then it returns, sleek and swift, before plunging once more into the deep.

[*missing text*]

248

I stagger to the ladder.

I cannot think straight.

I cannot see how this story will end for us all, or for you and me.

I may never make it back to you, Josie. If we survive the wrecking, we will most likely not survive what is waiting for us in the deep. I feel the quick rush of anger alongside my fear at the foolishness that took me so very far from you.

[*missing text*]

I am in the hold.

Water is pouring in as I scribble down the last of my love for you.

I think again of the old man. Give the creature a token and your life may be spared. I pull the letters I have written to you from inside my coat. They are a poor gift. Rough paper. Crude script. But they are precious to me.

The taper behind me flickers and will soon fade. There is little time.

A wine jug rolls across the floor and comes to rest beside me. And I decide. I will place my letters inside it and seal it with the wax Duncan gave me, melted down before the taper burns itself out. I will make the jug watertight. And when I fling myself overboard, I will carry it with me.

If I come face to face with a mermaid, I will hand her the jar, my heart bottled and stoppered and offered freely. And if she sees how much I love you, perhaps she shall speed me on my way.

I pray to God and all those other things that we do not understand that I will see you again.

Watch for me from your window, overlooking the sea.

Yours always and forever,
Edward

'Do you think it's true?' Callum said, as he came to the end of Edward's account. 'That it actually happened like that?'

Freya took a sip of her tea and thought of the old man from the earlier letter questioning the lines of history and myth and where one begins to turn into another. She replaced her cup on the table and shrugged noncommittally.

But Callum refused to be put off. 'I know, but what do *you* believe?'

Freya saw herself in the lighthouse tower surrounded by fog, or lying in bed just woken from sleep, hearing the same sound as the battle cry Edward had heard. Had it been her imagination? Was it, like so much else, simply in her head? She felt a cold shiver run through her. 'I don't know,' she said at last.

'Well, I think it's possible,' Callum said. He hesitated for a second before going on. 'And do you think Edward made it home to Josie? Or do you think he died?'

Freya thought of the blind seer, warning of a storm, of danger. And her thoughts turned to Torin. She blinked hard. 'I don't know,' she said again.

'I can't decide either. I think the old man sees death.

But Duncan, who also has the sight, thinks he will live. So which is it?'

'We'll never know, not for sure. There are practically no records of what happened to the *Speedwell* except for the fact that it was lost.'

'Well, I hope he survived and that he made it home to his family to tell the tale.'

Freya nodded, thinking of Josie and the baby, so far away from Edward in all but thought and memory, and the desolation that he felt on imagining them lost to him for ever. But perhaps that wasn't the end of his story. Perhaps it continued beyond the words on those pages. Freya saw Josie, in her small rooms in Plymouth, sitting by the fire as evening set in. She saw her look up surprised, at the unexpected knock on the door, and smile as her soldier opened it and walked back into her life after weeks of absence. Perhaps Josie ran to him, held him and he told her, in a way that he never had before, how much he loved her and what she meant to him. 'So do I, Callum,' Freya said. 'So do I.'

38

The ringtone crackled as Freya, lying on the sitting-room sofa, held the phone to her ear. She bit into a biscuit, looking out through the window into the blue of the afternoon. The deep azure of the sky melded almost seamlessly into the blue of the ocean. The weather was glorious and she had been outdoors for most of the day – walking across the island and then tidying the garden. For the first time since she had arrived, the plants and bushes had been pruned and neatened.

Just as she had decided that it was inevitable she would get voicemail, Marta picked up the phone. 'Hello.'

Freya smiled at the brusque efficiency of her voice. 'Hello, sis.'

'Oh hi, Frey.' Instantly there was a shift in tone. Warm and relaxed.

'How are you?'

'Oh, you know. Getting dumped on. Heaps of shit that no one else wants to deal with have suddenly gravitated towards my desk. But it always happens when someone leaves. Or when someone leaves in these circumstances,' Marta added, and then laughed. 'But that job that I told you about, the one I interviewed for and really wanted. Well, I got it.'

Freya smiled. That's why she was in such a good mood. 'That's fantastic, sis. Well done.'

'I know. Cool, huh? And it's only two weeks until I'm out of this place. I can't wait. I'm literally counting down the days.' Marta paused and took a breath. 'And how are you doing?'

'I'm fine.' She spoke to Marta almost every day so there wasn't much to update her on. She told her about Callum coming over and them reading the letters together. And then, perhaps because Marta was so upbeat, she told her about the blind old man's mention of the mermaid and Edward's revelation, in the final letter, of catching sight of one.

'Wow. Talk about the blind leading the blind.'

Instantly Freya wished she had kept her mouth shut. Why had she been so stupid as to divulge that? She felt anger growing inside her. Marta was always dismissive of things like this. How could she have thought she would be any different today?

'More likely Edward was panic-stricken and delusional on a sinking vessel. Or did he and the mermaid swim off into the sunset together?'

Marta started to laugh and Freya tried to make light of it. But what she had really been angling to say to Marta was that she felt a connection with this man. Even though they were separated by centuries and his world was gone, it was a world she couldn't help thinking resonated somehow with her own. And the feeling that she had had before, that the letters were somehow destined to come to her, was even stronger now.

'So what else is new?' Freya asked in an attempt to change the subject.

'Well, I've met someone.'

'That was quick work,' said Freya, surprised.

Marta laughed. 'I know. They say it often happens when you're least looking for it. It was just after I came back to London, actually. So we've seen each other a few times. His name's Rob and I really like him.'

Freya sat upright, registering this new and rather un-expected piece of news. 'Rob,' she repeated, looking out of the window and becoming conscious for the first time of an approaching boat. She squinted at it. If she was not mistaken it was Daniel's, and it was heading for the island.

'And I'm trying, this time,' Marta added, 'not to do my usual thing.'

Freya knew that this was unprecedented for her sister and she was irritated by the distraction of the boat. She stood and walked to the window to get a better view. Yes, it was definitely Daniel. Why was he coming here and what did he want?

'I even thought that you could meet him, Freya. Or that I could bring him to Ailsa Cleit sometime.'

'I would love that. You know I would. I'd absolutely love to be introduced.' As Marta chatted on, Daniel's boat drew ever closer. For a moment, Freya considered telling her sister the full story of the necklace. But she could hear

Marta's cool, rational voice telling her, in no uncertain terms, to give the bloody thing straight back to him. No, she didn't want to talk to Marta about it right now.

'Freya?'

She could see Daniel mooring his boat beside her own and jumping down onto the jetty. He began to walk swiftly up the hill. She felt the cold sting of fear in her veins. Her hand sought out her neck and she found herself walking to the kitchen door. Before she really thought about what she was doing, she turned the key in the lock. Then she pulled down the blind. At least it would appear as if she was out.

'Hello? Freya? Are you still there?'

'Oh hi, sweetheart. Sorry.' She went back into the sitting room and stood next to the bookshelves, out of sight of anyone peering in through any of the windows. 'I'm so happy that you've shared your news with me. You have no idea. I'm sorry to be so distracted. There's just someone coming and I need to go and get the door.'

'Oh, who is it?'

'It's Daniel,' said Freya. And as she said it she realised how ridiculous it was that she was hiding from him. But still she didn't move. 'So I've got to go. Can I call you back later?'

'Of course. I'll be in tonight. Is everything all right, sis? You don't sound quite right.'

'I'm fine,' said Freya, almost whispering now as she heard the clump of heavy men's boots along the garden path. 'Speak to you later.'

She hung up and waited. A few seconds later she heard a rap on the door. She felt her body tense. The knock came again. This time it was harder and more insistent. Freya realised she was holding her breath. She heard Daniel move away from the door, probably over to the kitchen window. Through it he would be able to see the kitchen and the sitting room. But not where she was standing, obscured by the wall and the shelves. She waited a little while longer, not daring to move. Perhaps he was walking along the outside of the cottage, peering in through the windows. She didn't like to think of it. A moment later another hard rap came against the kitchen door. Then the sound of the handle being turned and, when the door didn't open, rattled furiously.

Involuntarily Freya took a breath and put her hand over her mouth. She remained stationary until she heard his footsteps retreat. Then she stayed still for a further five minutes.

Eventually, when she was sure he was gone, she moved to the sitting-room window and, from its corner, watched his boat sailing away.

She breathed deeply and only then realised her hands were trembling. How ridiculous. She should simply have let him in and avoided all this drama. But she didn't want him asking to see the necklace again.

39

That evening Freya sat on the lamp-room floor, the necklace at her throat, a glass of wine and Sam's diary beside her.

There was only one entry left. Yet something in Freya baulked at reading it. Part of her couldn't believe that she hesitated – now she was so close to the end; so close, perhaps, to knowing what had happened. She had persuaded herself that it was her willpower, her immense discipline that had prevented her from galloping straight through the diary from beginning to end. But now she realised what perhaps she had known, unconsciously, all along. That in reading a little at a time, in delaying the arrival of knowledge, there had been solace. In not knowing there was also a kind of comfort.

She stood and made her way out onto the gallery, looking southeast towards the Torran Rocks. She could just make out the largest ones, where Jack and Sam had anchored. She tried to see further, to Jura and beyond, but the horizon blurred everything deep blue and charcoal. Moving back into the lamp room she sat down again. It was so familiar to her now, this place, floating somewhere between sea and land and air. It was her place, her home.

Mum will be home in three days and I am counting down the hours.

Even though I have had a great time with Dad, I have really missed her. Especially at bedtime. It's funny but I have missed the stories she reads to me even though lots of them are silly. I told Dad this and it made him laugh. He asked me which story I liked best. That was a difficult one as we have read so many. But then it jumped out at me – Beira, Queen of Winter. And I think it is Mum's favourite too. She always smiles when she reads it. Dad asked me to tell it to him. I couldn't remember all of it so I just told him the bits I could. They went like this.

It is winter. Beira is old and dark and fierce. Her beauty has faded. She remembers a time when she was fair, when the world was different and she is sad. Worse still, her reign is only just beginning. Every year it starts the same way, with her washing her great shawl in the sea. The place she chooses is between the western islands of Jura and Scarba, the whirlpool, the Corryvreckan. It is called that because the son of a king, named Breckan, was drowned in it, after his boat was tipped over by the waves.

Three days before Beira begins her washing her servants make the water ready for her and the Corryvreckan can be heard seething and churning for twenty miles around. On the fourth day Beira throws her shawl into the whirl-pool, and stamps on it until the edge of the Corry brims over with foam. When she has finished her washing she puts her shawl on the mountains to dry, and when she lifts it up, they are white with snow. That is how the Queen begins her reign.

As winter goes on, Beira grows older and angrier until at last her strength is spent. She cannot go on. But then she drinks from the Well of Youth on the Green Island, an impossibly difficult place to find unless you are magical and blessed. Then old Beira grows young and beautiful again with long flowing hair.

The End.

Dad liked the story. I think it also reminded him of Mum because he looked a bit sad. I think that he has missed her too. He asked me if I believed the tale of Queen Beira and I said Mum and I had talked about it and thought it was really a story about time and change and the seasons. I also said that Granddad and I had talked about the whirlpool as obviously it wasn't formed by an old hag washing her shawl. Granddad said it was because of the narrow strait between the islands, the underground rocks and pinnacles and the Atlantic sea currents that flow there. I said I didn't know about Breckan though and whether he had really died there or not.

Dad laughed at this and ruffled my hair, which is what he always does when I say something that he likes. Then he asked me if I'd like to go to the Corryvreckan as we hadn't been for a while. Perhaps the next day just before Mum came home so we could celebrate the story and her return – like that of Queen Beira.

I thought that was a brilliant idea. And I said it would

also be great if we could try and sail to the Green Island afterwards as Mum and I had often talked about it and how difficult it was to find.

And Dad laughed again and said that he would do his best. He asked where we should try to find it and we got out a map and had a look. I traced a line back from the Corryvreckan, back past the Torran Rocks and Dubh Artach where we had just been.

I told Dad that I thought our best chance of finding the Green Island was out beyond the black rock heading into the open ocean. Okay, he said, smiling. We'll go as far as we can. Weather permitting.

I'm so excited I'm not sure I'll be able to sleep tonight.

I wish Mum could come with us.

But I can tell her all about it when she's back.

40

The *Valkyrie* bobbed on the water in the heart of the Gulf.

Freya stared over the side of the boat. It was difficult to tell where the whirlpool ordinarily formed. The water was relatively still, but for the occasional eddy stirring here and there. She tried to see below the surface to the pinnacle of rock she knew was 30 metres down. But it was obscured.

She turned to check the tide clock attached to the doorway of the cabin. It was ebb of tide. She had timed her journey precisely to ensure there was no danger. Still it was hard to imagine, seeing the Gulf in its current placid state, how deadly this place could be at flow of tide and in high winds. Freya turned towards Eilean Beag, the islet off the coast of Jura. Perhaps that was where the *Speedwell* had met its end. It looked so innocuous in the still of the day. Gulls perching, sunbathing, silent but for the occasional flap of their wings. When the wind and tide were up it would be difficult, if not impossible, to get from there across the foaming gulf and on to land.

She sat down and took out Sam's diary once more. She had no idea what time of day her son and husband would have visited here. But she imagined they had come approaching high tide to see the best, most dramatic effects of the whirlpool. Then perhaps they had been caught out by the turn in the weather. But if they made it away from the whirlpool in time, they might have caught the Great Race, the large spill of high water out of the gulf of Corryvreckan onto the lower water to the west of Jura, and ridden that towards Colonsay. And then who knows how far they might have ventured before the storm hit. Beyond the Torran Rocks. Beyond the black rock. Perhaps even to the Green Island.

Freya put the diary down. She didn't really need to see it – she had read it over and over and it was committed to her memory. But she had reached the final chapter and still she didn't know where the last journey of her family ended. In all likelihood she never would.

For a long time she gazed over the water, looking at the sea caught between Jura and Scarba. She remembered having read about the documentary makers who had once thrown a mannequin, complete with life jacket and depth gauge, into the heart of the Corryvreckan. It was swallowed up and spat out far down-current, with a depth reading of over 250 metres, showing it had been dragged along the bottom of the sea floor for at least part of its journey. She closed her eyes and tried to rid herself of such thoughts. In their stead, she wanted to see her son and husband on their last day out together.

The sun was shining, although there was a tinge to the sky, a smell on the air that indicated to the wary that the weather might well change. She could see Sam standing at the back of the boat, in jeans and his favourite checked blue shirt, turning towards his father and smiling at him, his blond hair, blown by the breeze. She saw the scar on his forehead from a fall when he was four years old. She could almost smell his unique scent on the breeze. Milky sweetness, like almonds, mixed with the wildness of the Atlantic Ocean.

She could see Jack beside him: strong, protective, a larger version of his son; his blue eyes, often as unfathomable as the sea, now twinkling in the sunlight. She could see his lips, curved into a smile, hear his voice, speaking to Sam, telling him about the Gulf, pointing to birds flying close by. She saw them sail away beyond the reach of the whirlpool and caught Jack turning back to look towards her. Then she heard his voice, whispering, words for her alone to hear, words he once uttered to her in the darkness of night. And in the daylight beside the Corryvreckan, she surrendered to the ebb and flow of love and memory and longing.

Freya opened her eyes and looked at the clock again. She still had time before the flow of tide beginning at the southern end of the Strait of Jura reached here. But perhaps it was better to leave now. This was her final pilgrimage, she realised, the last time she would make a journey retracing the steps of her husband and son. She touched the silver necklace at her throat, worn as a token to Sam, and then zipped up her jacket. The breeze on the water was cold today.

As she went into the cabin to start the engine, she noticed another boat approaching from the northern coast of Jura. She hadn't noticed it before; didn't know how long it had been there or if it had only just now come into view. She watched it draw closer. It was Daniel.

'Hi,' he shouted, as he drew alongside her.

'Hi,' said Freya, smiling but she felt a flicker of fear move through her. 'What are you doing out here?' she asked.

'I know. Such an odd coincidence, right?' And then he laughed, awkwardly. 'Work, kind of.'

'Right,' said Freya, but for a fleeting second, as he tethered his boat to hers, she had an irrational thought that he had followed her here. As she walked towards him, she tried not to think about it.

'How are you?' he asked her.

'I'm okay,' she said. His eyes were flat, as unreadable as ever. 'I got to the end of Sam's diary. The last entry was about them coming to the Corryvreckan. So that's why I'm here. What about you?'

'Hmm. It's a bit of a long story.'

'Well, we have time.' Freya looked towards the tide clock and then back at him.

'I guess I've been thinking about the letters that I read the last time I came to your cottage.' He looked at her directly then, seemingly analysing her reaction. She met his gaze steadily even though her heart was pounding.

'Yes,' she said. 'I just finished reading them myself.' She paused, looking out over the whirlpool. 'And they end here, of course.'

'Exactly. I dropped by to see you the other day actually. I wanted to talk to you about it all. But I think you were out. The door was locked.'

'Oh. Then I must have been.' Freya met his eye again.

'I thought I remembered you saying you never lock the door. That it's not necessary around here.'

'No,' she said. 'I don't usually – although sometimes it's just instinct if I'm not thinking. A hangover from London.'

'And your boat was at the jetty.'

'Maybe I'd just gone out for a walk then.'

'Well, I scoured the island and didn't see you, so I don't think so.'

Something about the persistence of Daniel's enquiries, his tone, bothered her. He clearly suspected that she'd been at home. 'Oh well.' She said it lightly, trying to lift the unsettling mood. 'Perhaps a friend came to pick me up. Anyway . . . ' She let the word hang on the air, hoping to move the conversation on.

'Yes, anyway.' Daniel looked away from her, then out over the sea, playing with an object around his neck. Freya realised that it was the mermaid blade she had given him.

'Would you look at that?' she said. 'I like what you've done with this . . . ' She gestured to her own neckline and, as she did so, immediately remembered the silver necklace she was wearing. Instinctively, she touched the neckline of her jacket, which was obscuring it. She didn't want him to see it and for it to become an issue again way out here.

But Daniel, it seemed, was thinking of other things. 'I had some tests carried out on this. Like you suggested.'

'You did? What did you find out?'

'Nothing about the basalt – apart from the fact that the rock was local and old. But while they were running those tests, they discovered what they thought was a fish scale wedged into the base of the blade – here, where it splits into two parts.' Daniel leaned over towards her to show her. 'Tests on fish scales aren't performed often as they're difficult and time intensive. But they usually yield results. So here came the surprise. My colleague couldn't identify the scale. And that's not something that he's come across before. You can generally establish, at the least, the group of fish the sample came from. The best he could do was say it was probably akin to a porpoise or dolphin but wasn't a porpoise or dolphin. It was likely something undiscovered.'

'Wow,' Freya said.

'Mmm. So while we don't know what it is, we know it isn't something very ordinary.'

Freya looked at Daniel, but he was staring into the Gulf, completely preoccupied. 'What is it?'

'I think it started with the blade and your stories of mermaids out in the deep ocean. Then there was the inconclusive test on the fish scale. It all adds up, don't you think?'

'To what?'

'To the fact that I don't think the fish scale belonged to the fish that was hunted. I think it was from the fish that was the hunter.'

'That's quite a leap,' said Freya.

'Perhaps.' Daniel shrugged. 'But then the letters suggest something similar too. And now it all seems to me to point that way. And I'm a man of science.' Daniel laughed, but the sound was entirely devoid of joy.

Freya met his eyes. They were cold, and she realised for the first time that there was also something dead about them. Annalise's disappearance had killed something in him, something that perhaps he would never get back. Something perhaps he didn't want back. She wondered for a second if the same was true of her. That her restlessness – roaming the sea searching for something, her desire to be alone with the ghosts of the past – was actually a death wish rather than seeking to come to terms with things.

'I've been exploring the myths of the Scottish mermaid, the Ceasg, since all this other stuff came to light.'

Freya knew the tales, had been conversant with them since childhood.

'And I've heard that if the Ceasg is given a token or can be charmed by a person she may grant a wish. Have you heard that before, Freya?'

'Yes, I've heard it.' Freya thought of Torin, reciting stories over and over to her – both when she was little and again more recently. Edward also mentioned it in his letters.

'And it occurred to me that she couldn't fail to be captivated by a talisman – a thing of magic and beauty. You know what I'm talking about, of course.'

Freya looked at Daniel, a feeling of foreboding growing inside her.

'The Permian ring, of course.' He snapped the words out, impatiently.

Freya's fingers twitched and her first instinct was to touch the necklace at her throat. But instead she kept her eyes on Daniel.

'What do you know about the necklace?'

Freya swallowed. 'Not much. I was told that it was Viking and would have been buried with its owner in death.'

Daniel nodded. 'Who told you that?'

'A friend of mine.' Torin had seen darkness and sadness surrounding the necklace and had warned her of it. And yet, against his advice, she had continued to wear it. She blinked hard and went on. 'And I know that Sam found it under the sand at Balevullin Bay on Tiree. That's it. Why do you think it's a talisman?'

'Well, perhaps you can let me see it again, properly this time, and then I'll tell you.' Daniel smiled, but it had no warmth to it.

Freya's blood ran cold. How did he know that she was wearing the necklace? The only way he could was if he'd been watching her earlier and seen. Now she began to understand his true purpose for being here. For a moment outrage outweighed her fear. 'Have you been following me, spying on me?'

Daniel raised his hands. 'I'm sorry, Freya. But you gave me no choice. I came back to the house to ask to see it and you avoided me.'

Freya made a noise as if to speak but he raised a hand to her.

'Please, Freya, don't deny it. I can tell you're attached to it – because of Sam finding it. But now you'll have to let me see it.'

For a moment Freya thought about refusing. But what good would it do, to antagonise him out here, miles from anywhere? Her gaze moved past him, around the Gulf and beyond. There was no other boat, no one nearby. And although she usually relished such isolation, she realised that right now she found that prospect unnerving.

She unzipped her jacket and let him see the necklace wrapped around her throat.

Daniel reached towards it and stroked its silver. 'Like I said, when I first saw it at your house, it reminded me of another I had unearthed at a burial site. I couldn't be sure that it was the same one because this one's broken and the other one wasn't. But now I see it again, around your neck, I'm sure.'

Freya braced herself as he continued to touch the necklace, expecting him to try and take it from her. But he didn't.

'You see, I did a very reckless thing when I first saw this. I took it.'

'You took it?' Freya repeated. 'From an archaeological site?'

'I wanted Annalise to have it. I knew it would look so beautiful around her neck.'

So it had belonged to his wife. Freya felt breathless even

though his words were simply an affirmation of what she had known deep down.

'Even though I knew I could get into serious trouble. I didn't care. She was worth the risk. And she loved it and wore it all the time, even when she went swimming. So imagine my surprise when it turned up in your house.' He stroked the silver again, accidentally running his thumb over Freya's skin. His touch made her feel nauseous. 'You realise what this means, of course?'

'I don't,' said Freya.

'It means that it's charmed, blessed, something like that. I found my way to you on the night of the storm and, through you, the necklace found its way back to me.'

'Why didn't you tell me that you thought it was your wife's when you first saw it?'

Daniel shrugged. 'I was shocked and unsure. I couldn't think straight. And besides, you didn't want me to look at it properly.'

'But if you'd told me, I would have given it to you. Of course I would.'

Daniel's raised his eyes from the necklace to look at her. 'Would you? Would you really, Freya?'

'Of course,' she insisted again. Then she remembered how she had avoided him, avoided having the heritage of the necklace confirmed to her.

'Anyway, it doesn't matter. You can give it to me now. I've begun to think that, through this necklace, I might find a way back to her.'

'To Annalise? What do you mean?' Freya asked.

'Isn't it obvious?'

Freya shook her head.

'That if I give the symbol of my love, the necklace, to the mermaid, she will surely grant my wish to be reunited with my wife.'

Freya looked at Daniel, at his eyes burning with emotion. And for a moment she could almost see herself – trapped in her grief, imagining all kinds of crazy things. But she had never got so close to the brink; always, somehow, managed to pull herself back from there. Then she thought about Torin's warnings, that she should be careful of the past, stop dwelling always in the blackness there, that she shouldn't wear the necklace, a symbol of death at its most concrete. And then she heard Sam's words again, that there was danger, that death was stalking her. She had ignored them all. Freya wondered, as she looked at Daniel now, if she had more in common with him than she would like to admit.

He was still talking, pursuing his own thoughts, ' . . . And I think with the mermaid blade as well, I'll have two talismans. It can't fail really.'

Freya looked at the blade around his neck, a small and insignificant piece of chiselled rock. And she realised that she had to try and reason with him.

'But haven't you ever thought that you were saved on the night of the storm for a reason? To go on living.'

'No.' He shook his head. 'I realised that that was solely to bring me to you. And that.' Daniel pointed to the necklace and smiled at Freya. A happier smile than she had seen since she met him. 'Besides, I would go on living, but with Annalise. Come on Freya, tell me you haven't had the same thoughts.'

She looked over the side of the boat, at the water circling around them, gaining momentum with the flow of tide. She had determined that she would not be here as it got more dangerous and yet here she was. She remembered looking into the water at Dubh Artach, longing, in a way, to be swept out into the submarine valley, washed way out to sea, where she could join the gone and the lost. She had thought the same at the top of the lighthouse tower, as she felt the urge to jump. Perhaps in a way things had always been moving towards this point. She touched the necklace at her throat. It was the embodiment of death, wrapped tightly around her. And yet she had not shunned it; she had worn it like an invitation.

'I have.' She nodded and her eyes filled with tears. 'And yet . . . ' She stopped, struggling with herself. 'But I don't think this is something that you really want to do. Deep, deep down.'

'Trust me, Freya. It is. I've been stuck in this place for three years and I can finally see a way out. The letters were the final thing to show me that.' His eyes were shining, more animated than she had ever seen before.

Freya saw him then, perhaps properly for the first time. But it's not real, she wanted to say.

'So, I'd like it please.' Daniel touched the silver at her throat again, his fingers beginning to curl around the bands.

Freya took a step back from him. 'I don't think you should do this,' she said.

'Yeah, you've said that before. Come on, hand it over.'

'It's madness,' Freya muttered, holding her hand to her throat.

Daniel's eyes narrowed. Then he climbed over the side of his boat into Freya's. 'I'm getting tired of this,' he said, moving towards her until they were face to face at the stern. He held out his hand. 'Please give it to me. I don't want to hurt you.'

Freya's stomach twisted at the threat but she stood her ground and shook her head.

For a second Daniel paused. Then he grabbed her throat.

She gasped and strained against his hands. Even though part of her, the rational part, told her to simply surrender, to let him take the necklace and let him do what he wanted to do, the irrational part wondered perhaps if he was right, if here there was escape from pain, a way back to what she loved and had lost. And that part of her also longed to surrender to the deep.

As they struggled, she felt Daniel's fingers grasping the silver around her neck, trying to prise it free. She bent her head down and bit his hand. He recoiled and she took a step away from him.

'You crazy bitch, Freya. Just give it to me.'

'No,' she said defiantly. 'I won't. You're not thinking straight.'

Daniel took a step towards her and then slapped her

hard across the face. She was flung sideways and, before she could right herself, Daniel lunged at her, grabbing for the necklace. They both overbalanced, toppling over the edge of the boat into the water. As she fell, Freya hit her head, hard against the stern. The blow was unexpected, shocking.

She felt the cold water against her skin. Then nothing.

41

Freya opened her eyes. The darkness was the first thing she saw. If that was the right word. You didn't really see darkness, after all. You felt it. But this was a darkness punctuated with rays of shimmering light, falling softly from above, dissolving the black into iridescent blue and green. Where was she? Freya wondered. It was so beautiful, so intoxicating, this place. Then, in a flash, it came back her. The struggle, the fight, the falling, and suddenly she felt the cold pricking her body, the pain shooting in her head. As she looked up to the sunlight, now far above her, Freya realised. She was under the water.

There was a flush of panic and then the instinct to kick hard to the surface. But she resisted it. Instead she looked downwards and saw the pinnacle beneath her and, beyond it, in the ever-increasing blackness, the channel which plummeted down so deep. Freya felt the pulse of the water, its sensuous, arrhythmic heartbeat, catching her in an eddy, pulling her gently up and then more forcibly down in a sudden thrust.

The maelstrom was gaining force. She floated, her white hair spreading out around her, suspended somewhere between life and death. It was the choice she had struggled with, had anticipated, the taste of saltwater so often on her lips, catching at the back of her throat, erupting out of her dreams – the darkness or the light, the sea or the sky, death or life. There was tightness in her chest, the burning choke of white-hot lungs. She fought the urge to cough and gulp down water in the absence of air. And yet she also longed to do it. As she drifted further towards darkness, she looked for Daniel, but she couldn't see him, reached for the necklace at her throat, but it was gone, surrendered once more to the deep. What will my offering be? she thought, before the blackness closed again around her.

She drifted in and out of consciousness: one moment feeling the thrust of the water, upwards, pushing her towards the light; the next, the languid tug of the current at her heels, pulling her towards oblivion. How easeful it would be, she thought, to simply slip now into the dark. And yet. She opened her eyes, suddenly alert. She was still alive, she realised with a rush. Her breath was all but extinguished and yet she was alive. And there was something else. She felt it, she was sure of it. Something was watching from the darkness. Dreamlike images floated through her mind: her son's bedroom filled with water; something beyond her sight. And, as she continued to look, the darkness before her seemed to tremble and unfurl, a shadowy figure emerging from its clutches.

Perhaps it was death coming for her. Perhaps it was

nothing at all. She blinked. But she was not mistaken. The figure was moving closer, propelled towards her on the tide. And then she heard the noise, the sound that echoed through her dreams, the haunting, melancholy cry. Was it the sound of the whirlpool gathering force, or something else? As the figure moved nearer, she thought she could make out the form of a woman, gliding across the water with ease. She caught a shimmer in the darkness, a flash of light and gold. Was it the woman's hair, streaming behind her, or the last touches of sunlight flickering in the depths? Then came a glittering burst of silver, flashing past at speed. Could it be the Ceasg, a beautiful half-woman coming to take her life? Or would it spare her, recognising that her soul had already been touched too many times by death?

As Freya slipped towards unconsciousness, she thought she saw the woman's face, close now, her skin glinting with light in spite of the darkness, so close that her hair, rippling on the tide, intertwined with Freya's own. She reached out to touch the creature, but she was so weak her fingers brushed only through water. Was it an apparition, she wondered, down here in the deep? But then she heard the Ceasg's voice in her head.

For a moment she listened, and then the darkness claimed her.

42

Freya heard it first: loud, chaotic, bubbling, popping in her ears, a noisy rush of water around her head.

A moment later she burst, gasping, above the surface. Her eyes were wide open, shocked. She was still alive. Then thoughts rushed in. How long had she been down there? How had she survived? She coughed; deep, rasping breaths, filling the suffocating emptiness of her lungs, struggling to stay afloat, to resist the snapping downward currents. Her body was pulled one way, then back again on the surface of the water, caught – it seemed – in a powerful tidal flow, crashing outwards from the whirlpool. It was the Great Race, she was sure of it. If she could ride it out, she might even survive.

Every few seconds she was dragged down below the water, but somehow she always fought her way back up. She let the tide carry her, spewing her forward with its momentum. Gradually the churning din of the whirlpool faded, the tug at her heels lessened and she managed to stay afloat. As she glided, disoriented, eyes aching, head throbbing, body pummelled and exhausted, she tried to get her bearings. There was land around her, on either side of a channel, but she couldn't tell where it was. She turned her head back and forth, looking for a marker, something distinctive. But there was nothing. She let out a terrified, shuddering breath. She had no idea where she was and no will left to fight her way to solid ground. Fear clawed in her gut, tears pricked her eyes, but she didn't have the strength to cry. She turned onto her back and tried to float with the current. Less resistance, more surrender.

She felt dizzy and sick and her eyes grew dark, spots flickering across her vision. She feared that she would black out again. Perhaps she did. Perhaps she moved fleetingly in and out of consciousness. Images flashed: clouds fluttering at speed across a sky, blue shifting into grey, growing darker, the green and brown of hills with silver burns gliding down their sides, trees and bracken, the sea crashing onto rocks coated in kelp, wildflowers on the machair, a man waving to her, shouting out that he loved her, begging her to swim for home. What was real and what was not, what she saw and what was only memory or imagination, Freya ceased to be able to tell. Time had no meaning. How far she floated, supported by the sea, she did not know. Yet somewhere, in the midst of her isolation, she felt that someone or something was with her. That she was not alone. She caught it, in a blink of gold below the surface of the water, in a flash of scales and silver and light. And she heard its voice in her head.

She drifted past a cluster of rocks, spattered across the ocean. She thought of reaching out to grasp them but they disappeared too fast, too soon. They made her think of letters, stoppered in a jar and consigned to the deep. But they had been released, had they not?

She breathed deeply. Her chest stung and her head smarted. She was bone tired, her body freezing. She closed her eyes and didn't open them. She wanted to, but she couldn't. She had no strength left. Then she heard the ocean braying, felt it clawing at her. She was ready, she thought, to finally let go. But then she heard another voice. Her son's. Swim fast, Mum. The shore will be in front of you before you know it. And then, in a different tone: Mum, do you understand? There is danger for you here.

Freya's eyes snapped open. Her body was tingling but she was alert. She trod water for a moment and then looked around her. She had to get her bearings. But there was no land, no rock anywhere close. Further away she could see hills, but she had no idea where they were. She was out in open ocean, God knew where. She felt the panic lurking, longing to surge. It seemed hopeless. But then she remembered Pol's words. *The sea can be beautiful but it can also be frightening. I overcame the fear.* Freya swallowed and determined to do the same.

She turned in the water and then turned again. Nothing familiar. Then, as she stared ahead, into what seemed like nothing but sky, she saw it. A lighthouse emerging from the surface of the waves. A pale, rose-coloured tower, on the horizon at the very edge of her vision. It was her lighthouse, she was sure of it, beckoning her. East of it, she could see land, and beyond that high mountains. Mull, most likely. So that was north. At last she had something to grasp onto. She turned and looked south and west, and on the opposite horizon as she stared she caught a shadowy glimpse of Dubh Artach. She felt a tremor inside, much as she had when she was last there, and imagined the long, deep tunnel floating away underwater. With a clarity she had not felt in a long time, she knew that that was not the direction she would take. Instead she would swim north, towards home. The route, the quickest and most direct, was still imprinted on her mind from her recent journey to the black rock. She turned and began to swim, her strokes measured. She would follow the lighthouse as a guide, a marker, and she would swim as far as she could.

43

'Freya, is it you?'

She heard the voice first from a long way away. Her eyes were closed, she knew that much, and her clothes were wet, she thought, although she couldn't be sure exactly what she felt beyond pain. The voice came again. It was nearer this time and she could hear the crunch of feet running towards her. There was also the sound of water, lapping gently close by, the shingle shifting in the rise and fall.

'Freya, is it you?'

The voice was close now, almost upon her. She inhaled deeply and smelled the ocean, salt and seaweed. Then she opened her eyes.

'Freya?'

She could see a man running towards her. Then he was down on his knees at her side.

'Freya.'

He turned her over and the sky came into view. As he brushed the hair from her face she saw clouds like small puffs of smoke. The sky is on fire, she thought.

'Freya, can you hear me?'

She shifted her gaze to the man. He had kind grey eyes, but they looked anxious, the lines at their edges pronounced. And his body was taut as he repeated her name over and over.

She managed to nod her head. Just a fraction but it hurt her. She tried but she couldn't speak. So she smiled instead.

The man took a sharp intake of breath and then released it. It felt to Freya as if he had been suddenly deflated, his tension dispelled onto the air. Then he smiled back. His eyes lit up when he did that. 'Jesus, Freya. You had me worried sick. And Torin. He sent me over to check on you.'

He took off his jacket, rolled it up and put it under her head. He examined her as he did it. 'You're bleeding, Freya. What happened? Where's your boat?'

'Corryvreckan,' she managed to get out.

Callum's eyes rolled, concern overtaking them again. 'Jesus. And you made it back here. How the hell . . . ?' His words stuttered to a halt. 'Are you okay?'

She looked at Callum again. 'I am now,' she said, and reached for his hand.

He took hers, squeezed it and smiled again. Then he grabbed his phone.

'I think we need to get someone out here to have a look at you. And you know I'll never be able to get any service down here.'

He fiddled around for a moment or two before giving up. Then he pulled off his sweater and covered her with it. 'I'll have to go up to the house. Use the phone there. Don't you be going anywhere while I'm gone. Promise?'

Freya smiled but felt a ricochet of pain through her head. She winced and tried to lie still.

'Aye, don't move, don't try and speak.' Callum jumped to his feet. 'I'll be back in a minute and I'll bring blankets and water.' He started to leave but then turned back to her as if something had just occurred to him. 'I almost didn't recognise you. With your hair and everything.'

Freya frowned as she watched him turn and run up the beach to the cottage. What was he talking about? She reached and took a strand of her hair in her hand. What she saw she couldn't believe. It was black. She took another strand and then another. But it was the same. Her hair was black once more. She thought about the Corryvreckan: a flash of silver in the deep, golden hair interlinking with her own.

She felt another stab of pain in her head and closed her eyes. Out of the darkness of her mind a beach appeared, an arc of bright white sand, and behind it a swathe of green machair. From a corner of the beach a young boy came running, stumbling over the rocks as he approached the water's edge, laughing at his own clumsiness. His blond hair was whipped by the wind and his eyes were bright, shining with delight. He looked at her and smiled. I love you, he called out, and she repeated the words back to him. Then the boy turned and shouted out to the man who was following behind him, a tall man with the same eyes, once icy blue but now warm. The man and the boy stood side by side on the beach looking at her for a moment. Then they turned and carried on until they disappeared from view. Freya smiled. It was a special place they had found, that was what she told herself, a place always bathed in sunlight, with a magical spring that kept its inhabitants for ever young. The Green Island. It was a place she too would like to find one day.

She opened her eyes again and, as she lay staring at the sky, she realised something else. It wasn't just her hair that had changed. She felt different too. The darkness inside her had shifted. The pain was still there – would no doubt always be there. But intermingled with it was something else she hadn't felt for a long time. Hope had returned.

44

Freya heard a whirring sound. She opened her eyes and realised that she was still lying on the beach. She had no idea how long she had been there, but she caught sight of Callum, a blur of motion, running back towards her.

Then she saw blades circling above her, heard their deafening roar. A helicopter. She felt the presence of people nearby, hands softly touching her head, lifting her, strapping her onto something – a stretcher, most likely – and raising her up. Then she was weightless, flying – almost the same sensation as floating below the surface of water. Suddenly afraid, she cried out for Callum. After a moment she felt his hand upon hers, caught sight of his face above her smiling, his mouth uttering words she couldn't hear above the hum of the rotor. Her panic abated and she closed her eyes, exhausted, overcome.

The room was quiet, save for the intermittent beep of machines. It smelled vaguely of bleach and had a bare feel, with two narrow, empty beds opposite hers. She was in hospital, her left hand hooked up to a drip, her head thick and throbbing. Callum was sitting in a chair beside her, flipping through the pages of a magazine. But Freya knew, by the speed with which his eyes passed over the words, that he wasn't concentrating on any of it. She smiled, feeling a rush of emotion.

'So, what brings you here?' Her voice was hoarse but she managed a smile.

'Oh, I love a visit to the community hospital when I'm in Craignure,' Callum joked. But there was relief in his tone. 'How you feeling?'

'Like shit.'

He smiled. 'Well, that's to be expected. You had head trauma and hypothermia. But neither too serious. Miraculously. And the coastguard got to you quickly and brought you here. Amazing considering. I mean, the Corryvreckan . . . ' Callum muttered.

'Did they find Daniel?'

Callum shook his head. 'No. I told the coastguard about your boat and they found his alongside yours. But there was no sign of him.'

'Tell them they need to keep searching,' Freya said, and then was overcome with a rasping cough.

'They're already doing it. But I'll tell them again,' said Callum, passing her some water and supporting her head as she drank. 'What happened out there?'

Slowly Freya told Callum the bare bones of the story. The necklace, the fight, falling overboard. Then she remembered what she had seen, or thought she had seen, there.

'Do you remember what we talked about at the Treshnish Isles?'

Callum nodded.

'While I was in the water at the Corryvreckan, I thought I saw something in the darkness that swam towards me. Something that your great-great-grandfather had also seen sitting on his fishing baskets off the coast of Muck.' Freya looked at Callum and his eyes widened. 'I felt a presence. It spoke to me, helped me.' She waited for Callum to say something to contradict her, to say that it was the coldness of the water making her hallucinate, the light and shadow of the underwater world creating apparitions. But he was silent, running his fingers over her hair. 'You do believe me, don't you?' she said at last. She felt tired, drained from the effort of speaking.

'I believe you,' he said softly. 'Don't worry. It'll all be fine. Your parents and sister are on their way. But for now you need to sleep.'

And as her eyelids flickered and closed, Freya saw a sudden flash of silver, swift and darting.

Then the darkness came.

45

Freya stood on the lighthouse gallery, looking out over the ocean. It was late but the sky was still a vast pale blue hanging over the sea. She had watched the moon rise, her hands wrapped around the metal railing, and she had realised for the first time that her eyes were no longer searching for a boat bringing her loved ones home. She had accepted that they would not be coming back.

Her thoughts turned to Daniel. It was now two weeks since the incident at the Corryvreckan and his body had not, as yet, been recovered. He was gone. She knew it with certainty. Like Daniel's wife before him, like her husband and child. He was not coming back. The sea had taken him. Perhaps it was as simple as that. Or perhaps the Ceasg, if such things existed, had taken pity on him, on his grief-stricken madness, and granted him his wish to be reunited with his wife. Perhaps.

Freya gazed out over the emptiness of the ocean, an unusual feeling of calm upon her. She could hear the sounds of her family below: the high-pitched squabbling of her mother and sister, the lower tones of her father and Torin, no doubt discussing the truth or fiction of some Nordic tale. And then there was Alister, his voice soft yet discernible, talking on his favourite subject to Rob, Marta's new boyfriend, a curator at the British Library.

Footsteps on the stairs disturbed her. A moment later Callum appeared, blond hair unkempt, frowning and breathing hard. But as soon as he saw her, his face broke into a smile. He came onto the gallery and stood beside her. 'I got lobsters and razor clams. And some cod just off the boat. We could have a barbecue if you fancy it.'

She smiled back at him. 'That sounds great. Is everyone okay down there?' She tilted her head towards the stair-case.

'Ah, sure. They're having a grand time.' After Freya's 'accident', as they had taken to calling it, her family had descended on the lighthouse. And she liked having them here. The irony, she told only Callum, was that for the first time since Sam and Jack had died, she was also fine to be alone. There had been a sea change within her since that day at the Corryvreckan. Whatever had happened there, a pilgrimage had been completed. She had followed Jack and Sam on their journeys and had made one of her own back again. Everything here had played a part, she thought, even Daniel. Perhaps him more than anything or anyone else. She was right to have stayed.

'It's miraculous,' Callum said, reaching out to touch the ends of her hair. Like everyone else, he still struggled to believe it possible. And he was more superstitious than most. 'Just like Beira,' he said, not for the first time.

Freya nodded, remembering Sam's words about the queen's transformation.

Do you believe in magic, Mum? he had asked her.

Perhaps, she had replied.

But now her doubts had all but vanished.

Callum made a move for the staircase. 'Will you be down soon?'

She nodded, following him into the lamp room. 'Just as soon as I've finished reading.' She pointed to Sam's diary on the floor.

'Okay. But don't be too long or they'll be up here dragging you out.'

'I won't,' she said, smiling.

When he had gone, Freya sat down on the lamp-room floor and opened the diary. She looked once more at the page that two weeks ago she would have sworn had no writing on it. And there, in the uncertain hand of her son, she read the words once more that she felt had been written just for her.

We are at peace.

ALSO AVAILABLE IN ARROW

The Medici Mirror

Melissa Bailey

*'I have heard, but not believed, the spirits of the
dead may walk again...'*

A hidden room

When architect Johnny Carter is asked to redesign a long-
abandoned Victorian shoe factory, he discovers a hidden room
deep in the basement. A dark, sinister room, which contains a
sixteenth-century Venetian mirror.

A love in danger

Johnny has a new love, Ophelia, in his life. But as the pair's
relationship develops and they begin to explore the mystery
surrounding the mirror, its malign influence threatens to envelop
and destroy them.

A secret history

The mirror's heritage dates back to the sixteenth century, and the
figure of Catherine de Medici – betrayed wife, practitioner of the
occult, and known as the Black Queen.

The Medici Mirror is a haunting story of jealousy, obsession and
murder; of the ability of the past to influence the present; and of
love's power to defeat even the most powerful of curses.

arrow books

THE POWER OF READING

Visit the Random House website and get connected with information on all our books and authors

EXTRACTS from our recently published books and selected backlist titles

COMPETITIONS AND PRIZE DRAWS Win signed books, audiobooks and more

AUTHOR EVENTS Find out which of our authors are on tour and where you can meet them

LATEST NEWS on bestsellers, awards and new publications

MINISITES with exclusive special features dedicated to our authors and their titles

READING GROUPS Reading guides, special features and all the information you need for your reading group

LISTEN to extracts from the latest audiobook publications

WATCH video clips of interviews and readings with our authors

RANDOM HOUSE INFORMATION including advice for writers, job vacancies and all your general queries answered

Come home to Random House

www.randomhouse.co.uk